CATCH!

C & C Muirhead

Copyright © 2025 C & C Muirhead

All rights reserved.

ISBN: 9798302507105

DEDICATION

All proceeds from the sale of this book will be donated to support the excellent work of the West End Refugee Service (WERS) in Newcastle upon Tyne. Long may WERS continue to make a positive difference to the lives of refugees and asylum seekers in the region.

CONTENTS

Acknowledgements	i
Map of Sicily	ii
Map of Siracusa	iii
Prologue	1
The First Weekend	3
Monday 23rd October	19
Tuesday 24th October	37
Wednesday 25th October	65
Thursday 26th October	95
Friday 27th October	119
Saturday 28th October	139
Sunday 29th October	169
Monday 30th October	229
Epilogue	251

ACKNOWLEDGEMENTS

With special thanks to Kumoi K F Ngeenguno for his design of the cover of this book. Thanks also to Alison Wightman for her helpful feedback on the final draft of this book.

The maps of Sicily and Siracusa are based on Shutterstock vectors 1937900428 and 2470230289 respectively, purchased from Shutterstock under Standard Licence (www.shutterstock.com).

MAP OF SICILY

The Italian name for the city of Siracusa is used throughout the book, rather than the English name Syracuse.

MAP OF SIRACUSA

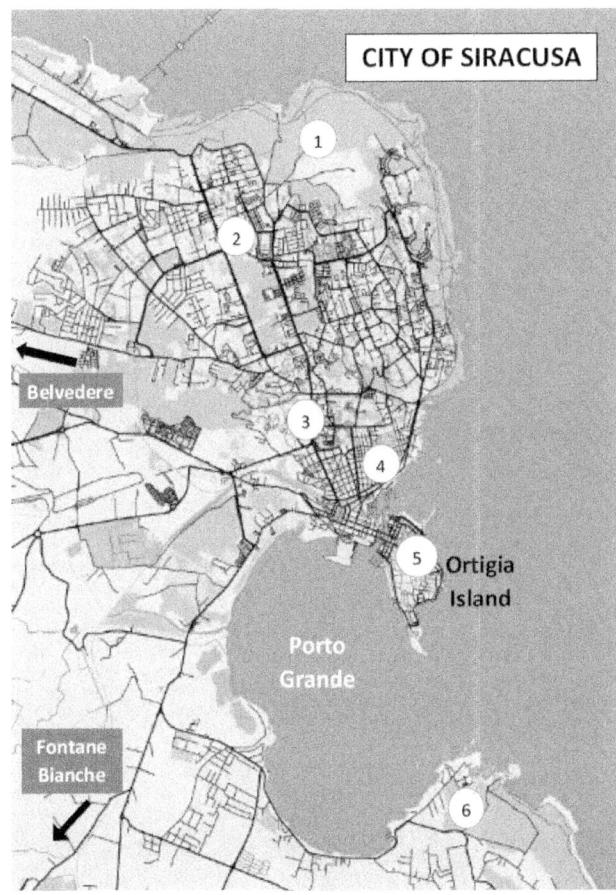

Key to locations, fictional and otherwise, in the book:

1. Villa Santa Panagia
2. Police Headquarters
3. Rosa's apartment
4. Mikey's apartment near Piazza Santa Lucia
5. EasyWash Launderette
6. Franco's House

PROLOGUE

"DANI, DANI!"

The young man looked up towards the thousands of gleeful fans, sat in the middle of an otherwise empty stand, calling out his name. Normally practice sessions for a baseball game would attract a few tens of supporters, but Dani's team – the Bakerside Bats – were just a couple of days away from the start of their biggest ever competition: the World Series. Interest in the Bats in this part of California was sky-high.

Dani turned his attention to the huge player who was standing a few yards away from him, swinging his bat nonchalantly. Over the previous couple of years, Dani had pitched countless balls during practice sessions. But today was different and not just because of the World Series. The images he had seen on his phone just half an hour earlier were still pounding in his head.

He took a deep breath, looked around at his teammates stretched across the baseball field, then turned, drew back his arm and hurled the baseball towards the batter.

WHACK!

The batter hit the ball perfectly. He didn't bother to move, clearly thinking that he had hit a home run. Dani watched the ball arc into the sky ... and fall.

And fall.

The ball's going to land in the stand at the far end of the field, thought Dani – it will be a home run. Suddenly, however, a fielder leapt athletically into the air.

CATCH!

Dani's fans screamed their delight as the fielder fell to the ground with the ball firmly in his grasp. The batter shook his head and walked slowly off the field.

One of the Bats' coaches walked over to Dani and slapped him on the back: "Great job!" Dani forced a smile but said nothing. "Mamma mia!" he thought, "what am I going to do on Sunday?"

THE FIRST WEEKEND

CHAPTER 1

It had all started late on Friday night, long after Franco had gone home. Around 11.30pm the police headquarters in Siracusa, Sicily, had answered a phone call from mainland Italy. The caller, a concerned father, had just taken a frantic call from his son in the USA. The lad had received a message telling him that his mother had been abducted earlier that day from a launderette in Ortigia, an island appended to the city of Siracusa.

Next morning, *Commissario* Franco Spina, Head of Criminal Investigations for Siracusa Province, arrived punctually for work at the police headquarters. It was precisely 7.30am. Some would say he was obsessively punctual, certainly by Sicilian standards. And Franco was 100% Sicilian, born and bred. The Spina family had lived in the south of Sicily for generations.

Within minutes of arriving, he was sitting at his desk, laptop open, examining some photos. He looked closely at the screen, trying to pick up clues about where the photos had been taken. Unfortunately there was little to go on – an ill lit room with no furniture apart from one plain, wooden chair. Zooming in on the chair, he recognised the simple, rustic Sicilian style. He also noticed splashes of what looked like white paint on the woodwork and wondered how those had got there. A pale coloured wall in the background looked bare. But in one of the corners he could just make out the logo of a well-known Sicilian plasterboard manufacturer. He looked again, yes, this was a makeshift wall – possibly a new build. The floor also looked bare. There were no discernible signs of flooring of any sort.

Sitting across from him on the other side of the desk was the police officer who had been on duty the previous evening and had taken the phone call. Franco looked up from the screen.

"So, Pappalardo, what do we know about this woman?" he asked, referring to pictures of a rather anxious but otherwise healthy-looking woman, who was perched on the wooden chair. She looked about the same age as Franco himself – early forties. He noted that she was dressed in a warm looking quilted jacket.

"We know that it's Roberta Montanari, *dottore*. She runs a launderette in Ortigia." Ortigia was the ancient part of Siracusa. Franco knew it as a popular tourist attraction, especially with cruise ships. Much of Ortigia was a UNESCO world heritage site and for those with money, it was an increasingly sought-after holiday destination. Several launderettes had sprung up in Ortigia in recent years. Franco was aware of that, and had often wondered what sort of customers these places served.

"Signora Montanari is well known in Ortigia," the officer continued.

"Really? Why is that?"

Pappalardo sounded surprised at Franco's question. "Her son is Daniele Montanari! He's a famous baseball player!"

Franco remained impassive at this point. His knowledge of baseball, or of any sport for that matter, was limited. But Pappalardo didn't need to know that. "Was it Daniele or his father who sent us these pictures?" he asked.

"Daniele sent them to his father and Montanari senior then forwarded them to us, *dottore*."

Interesting that the son had gone through his father, thought Franco. Why had he not contacted the police in Siracusa directly?

"OK Pappalardo. Get me Montanari senior on the phone! And bring me a coffee."

In the meantime, Franco instructed his deputy, Giovanna Campisi, to contact the company that owned the launderette. If the woman had been abducted from the launderette, somehow they would need to gain access to the premises before it opened up again.

The phone call with Tommaso Montanari was brief. He came straight to the point, informing Franco that the abductors were blackmailing his son. With barely concealed panic in his voice, Tommaso explained that any obvious police involvement could jeopardise Roberta's life, not to mention his son's career. To put it bluntly, the Bakerside Bats, his son's team, had to lose the forthcoming World Series – otherwise it would be curtains for Roberta. The police chief instantly put two and two together: there had to be a link to gambling. He also quickly understood the delicacy of the situation, especially from the son's point of view.

The conversation revealed that Tommaso lived in the North of Italy, near Parma. He and Roberta had divorced four years ago – after their son, Daniele, had left home to take up a baseball scholarship in the US. Roberta had then moved south to Sicily. Tommaso thought she had been working at the launderette for about three years. Concluding the conversation, Franco gave Signor Montanari a private non-traceable number to use for future calls. Franco would need to be kept informed of all future contact with Daniele. The number was for a second SIM card on Franco's work phone. The police chief would set up his phone so that he could be notified immediately of any calls or messages to that number. As a further precaution, he and Tommaso agreed to use WhatsApp for sharing messages and pictures.

After the call Franco decided to see the launderette for himself. He lost no time driving the short distance over the bridge from the modern city of Siracusa into Ortigia. The streets were busier than usual on a Saturday morning and he disliked having to slow down to allow crowds of tourists time to cross the road. Didn't these people realise he had a crime to solve? It took him 15 minutes to finally reach his destination. He hadn't banked on the crowd of onlookers when he turned his vintage Alfa Romeo into the narrow street where the launderette was located. Rather than risk any damage to the car, he decided to park at the top of the street and walk the short distance down to Roberta's place of work.

Approaching the launderette, he noticed that the shutters were down. A small crowd of curious onlookers who had gathered outside the entrance was turning vocal. The rather hapless looking young man who was attempting to put up a sign seemed to be the centre of attention and the focus of noisy protest and disgruntlement.

"Hey mister, when are they opening up?"
"I've been waiting here half an hour."
"What's going on?"
"Can we come in now?"

Blocking out all the babble that was going on out front, the police chief shot down a narrow lane at the side of the launderette and round the back of the building. Giovanna was waiting there for him, holding a key.

"Nice work, Gio. Let's take a look inside."

"There's something you need to know boss." Giovanna looked at him meaningfully. "The launderette is owned by a company called EasyWash. I phoned them about access to the back door –"

"And you got the key from the rep who's out front at the moment?"

Giovanna nodded. "EasyWash were only too willing to help."

She paused before coming to the point. "They received a text from Roberta Montanari earlier this morning."

Now she had Franco's full attention. "Go on," he said.

Giovanna consulted her notebook and read out the message: *"Sorry for short notice. Taking two weeks holiday. Ciao, Roberta."*

Franco's brain went into overdrive. Mindful of his conversation with the troubled Tommaso Montanari and the photos that had been sent through, this text message didn't make any sense. It had to be a hoax, surely? Giovanna was watching him intently, poised for instructions from her boss.

"OK, Gio, we are going to need recent photos of Roberta Montanari. Check that she is in fact the woman in the photos we were sent through. And see if you can trace where the text message came from. Which phone? Which location?"

His deputy nodded.

Feeling ready for action, Franco turned to face the back entrance to the launderette. "But first of all, let's see what's behind this door."

Closing the door behind them, the pair found themselves in a back room. They set to work examining the space for any possible clues as to the disappearance of Roberta Montanari. It was quite a small room with a lot of natural light coming from the back window. Detergent bottles and cardboard boxes lined one wall, all neatly stacked. There was a small toilet cubicle in one corner and next to it a sink. A single mug stood upturned on the draining board. Against another wall stood a table with two plastic chairs. The table was empty.

Moving through to the public part of the launderette, the pair of them had to adjust to the lack of light there. Switching on his torch, Franco took a moment to take in his surroundings. He noticed how neat and tidy everything looked: the cleanliness of the self-service machines and surfaces, the instructions for customers clearly posted on the walls, and the organisation of the public space into a seating area with coffee machine and coin dispenser and a folding area with carefully stacked baskets. Evidently Signora Montanari ran a very orderly business. Unless he was mistaken, she had left things in exactly the same way she would expect to find them when she arrived for work on Saturday morning.

Pointing to the shutters, he asked Giovanna "Do you think those are closed from the inside or outside?"

"Definitely from the outside," came the confident reply.

"That's what I think too. So, Signora Montanari closed shop herself before leaving on Friday. Or did someone else? See what you can find out Gio – make a few inquiries in the street. Did anyone see anything? Notice anything unusual? "

"Leave it to me, boss."

Franco had already briefed his deputy on the delicacy of the situation. He knew he could rely on her to make up a plausible story for her inquiries, without betraying her police identity. But sometimes *Commissario* Spina just couldn't help himself, he liked to be thorough.

"And be discreet, Gio! For now at least, we need to treat this as a very delicate situation. No police references – that's an order!" were his parting words to his deputy.

Giovanna nodded knowingly.

Later that afternoon, back at police headquarters, *Commissario* Spina spoke on the phone with the director of EasyWash Sicily, a Signora Lombardi. She confirmed that the email from Roberta had been very out of character. Signora Montanari was in the habit of giving her employer plenty notice before taking time off. Normally, she took a few weeks leave in the summer, and then again around Christmas time in order to visit her son in California. Signora Lombardi was not aware of any reason why Roberta should suddenly disappear like this. There were no problems or health issues that she was aware of. On the contrary, Signora Montanari loved her work. She ran the launderette single-handedly, and got on well with customers, locals and tourists alike. Franco listened. He was now more convinced than ever that the text message did not make any sense.

"Signora, tell me please in confidence, do you really believe that Signora Montanari has gone on holiday?"

Signora Lombardi replied without hesitation. "No, *commissario*. I think Roberta might be in some kind of trouble. Please, can you help?"

"We will do our best, Signora. Do you have any idea what kind of trouble that might be?"

Unfortunately, that question drew a blank. Instead, Signora Lombardi turned the conversation round to the challenge of finding a replacement for Roberta. Franco listened. The director sounded dejected, explaining that EasyWash would need to close down their Ortigia branch for the time being. Roberta Montanari was a highly valued launderette operator, a frequent recipient of the EasyWash employee of the month award. She would be very difficult to replace. And certainly not at short notice.

Franco had heard enough for now. "Signora, I give you my word. If Roberta Montanari is in trouble, we will do our utmost to find her. But for now, it is imperative that we observe discretion. After all we are both professionals. Can we please agree to go along with the text message – if anyone asks, Signora Montanari is on holiday." Just in time, he stopped short of adding 'that's an order!'

Signora Lombardi was gracious in her reply. "Thank you *Commissario* Spina. I understand the delicacy of the situation. You can count on my discretion.

Giovanna meanwhile had been busy.

Late afternoon, Franco summoned her to his office for an update. She reported back that the rather anxious looking woman in the photos they had been sent was indeed Roberta Montanari. All the photos that Giovanna had managed to look at confirmed this. The text message had been traced to Catania Airport, where it had been sent at 6am that morning using Roberta's phone. Giovanna doubted that the phone was still in Roberta's possession. But she had tried the number anyway – it was switched off.

These findings confirmed what Franco had already

hypothesised. There were no surprises in what he heard from his deputy. But Franco still liked to know when he was right. "Good work, Gio," he said. "Anything else to report?"

"There is one thing, boss. I went round to the address where Signora Montanari lives – one of the new flats near the city centre. And I spoke there with a neighbour."

"And what did the neighbour have to say for himself?"

"Actually, boss, it was a woman. A very large woman with lots of curly hair, by the name of Rosa Mangiafico."

"Mangiafico," repeated Franco, "where do I know that name from?" He beckoned Giovanna to continue.

She consulted her notes. "I told her I was an EasyWash rep and was looking for Roberta Montanari. Fortunately, this Rosa was pretty chatty. Told me she hadn't seen Roberta since yesterday morning."

"Friday morning?"

"Yes, boss. Except she didn't actually see Roberta then, she heard her leave. Apparently, Rosa heard Signora Montanari say goodbye to Lola."

"Lola?" Franco raised an eyebrow.

"Roberta's cat."

Franco disliked cats at the best of times. He did his best not to roll his eyes at the thought of someone actually speaking to one.

"She's a lovely, white fluffy cat! Spoilt rotten by the looks of things. Apparently when Roberta's not there Rosa looks after Lola – feeds her, plays with her, empties her litter – that sort of thing".

Franco was starting to feel exasperated. "What else did you find out?"

Giovanna smiled. "Rosa has a spare key for Roberta's apartment!"

Franco's ears pricked up. "Well done, Gio. And were

you able to get into the apartment?"

"Didn't even need to ask, boss. Rosa suggested we both take a look! Very, very tidy flat. Nothing looked out of place or tampered with, just like the launderette."

Franco nodded. "What about Roberta's passport?"

"Not easy, boss, with Rosa standing next to me most of the time!"

"Go on."

"I did make an excuse to use the toilet and managed a quick look around Roberta's bedroom, checked a few drawers. Let's just say, if her passport is in the flat, then it's not in an obvious place."

"And no sign of Roberta?"

Giovanna shook her head.

Franco took stock. Signora Montanari wasn't at the launderette, nor was she at home; there was no obvious sign of a break-in in either location. It was clear from the photos and from his conversation with EasyWash that they were dealing with a missing person investigation, possibly something more sinister, and a situation that required delicate handling. Added to which, time was of the essence. The World Series was starting soon. In fact, the opening game was scheduled for Sunday evening, US time or early Monday morning, European time. Tommaso Montanari had pointed out to him the best of seven rule – the bottom line being that the World Series could be all over by Thursday!

He could see that Giovanna was waiting for a response from him. "OK, Gio. Let's call it a day for now."

Next day was Sunday. Franco didn't consider himself a religious man. But he liked to keep Sunday special and always looked forward to Sundays as a day of calm. He liked to start the day with an orderly breakfast, sitting at his kitchen window watching the sea. Siracusa was not visible from here, hidden around the headland that twisted from his house around to the bay that separated Siracusa from the rural area where he lived. He would be heading towards the metropolis later. He wanted to take a look at a classic car rally that was taking place in Ortigia that weekend. But first things first – coffee. He carefully measured the freshly milled coffee beans into his state-of-the-art coffee machine and stretched contentedly, letting the aroma fill his senses. Within seconds the machine had pinged, letting him know that his double espresso was ready. He poured it into his beloved blue *'papà'* mug and wandered over to the kitchen table where an opened tin of his favourite biscotti biscuits was waiting for him. Dunking a biscotto into his mug, he gazed out to sea.

This was as close as he ever got to switching off from work. At times like this, he was happy to let his thoughts wander. But before long *Commissario* Spina found himself returning to the conversation he had had the previous day with the woman from EasyWash, Signora Lombardi. It had been a pleasant enough exchange. More than anything else, he had been struck with how openly she had talked about her employee, Roberta Montanari. It was clear that she valued Signora Montanari very highly. Franco wondered if he could talk as insightfully about the strengths of his own squad. In all honesty, with the exception of Giovanna, his trusted deputy, he might struggle to identify many strong points. Mesmerised by the incoming tide, clearly visible from his window, he let his mind wander again. This time, it came to rest on something of a stumbling block. Franco reminded himself of a staffing issue within his own squad that he really needed to resolve.

Detective Mikey Ricci had recently joined Franco's

squad, from Rome. His reputation had preceded him. The previous year in May there had been a big story among the police fraternity, involving the theft of a Sicilian masterpiece from a gallery near Palermo. Working undercover, on a cruise ship, Ricci had been key to the arrest of the art theft gang and, more importantly for many Sicilians, the safe retrieval of the painting. At the time, he had been feted as a hero in Sicily. Franco remembered well the press coverage and the banter among his colleagues, especially the more junior members of the squad. By the time Ricci arrived in Siracusa, 16 months later, the fuss had started to die down – thank goodness. The last thing *Commissario* Spina wanted was a superstar on his team. He expected everyone to pull their weight, no one was bigger than the team.

Nevertheless, Mikey Ricci's transfer to Siracusa had not been without its challenges for *Commissario* Spina, his line manager. The truth was that Franco was becoming increasingly frustrated with what he perceived as Ricci's lack of organisation and his rather chaotic lifestyle. So, up until now, he had tended to assign Ricci to minor cases. But there was a limit to the number of stolen cars that needed investigating.

What would Signora Lombardi do in my situation, mused Franco, recalling his phone call with the EasyWash director. In the world of EasyWash, it appeared that an ability to get on with people was an asset. Hadn't Signora Lombardi said as much herself? She'd certainly made it clear that Roberta's ability to get on with a wide range of clientele was what made her almost irreplaceable. No doubt Signora Lombardi and Ricci would get on like a house on fire, he thought, munching on a second biscotto.

He had to concede that Ricci certainly got on well with people. In fact, that was part of the problem. Ricci never seemed to get on with proper police work – too busy socialising, and not nearly enough attention to detail for Franco's liking. But was it possible that Franco's concerns about Ricci's approach to police work had blinded him to the younger man's undoubted strength – his ability to get on with people? It seemed that Ricci possessed precisely the sort of interpersonal skills that EasyWash were looking for.

BEEP! BEEP! An intermittent buzzing noise interrupted Franco's musings. He glanced at the notification on his smartwatch: just half an hour till the opening of the car rally in Ortigia.

He parked his car on the outskirts of Ortigia and walked the short distance to the rally. The main shopping street, Corso Matteotti, had been closed to through traffic. About twenty classic cars lined one side of the street. Franco immediately picked out a few that were of particular interest, including a 1988 Lamborghini Countach, gleaming scarlet in the Sicilian sun. Ever since he'd learnt to drive, he had dreamt of owning such a beauty.

The street was filling up with people. There seemed to be a good mix of locals and visitors, some were interested in looking at the cars, others were more intent on shopping and speaking with friends. Franco didn't speak to anyone, he didn't feel he needed to. Across the street from the cars, mingling with the car owners, he recognised a few familiar faces – fat cats all of them. No doubt they recognised him, too. They were known to Franco as loan sharks, extortionists and worse. Reminding himself that he was off duty today, he avoided eye contact with them.

For the best part of an hour he indulged his passion, admiring the workmanship on show, examining the cars from every possible angle, and taking a few well-crafted photographs of rare design details he had discovered. But he kept coming back to the Lamborghini, his idea of perfection on four wheels.

By 11.30am Corso Matteotti was packed. Franco escaped to the Lungomare, the road running next to the sea. It was quiet there save for the occasional tourist, ambling around the edge of the island. He had lunch in one of his favourite fish restaurants overlooking the bay. Then drove the short distance to a marina where he parked his car.

Picking up the occasional flat stone from the shore, he skimmed it masterfully across the surface of the water. He had learnt his skill as a boy, growing up in Southern Sicily and the satisfaction of watching a streak of seven or eight bounces had never left him. These days he found that the act of skimming stones helped him to focus. Thus he spent the best part of an hour mulling things over. He considered the case and his staffing dilemma from different points of view. They might just have four days to find Roberta Montanari.

Finally, just as the sun was starting to disappear from view, Franco was ready to head for home again. Time was now of the essence. But he was satisfied that he had found a way forward, a way of turning the Ricci situation to his advantage and perhaps even helping the investigation at the same time. *Commissario* Spina and his squad would find Roberta Montanari, the irreplaceable employee, and in exchange EasyWash would take on a substitute to run the Ortigia launderette – someone highly recommended by the *commissario* himself. That evening he started to put his plan into action so that the launderette could open again on Monday morning.

… MONDAY 23RD OCTOBER

CHAPTER 2

"*Ciao*, Mikey!" There was a tone of surprise in the barman's voice. "You're early today."

Mikey glanced at the bright orange-coloured clock on the wall and laughed. "Yes, 7 o'clock is early for me! I've got a long day ahead …"

Mikey walked towards the counter, aware that he and Antonino were the only people in this normally busy café. "The usual, please," he continued.

Antonino had already started to prepare the espresso. Mikey had been a customer for less than two months, but Antonino knew that Mikey always started the day in the same way.

"So, what have you got on, today?" asked Antonino, with a hint of a smile. That's progress, thought Mikey; perhaps Antonino's normally dour demeanour was starting to brighten up?

"I'm starting a new job," responded Mikey. "Over in Ortigia."

"Oh," said Antonino, as he placed the espresso on the gleaming counter. "In a hotel?"

Mikey picked up the espresso and downed it in one – so good! "No. I'll be my own boss – for a change!"

Antonino smiled broadly. "Being your own boss – that's not always a good thing!" He pointed to the empty cup. "Another one?"

"Not today," said Mikey, slapping some coins on the counter. "I'm late already. *Ciao*!" He dashed out of the door, almost bumping into a smartly dressed woman who would be Antonino's second customer of the day. Mikey didn't recognise her but guessed that she – like many others in this area of Siracusa – would be catching the early morning coach to Catania for work.

It still wasn't fully light when he jumped into his red Cinquecento, turned on the ignition and headed into the quiet streets of the city's Borgata district. Mikey was still getting used to the road layout in Siracusa. However, he and Totti – the name that Mikey had given to his car in honour of his favourite-ever AS Roma footballer – had been together a long, long time and Mikey felt instantly at home whenever he was behind the wheel of Totti. Looking towards the stadium where the local football team played, Mikey wondered whether he should start watching matches there. Then he glanced at his bracelet, decorated in the colours of his beloved team, and thought not; once a Roma supporter, always a Roma supporter!

Next on the route was the square named after Siracusa's patron saint: Santa Lucia. Mikey had visited the Basilica that dominated the square a few weeks earlier, not for religious reasons, but to look at Caravaggio's painting of Santa Lucia. A painting that Mikey had seen some time earlier, in another part of the city …

Mikey was still musing about his first visit to Siracusa

when he and Totti reached the bridge that connected the Sicilian mainland with the ancient part of the city: the island of Ortigia. The traffic was light, so he had time to glance at the statue of Archimedes, the Greek scientist who had tried – in vain – to protect his city from the Romans more than two millennia earlier. Mikey recalled hearing Archimedes' story from the enthusiastic and engaging American art historian whom he had met during that first trip. Well, thought Mikey, at least Romans seem to be more welcome here nowadays!

Once over the bridge, Mikey headed east, spotting vendors offloading from trucks the fruit, vegetables and other produce that would shortly be placed on display in Ortigia's vibrant daily market. He also saw crates of freshly caught fish and seafood being carried in the same direction. Normally Mikey would delight in the chance to wander around the market, wondering which of these delights he would choose for dinner back in Borgata. But not today, nor for the time being.

Mikey was running late. However, starting the day with an espresso had been an absolute must. And when he reached Belvedere San Giacomo, the view out to sea caused him to brake and turn around, before parking Totti next to the esplanade. He grabbed his camera from the boot, then raced to the railing, several metres above the lapping waters of the Ionian Sea.

This was a first for Mikey: the first time he had seen a Siracusan sunrise. Previously, he had either been in bed or in the bathroom carefully trimming his moustache when the sun rose. But, as October inched towards its conclusion, the days were slowly starting to shorten. Mikey noticed that the sea was relatively calm today, in contrast to the wild waves that had battered the seawalls in recent times. On the horizon, a band of orange was gradually widening, erasing the darkness above and lighting up a few small fishing boats bobbing on the water. Mikey clicked the camera shutter continuously as various shades of orange and yellow and sea started to fill the sky and then the full shape of the sun finally came into view. Glancing to his right, Mikey saw people gathered at a nearby look-out point, Forte Vigliena, enjoying nature's spectacular start to the day. A few joggers and power walkers had also stopped briefly a few feet from him, to take in this enticing scene.

Mikey pulled out his phone and checked the time: 07.20! He needed to get a move on. After throwing his camera back in the boot, Mikey leapt into Totti and sped off, just missing a car that was travelling in the same direction. Realising that he was now in a one-way street heading away from his destination, he checked the map on his phone and quickly worked out how to revise his route. A few minutes later he arrived in via Verona, a quiet side street. Fortunately, there was just enough space to park Totti between a silver 4x4 and a shiny blue Toyota. He sprung out of his car and headed towards a shuttered building. He removed a handwritten note *CLOSED UNTIL MONDAY MORNING* that had been stuck on front of the building, pulled out a set of keys, and opened the shutters. A short man with greying hair and a sullen expression was standing nearby with a large plastic bag of washing.

"*Buongiorno!*" said Mikey in a bright and breezy voice. He held out his hand as he approached the man. "Sorry for the delay. My name's Mikey!"

"*Giorno,*" murmured the man, who – rather than reciprocating Mikey's gesture – raised his hand to his mouth and took a long drag on his cigarette.

Hmmm, thought Mikey. This could be a difficult job.

A couple of hours later, Flavia arrived in via Verona. As soon as she turned into the street, she saw that something wasn't quite right. Normally Signora Montanari would have opened the launderette three hours earlier and the chairs would be out, a sign that she was ready to welcome customers. But that hadn't happened today. Maybe she's not opening today, wondered Flavia. Or maybe she overslept? Hope she's ok, thought Flavia. She liked Roberta. The two had been good friends ever since Flavia started using the launderette about three years ago, when she moved to Ortigia. She looked forward to their weekly chats.

She scooted down the street towards the launderette. Roberta's car was there in its usual space, neatly parked within the painted lines. The blue Toyota always looked in immaculate condition. It wasn't a flashy car, but Roberta looked after it well. This was in contrast to the rather bashed-looking red Fiat that was occupying Flavia's usual space opposite the launderette. Not great parking, she thought. She decided to leave her electric-powered scooter on the empty pavement outside the launderette for the time being – at least until she had loaded her washing. But she didn't dare leave it there much longer than that. She would need to move it. This was a bit of a nuisance as she had planned to spend the next hour in the launderette catching up with Roberta and taking advantage of the free Wi-Fi – she desperately needed to get on top of her overflowing email inbox. However, the police were pretty strict on illegal parking in this part of town, she didn't want to risk another fine. Not today.

Picking up her brightly coloured, retro-look laundry bag, she made her way towards the entrance to the launderette. There were two doors for customers to use. Normally both were wide open – no negotiation required. But today was different. Flavia tried to push the first door open, then the second. They didn't budge. Someone must have locked them, she thought. And it was difficult to see through the glass pane as both doors were steamed up. Putting her ear to the door, she could vaguely make out the familiar sound of the washing machines turning and churning. *Mamma mia!* What's going on in there, she thought, banging on the door with her fists. Has there been an accident? Is Roberta OK?

"Roberta! It's Flavia, open the door!"

"*Ciao*, Flavia! What's up?"

She turned to see white haired Luca Carusa, waving in her direction as he crossed the road to join her. Luca looked after the small art gallery on the other side of the street. Flavia was a regular customer; she took a keen interest in the exhibitions that he curated and – like him – was keen to do her best to support up and coming artists.

The pair embraced as friends. "*Ciao*, Luca! There's something strange going on ..." Flavia started to elaborate on the turn of events. However, she had not got very far when the launderette door that Luca had been leaning on was suddenly pulled open, causing him to lose his balance as he fell backwards. Fortunately, the brightly coloured laundry bag was there to break his fall and Flavia dived forward to help him to his feet again. However, the suddenness of her actions and the impact of heaving the man to his feet was too much of a strain on the fragile necklace she had been wearing. Snap! The necklace burst, releasing a sudden cascade of boldly coloured beads that bounced down onto the pavement and started to disappear down the street.

All thoughts of the launderette flew from her mind as

she frantically tried to recover the precious pieces. The beads meant everything to her, and it broke her heart to think she may lose even one of them. Each had been lovingly polished by hand from local Sicilian glass and pebbles, washed up on the shore. Each had been carefully chosen to go together in a stunning necklace, designed specifically to flatter the fuller figure. She ran after the trail of baubles down the street away from the launderette, paying particular attention to the gutters. Bending down she picked up what beads she could find and placed them in the pocket of her flowing dress.

So focused was she on retrieving her precious pieces that she didn't immediately notice the stranger standing next to her. It was only when she stood up to give her aching back a rest that she saw an outstretched hand offering her a small hoard of turquoise, green and white beads. Her eyes lit up when she saw them, and she raised her gaze to find out the identity of her good Samaritan. He was a bit taller than her but not by much. Dark curls framed his Latin face and his lips curved in a smile beneath a well-groomed moustache. She stood there transfixed. For a split second, time seemed to stand still. Then Flavia sensed that there was something behind the smile. She followed the direction of his gaze. So that's why he's smiling, she mused.

"*Grazie mille,*" she smiled back, nonchalantly removing a large stripy bead that had been lodged in her ample cleavage.

"My pleasure," he replied, looking her in the eye now and revealing the full extent of his smile. "Have you found all the beads that tried to escape?"

Flavia smiled at the image this conjured up. "It's fine, I think I've got most of them. But I need to get on with my laundry now. Thanks again for your help."

"Oh, you're going to the laundrette! I'm going there too!"

"Let's hope there are enough machines for both of us! Do you have much washing?"

"Actually, I'm working there. My name's Mikey."

"Nice to meet you, Mikey. You say you're working at the laundrette? Then you must know Roberta?"

"Actually, we haven't exactly met. She's on holiday at the moment and I'm deputising for her."

Flavia was confused. Why had Roberta not mentioned this to her last time they had met? And why had Roberta left her beloved Toyota parked at the laundrette? There seemed to be something very odd going on.

Now it was Monday afternoon. *Commissario* Spina stood looking out of his office window. The police headquarters were located in the centre of Siracusa. Below him the sprawling metropolis was slowly waking up again after the midday siesta. Deliberately ignoring this, Franco raised his eyes to the volcanic mountain, looming majestically on the horizon. On a day like this Etna was clearly visible to the north of the city, despite the 60 kilometres that separated them. Franco thought of his daughter who lived just a short bus ride away from the volcano, in downtown Catania. She would be making her way home from school about now. He sensed that Etna united the two of them. It was comforting to think that both of them might even be looking at Etna at that same moment in time. Although not a superstitious man, the sighting of Etna felt to him like a good omen. After the events of the weekend, he felt he could use a good omen.

He left the police headquarters and drove to the courthouse where he had been called to give evidence in a drug smuggling case. He enjoyed being behind the wheel and was glad to get away from the confines of his office. Leaving the main thoroughfare, he took a slight detour. He parked his beloved Alfa Romeo in the shade of a new block of apartments. This was where Signora Montanari lived. He looked up and nodded in approval. They hadn't done a bad job of the new building. Unlike some of the monstrosities elsewhere in the city, this block was just a few floors high. It formed an extended crescent shape that curved around a green area with benches and a small fountain. He liked the symmetrical shape and the distinctive red brickwork; and noted that the area was surprisingly quiet. He looked up at the walls of the apartment block and of surrounding buildings: no CCTV cameras. A pity, he thought.

Then he spotted a young man leaving the block, laden with rubbish bags. Franco jumped out of his car.

"Let me help you," he offered and opened the gate.

The young man gave a nod of appreciation.

Franco waited until the bags of rubbish had been deposited. "I'm looking for Roberta."

"Roberta Montanari?" asked the man.

Franco nodded.

"Don't think you'll find her here today. I heard she's on holiday. Lucky so and so! Probably gone to see Dani – her son."

Franco smiled. Word had spread quickly.

"I guess so," he replied. "Her son plays baseball in America, doesn't he?"

"That's right! Dani's team, the Bats, won the first game in the World Series last night." The man looked over his shoulder at the apartment block, then turned back towards Franco: "I don't want to mention it to my fiancée, not yet anyhow, but I've bet 1000 Euro on the Bats winning the World Series! They're favourites, so I didn't get great odds for the bet, but I'm certain they're going to win! I'll use the winnings for our honeymoon; we're hoping to go to the Maldives."

Franco nodded, then returned to his car and headed back to police headquarters.

Four hours later, the skies over Siracusa had turned dark. Mount Etna had long since disappeared from view and Franco was in evening mode. Unlike many of his compatriots, he had already eaten his final meal of the day and drunk his final coffee. He organised his desk for the following morning, checking that everything was lined up exactly where he wanted it to be: pen pot, calendar, photo of his daughter and clean coffee mug. Then he looked at the clock on his office wall – 8.30pm. Time to leave. He had a meeting ahead of him – in Ortigia.

It had been a long day. Mikey pulled down the shutters of the launderette and – having locked them – turned to look up via Verona. Through the darkness he saw a light coming from a bar at the top of the street, accompanied by the distant sound of chatter and laughter, but otherwise all was quiet. Crossing over to Totti, he noticed that the shiny Toyota he had parked next to that morning was still there, directly below a streetlight. He glanced inside and was struck by the lack of clutter. The only thing that stood out was a pair of sunglasses on the dashboard. Mikey walked on towards Totti, sat down in the driver's seat and turned on the ignition. A 90s hit tune on Radio Italia immediately filled the car and he sat back for a few seconds, letting the music ebb through his mind. Then he checked his phone: the message was succinct – *I'M WAITING*. Better get a move on, thought Mikey.

Totti sped out of via Verona and followed the Lungomare, along the seafront. This was the same road

Mikey had taken on his way to the launderette that morning, but now he was heading back towards the Sicilian mainland. Before he reached the bridge, he turned off into Talete, an underground car park close to the port. The car park was often used at weekends by visitors to Ortigia, wishing to avoid the restrictions on vehicle access to the oldest parts of the city. However, on this Monday evening in October, it was nearly deserted. Mikey parked Totti close to the entrance, then walked outside and up a slope onto the roof of the car park – a large open square, bordering the breakwaters that ran along the eastern side of Ortigia. Unlike the car park, with its strong lights and echoing concrete walls, the night-time darkness of the square and the crashing sound of the now-turbulent sea would make it easy to have a private conversation.

Mikey strode towards a seat close to the breakwater and sat down next to his boss. "*Ciao!*" said Mikey. *Commissario* Franco Spina, who had been gazing out to sea, turned to him. "Evening. What have you got for me, Ricci?"

Mikey had been fully aware since his arrival in Siracusa that Franco didn't indulge in small talk. In Rome, Mikey had often chatted about other things before getting down to business, which gave him more time to decide what to say. In his new job, however, he had to be fully prepared ahead of meetings with his boss. Easier said than done, though. Mikey had been wracking his brains shortly before leaving the launderette, wondering exactly what to say – and what not to say, too.

"It's been an interesting day," he started. "I hadn't realised how many people would use the launderette! And they're quite varied, too."

"In what way?" Franco rubbed his neatly finished goatee beard. Mikey looked carefully at the beard. Very good, he thought – maybe he should try one sometime? Or would it compete with his beloved moustache?

"Ricci?" Franco's voice brought Mikey back to the present.

"Yes, *dottore*. Well, as I was saying –"

"It's been an interesting day," Franco intervened. His expression had now turned quizzical.

"Indeed! Many different characters. A launderette is a really good place to speak with people. I mean, some of them just turn up, put their washing in the machine, disappear for half an hour or so, come back to collect their things and head straight off with a rushed '*Ciao*' at best! But many are happy to wait for their washing. Several people told me that the free Wi-Fi at the launderette is a big attraction. I was chatting with a student who's based at the Architecture Department here in the city. It's part of –"

"The University of Catania," interjected Franco. "It's an excellent university."

Mikey noted a tone of pride in Franco's voice; perhaps he had studied there too?

"Anyhow," continued Mikey, "this guy's a big baseball fan. He was wearing a Bakerside Bats shirt today and Dani Montanari is his absolute hero. He showed me this video of last night's game on his phone – the first match of the World Series."

"Ah," said Franco, "I hear that Dani's team won." The *commissario* said all the right words but Mikey could tell that he was uninterested.

"Yes, that's right. There was a fantastic finish to the game! The Bats' opponents, the Kentucky Kats looked as though they were going to win, but then Dani got their main batter out. His teammates went berserk!"

"How did Dani seem at the end of the match?" Franco

appeared more interested now.

"He was smiling, but I had the impression that –"

"The smile was forced, he didn't mean it?"

"Possibly," replied Mikey. "Hard to tell, but he seemed lower key than his teammates. To be honest, it was a brilliant catch by one of his colleagues that got the batter out."

"OK," said Franco. "Tell me more about who you met at the launderette."

"There were quite a few foreign tourists who are staying in Airbnb's. Americans, French, Britons. I spoke with a charming couple from ... now, where was it? Ah, yes, Scotland! They're regular visitors to Siracusa and have used the launderette frequently over the past few years. They'd often spoken with Roberta, usually to pass the time of day, although they didn't know her that well. But then ..."

YOWWWW!

Mikey turned to see a black cat a few metres away, screaming in a high pitch. Franco jumped up and raced towards the feline invader, shouting and shooing it away. The cat fled into the darkness.

"There are cats everywhere around here," lamented Franco, sitting back down again. "I do like Siracusa, but those cats –"

"Absolutely!" said Mikey, deciding that it was his turn to interrupt. "I can't stand them either. Give me a dog any day! Anyhow, back to the launderette. I met a lovely lady called Flavia. *Bella donna!* She lives nearby and is a regular customer. She knows Roberta Montanari well and was very surprised not to see her today. Flavia had passed by the launderette on Friday and stopped for a chat. Roberta had seemed fine then and there hadn't been any suggestion that she was going away. In fact, Flavia showed me Roberta's car, which was parked in its usual place just across the road. It's a blue Toyota."

Feeling proud of his foresight, Mikey recited the car registration to his boss, who entered the details into his phone. "That's highly useful, Ricci," said Franco. "Good work! We'll follow this up."

Putting his phone away, Franco continued. "This Flavia could be useful for the investigation. Gain her confidence, Ricci. We need her onside. Find out what you can but dissuade her from reporting Signora Montanari as a missing person – that's an order!"

"I'll do my best, *dottore*. She told me that she has a small jewellery shop just around the corner, in via Vicenza. If she doesn't drop by tomorrow, I'll nip out and visit the shop." Mikey chose not to say that he'd also like to find out more about Flavia.

"Anything else?" Franco glanced at his smartwatch, then at the raging sea, before turning back to face Mikey.

"Yes, Flavia introduced me to Signor Carusa – an elegant gentleman, he runs an art gallery in via Verona, just across the road from the launderette. We didn't speak long, so I'll try to have a longer chat with him tomorrow. Apart from that … oh yes, I saw a priest walking past a couple of times. He looked preoccupied."

"You're telling me that you saw a priest? This is Italy, Ricci! This is not news!"

Mikey gulped. "Of course, *dottore*. Of course. But there was something in his expression; he looked worried." Mikey didn't mention the priest's designer trainers, which had also caught his attention – *bellissime*! He knew that talking about shoes – even beautiful ones – might just tip his boss over the edge.

"OK, keep an eye out for anything strange," responded Franco. "We'll meet here at the same time tomorrow, but if anything comes up in the meantime, message me."

"Of course! How's the rest of the investigation going?" asked Mikey.

"Slowly. But we're going to solve this."

"Let's hope so. By the way, the student I spoke to today told me that Dani will be playing again tonight."

"Really!" Franco sounded interested again. "What time is the game?"

"It'll be in the middle of the night, our time. We'll know the result tomorrow morning."

Franco nodded slowly. "I wonder what will be going through the young guy's mind?"

Mikey stroked his moustache, then replied, "I'm sure he'll be thinking about his mother."

The two men stood up, said good night and walked back to their respective cars. Mikey took a moment to contemplate the old buildings ahead of him, lit up by streetlights. Who would have thought that in the 21st century, this ancient jewel of the Old World would be so closely connected to a sports spectacular in the heart of the New World? He slid back into Totti, relieved that the meeting hadn't gone too badly. He headed back to Borgata, seeking a snack then a good night's sleep.

TUESDAY 24TH OCTOBER

CHAPTER 3

Tuesday morning had started quietly at the launderette. After the first customer had loaded his washing and walked to the bar at the top of the street, Mikey was left on his own. He gazed at the washing machine as it turned around and around, with shirts, underwear and trousers slowly rising, then falling, before rising again. The effect was quite hypnotic. He must have had his eyes fixed on the machine for a couple of minutes or so before the trance was broken. "*Scusi! Scusi!*"

Mikey turned to see a lady, brightly dressed, possibly in her early 50s, waving at him from the other end of the launderette. "How can I get change, please?" she asked. Sounds like she's American, thought Mikey. He recalled the many accents he had heard every day in Rome, from the shiploads of tourists who passed through the city. Perhaps she's from New York?

Sure enough, when Mikey got talking to the lady – who introduced herself as Lauren – it turned out that she was from just outside New York, that she had moved to Siracusa a couple of years previously, that she loved her new home, that she **loved** the food here, that she didn't miss the freezing winter weather back in New York, that ...

As Lauren continued her life story, Mikey smiled and nodded whilst collecting her 10 Euro note and putting it into the change machine near the launderette's counter. CHING, CHING! The sound of the falling coins briefly interrupted Lauren's flow, before she resumed at the same rapid pace. After a few more minutes, during which she listed her favourite restaurants in Ortigia and which to avoid, Lauren loaded the washing machine next to the one Mikey had been gazing at earlier, shut the door, put in the money and pressed the 'go' button.

"I need to get to the market before all the best swordfish has gone! Great to speak with you, Mikey!" With that, Lauren waved, then trotted down via Verona.

Mikey shook his head. He had always thought of himself as being chatty, but Lauren had totally outshone him. Never mind, he had enjoyed listening to her and picking up some useful tips for eating places.

Standing at the door, he looked out into via Verona. As on the previous morning, he had parked Totti next to the blue Toyota. Mikey saw a traffic policeman walking slowly along the street, checking that vehicles had the permits needed for parking in this part of the city. Mikey had been given his permit when he had collected the keys for the launderette a couple of days earlier. He had also seen a permit on the windscreen of Roberta's Toyota, when he had passed by the car the previous evening. He watched as the policeman looked carefully at the exterior of the Toyota, then peered inside, before writing something in his notebook. This wasn't a routine inspection, in Mikey's opinion, but rather one instigated by Franco. Mikey turned to his left and looked across to Signor Carusa, who was standing at the door of his gallery. As they waved to each other, Mikey hoped that the traffic policeman's investigations weren't attracting undue attention.

"*Ciao*, Mikey!" Mikey recognised the young man ambling down the street towards him, proudly wearing his Bakerside Bats shirt. "*Ciao*, Marco!" he responded, as they clasped hands.

Marco was the architecture student that Mikey had told Franco about. Today Marco didn't have any washing with him; instead, he asked if he could use the Wi-Fi at the launderette. "Of course," responded Mikey, keen to discover more from this baseball devotee. "How did last night's game go?"

Marco grimaced. "Badly! I've heard the result, but I wanted to see the highlights." Stepping inside the launderette, Marco took out his phone and quickly navigated to a sports website. After a few seconds, both he and Mikey were transmitted from a sunny Sicilian morning to a dark, rainy evening in Kentucky.

Mikey was immediately struck by the noise. He was used to loud cheers – and groans – from his many visits to the Stadio Olympico in Rome, watching his beloved AS Roma. Nevertheless, the supporters in this baseball stadium were making a huge racket. And, although Mikey's knowledge of the game was patchy to say the least, the reasons for their cheers were obvious. The highlights showed a batter hitting a ball high into the sky and into the screaming crowd; then another batter doing the same; then another.

Marco shook his head. "I can't believe that the Kats are scoring so many runs! Dani is normally a very reliable pitcher; plus, he played well in the first match." Mikey saw a young man standing in the centre of the field, with his hands on his hips, wearing the same shirt as Marco. Mikey had seen photos of Dani in *La Gazzetta dello Sport*, whilst flicking through his favourite newspaper in search of the latest football news. However, this was the first time he had seen him playing. The body language wasn't good; Mikey could tell that Dani didn't want to be there. And Dani's coach didn't look happy either.

"Look," said Marco, pointing at the screen, "it's only the 4th innings and they're taking him off!" The highlights showed Dani walking disconsolately to the bench, as one of his teammates took over as pitcher.

"Is that unusual?" asked Mikey. "To be substituted in a game?"

"No, it isn't. In fact, all teams replace their starting pitcher towards the end, and bring on a relief pitcher, a fresher player who can close out the game. Each team has nine innings in a game and the starting pitcher is normally replaced after the 6th or 7th innings. But Dani was taken off in the 4th innings! I can understand why the Bats did that, though. Dani conceded two Grand Slams!"

Mikey looked at Marco, perplexed. Grand Slam? Is that something to do with tennis, he thought.

"Ah, sorry, I should have explained," continued Marco, who then rewound the video and pointed to the screen. "In baseball there are four bases; first, second, third bases, plus the home plate. They're shaped like a diamond." Marco pointed to their positions. "You can see that the Kentucky Kats had a player on each of first, second and third bases. This was a really dangerous situation for Bakerside, because all of these Kats would score a run if they could get back to the home plate. And that's just what happened." Marco restarted the video, showing Dani pitching to the Kats player standing on the home plate. Mikey was a baseball novice, but he fully appreciated the batter's strength and timing as the ball flew like a rocket into the night sky and dropped into the middle of the elated Kentucky crowd.

"So," said Marco, "the batter got a home run and ran around the bases unopposed. Not only that, but his teammates on the other bases all made it home too. That's a Grand Slam – four runs from just one strike of the baseball! It's one of the reasons I love the sport; games can turn around so quickly."

Mikey nodded. He wasn't sure he understood the game fully, but he had a better idea now. "Did the Bats do better after Dani was taken off?"

Marco forwarded the video towards the end of the highlights. "Not much," he replied. "We were already losing by 9 runs to 1 when Dani was replaced. It ended up 10 to 3. We weren't likely to get back into the game after such a poor start, but at least it didn't get any worse."

Mikey was momentarily distracted by the return of the first customer, who walked past and opened the washing machine that had previously captured Mikey's attention. Now, however, he wanted to speak more with Marco. "So, both teams have won one game now. What happens next?"

"There's a break today. Both teams will travel to Bakerside and they'll play there on each of the following three days: Wednesday, Thursday and Friday. During the night, our time."

"Will they play any more games in Kentucky?"

"Possibly. It depends on how the next three games go. To win the World Series, you need to win four games out of a possible seven. If neither team wins all the next three games, then they'll return to Kentucky and play there on

Sunday."

"Will that be the final match?" asked Mikey.

"It depends. If the score is 3-3 after that, then the deciding match will take place in Kentucky next Monday night. But I'm hoping that it won't come to that! We'll have home advantage for the next three games. If we win them all, then we'll win the World Series!"

Mikey turned his head slightly towards the customer, who was standing a couple of metres away, holding his full laundry bag but showing no inclination to leave. Maybe he's interested in this conversation, thought Mikey. However, before he could ask the customer whether he was a fan of baseball, the man pulled out his phone and started scrolling down the screen.

Mikey turned back to Marco. "What about Dani?" he asked. "Will he play in these matches?"

"Perhaps," responded Marco. "During the World Series, teams rotate the starting pitcher, so the Bats will probably use someone else in this role for the next game or two. However, Dani might be brought on as a relief pitcher – and I'm sure that by Friday he'll be back as starting pitcher! I know last night was bad, but Dani's played so well this season; we really need him. It would be wonderful for Signora Montanari to see Dani winning the World Series for the Bats! I've been coming to this launderette since the start of September, when I started my studies, and the signora is always telling me how proud she is of Dani. She's a lovely lady. I guess she's out in the US at the moment?"

Out of the corner of his eye, Mikey realised that the customer was still standing in the same position, looking at the screen of his phone.

Mikey replied, "I guess so. She's definitely on holiday."

Marco's phone beeped. "Sorry, I've got a lecture in 10

minutes! It's been great chatting with you." A quick handshake with Mikey and then Marco strode briskly up the street. At the same time, the customer silently exited the launderette and walked in the opposite direction.

Mikey sighed. Friday, he thought. The World Series could all be over by Friday – and this is Tuesday. He would have to ring Franco and let him know. He imagined how his boss would react when he heard the news: Signora Montanari had to be found before the end of the World Series and Mikey needed to find some leads – asap!

Franco glanced at his watch: 12.30. Thirty minutes to lunch. Not 20 minutes, not 40. No, unless he was out on a case, lunch was always at 1 pm. He didn't have a large lunch whilst on duty: perhaps a small pasta dish or just a *panino*, enough to tide him over until the evening. Franco would have to leave his office in 10 minutes' time, so he had the opportunity to reflect on the call he had just received from Ricci.

To be honest, he hadn't taken in all the details that Ricci had blurted out. Franco had tried to convince Ricci to slow down, but he seemed to be in a rush; something about an American woman returning to the launderette and needing to finish the call before then. However, there were a few key points that Franco had taken in: that Dani's team had lost last night and that Dani hadn't played well; that Dani probably wouldn't be playing a major role in the next couple of matches; but that Dani would likely be centre-stage on Friday evening – and that this could be the final match. So, there might only be three days left to find Signora Montanari and free her. Franco felt sympathy for the kid; he didn't envy his predicament.

Franco had instructed his deputy, Giovanna, first thing that morning to conduct further inquiries in the area around the launderette. They had arranged to meet to discuss progress over lunch. He would have been happy to give her a lift to the trattoria, but she had texted earlier to say she would meet him there. Franco wasn't totally surprised; Giovanna often went for a run around the middle of the day. However, reaching this particular location would represent a serious work-out.

Another check of his watch: 12.40. Franco pulled on his tailored jacket and headed out of the office. Within a couple of minutes he was sat in his beloved Alfa Romeo, taking a moment to run his hands over the leather steering wheel: he enjoyed the feel of the leather. Then he fired the car into life and headed out onto the busy roads of the modern centre of the city.

As he waited at traffic lights just outside the police headquarters, Franco tried to shut out the toots from cars queued behind him, whose occupants – like himself – were keen to sit down for lunch asap. He surveyed the scene outside: people filing out of shops shortly before they closed at 1pm and putting on sunglasses to reduce the glare from the Mediterranean sun that – even at this time of year – could still be strong. Franco glanced at the multitude of posters stretching along the side of the street, proclaiming the virtues of candidates for the council elections taking place in a few weeks' time. His gaze fixed on the smiling face of a bald-headed man in his early 50s: Alfonso Bellotto. The owner of Bellotto Construction, the company responsible for many of the developments that had gone up in and around the city in the past 10 years. A wealthy man who was now entering politics, singing the praises of the popularist far-right party which wanted to make Italy great again – principally by expelling refugees and demonising anyone not deemed to be patriotic. Franco shook his head; Bellotto and others in the party never mentioned the name Mussolini, but Franco had no doubt as to who had inspired their policies.

The lights turned green. Franco turned away from the main thoroughfare and headed uphill. Within a couple of minutes, he had left behind the hustle and bustle of the city and was driving past the scrubland and white rocks that made up much of the countryside in this part of Sicily. As he neared the top of the hill, he saw a sign to the right that he had passed many times in the past: *CASTELLO EURIALO*. Franco had, on several occasions, thought about visiting the ruins of this castle, constructed by the Greeks when they had ruled the island 2400 years previously. According to legend, Archimedes had placed a giant mirror here in 213 BC and shone it down on the Roman ships that were attacking the city, setting the ships on fire. Franco smiled; he could do with Archimedes' mirror now, to shine some light on this investigation. But a visit to the castle would need to wait for another day.

The surroundings changed once more, as Franco's Alfa Romeo entered Belvedere, a suburb of Siracusa. Most of the buildings here were relatively modern; many were the homes of workers at the large petrochemical complex spread along the coastline to the north of the city. The suburb was also close to the *autostrada* that Franco used frequently; both heading northwards to see his daughter in Catania, and southwards to visit his parents and brother, who lived near the ferry port at Pozzallo. Belvedere also had the advantage – in Franco's view – of being quiet and free of tourists, in marked contrast to Ortigia and the surrounding area. He reflected on the frequent traffic jams encountered on the daily commute from his home on the coast just to the south of the city; perhaps Belvedere would be a better place to base himself?

Franco switched his attention towards finding a parking space in the main street, close to Trattoria Gelone. He was in luck; there was a space just outside the entrance. Before getting out of the car, he checked his phone and read the text that had come in a few minutes earlier: *I'M HERE*. He smiled once more; if only everyone could be as reliable as Giovanna.

On entering the trattoria, Franco looked first at the clock on the wall: 1 pm, on the dot. Then, he smiled at the waiter, Davide, who in turn pointed to a table next to the window of the otherwise-quiet dining room. Sat there, dressed in a light-blue tracksuit and sipping a glass of mineral water, was Giovanna, who greeted Franco with a smile as he approached and sat down next to her.

"*Ciao!*" said Franco. "It must have taken you some time to get here!"

Giovanna laughed. "Well, it was about an hour, but I really enjoyed it! There were some great views down towards Ortigia and the Porto Grande as I neared Belvedere. Plus, I didn't have time for a run this morning, so it was good to fit this in."

Franco recalled the stunning views down to the large sheltered area of water next to Ortigia from his previous visits to Belvedere. Another reason to live here, he wondered. But immediately he shifted his focus. "*Siracusana*," he said, turning towards Davide, "and mineral water – with gas." "Same for me," added Giovanna. Davide nodded and headed to the kitchen, unsurprised that Franco had requested his favourite pasta dish.

"So, what have you got me for, Gio?" Franco turned his attention back to his trusted colleague.

"A mixed bag, really. I checked via Verona and the surrounding streets this morning. I spoke with the traffic cop who I'd asked to inspect Signora Montanari's car. Nothing strange that he could see on the car's exterior or inside the car. I did wonder whether there's anything of interest in the boot; I might check that out tonight, when things are quieter."

"Yes," said Franco, "but be discreet. Wait until it's dark."

"Of course, boss. I also popped into the art gallery opposite the launderette and had a chat with the owner, Signor Carusa. He seemed a nice guy. I think he thought I was a potential customer! In fact, I had the impression that he was very keen to sell anything, even a very small picture."

"Does he have financial problems?" Franco had taken off his jacket and was sat, elbows on the table and hands under his chin, looking intently at Giovanna.

"Yes. He didn't say anything, but I checked his accounts when I got back to the office. The gallery's had significant cashflow problems for the past couple of years. Seems like they're only just getting by."

"Hmm", responded Franco. He wondered if Carusa might have turned to gambling to raise extra funds. Or might he have been willing to pass on information about Signora Montanari's movements in and around the launderette to someone offering a lot of money? "Carusa is a potential lead," said Franco. "Ricci will be speaking with him and try to find out more. Anything else from you, Gio?"

"You remember there was a lane running along the side of the launderette? That's how we reached the back door on Saturday. Well, I thought I would check it out, in case –"

"There was something we missed there?"

Giovanna smiled, she was used to Franco finishing her

sentences. "Indeed. Well, there did seem to be something. About five metres into the lane, I spotted a short red line on the wall. Difficult to be sure, but it could be –"

"Blood!"

"Maybe. I tried to take a sample from the wall, but it might not be enough for Forensics to use."

"It's worth trying. Anything else?"

Giovanna sipped from the glass of mineral water in front of her, before responding. "Yes, boss, there's something else. I went into the bar at the top of via Verona. I overheard an elderly man chatting with the barman. Incidentally, they do great coffee there!"

Franco raised his eyebrows but said nothing.

Giovanna continued. "The man lives in a flat towards the bottom of via Verona. He had been watching football on the TV on Friday evening and had gone to the kitchen to get a drink when he heard a noise outside; this would have been shortly after 8pm. When he looked out, the middle of the street – between his flat and the bar – was in darkness. He had gone back to his living room to watch the second half of the match and hadn't thought much more about it. However, when he happened to look out from his flat on Saturday evening, the streetlight was back on. The guy was impressed that it had been repaired so quickly."

"*Siracusana!*" Davide's arrival with two delicious-looking plates of spaghetti, aubergine, tomatoes and anchovies immediately captured both Franco's and Giovanna's attention.

"*Buonissimo!*" Franco smiled broadly at Davide. This dish was an absolute winner in Franco's eyes, particularly at Trattoria Gelone. Giovanna smelt her dish. "Lovely!" she said. Then, twisting her fork into the dish, she continued her story.

"After I left the bar, I rang the council and asked about the streetlight in via Verona. They had received a report of a broken light, and when they visited on Saturday to repair it, they found that the light had been vandalised."

Franco swallowed a beautiful combination of pasta and anchovies, then responded. "Sounds as if someone wanted that light out on Friday evening."

"Indeed. One more thing, boss. I was flicking through the newspaper this morning and I came across a photo of Rosa Mangiafico. She had been at a dinner of local dignitaries a few nights ago."

"Why would she have been there?"

Giovanna turned and pointed out the window. "She was arm-in-arm with him!"

Franco looked at the smiling face on an election poster on the other side of the street. "Alfonso Bellotto," he murmured. He took a deep breath. This case was getting complicated.

CHAPTER 4

"*Ciao, ciao,* mamma!" Flavia switched off her phone and placed it on the counter. She was sitting behind the glass counter in her small shop, gazing at the street ahead of her. She had opened the shop here two years previously, specialising in handmade jewellery, using her own designs and natural Sicilian materials. She relied on tourists to keep her solvent, wealthy tourists who didn't mind spending triple figures on a trinket or two to remind them of *la bella Sicilia* and at the same time support local traditions and the local economy. So far, so good – at least she was managing to make ends meet.

It was well past 4pm, her 'official' opening time, but she was in no rush to open up again after the lunch break. She popped the last bit of a large *cannolo* she'd bought for lunch into her mouth and munched away contentedly, savouring every last taste of ricotta and pistachio. She swept her tongue around her teeth, making sure that she didn't miss a single morsel of the sweet delicacy. Her eyes were glued on the dark, curly haired individual lurking outside her shop window. She'd been watching him now for about ten minutes. If she wasn't mistaken it was the guy from the launderette – the one who was covering for Roberta. But what was his name again? She had a feeling it began with 'M'.

She smiled, remembering how he had helped her with her 'escaping beads' the previous morning. Mind you, he had looked a bit out of his depth afterwards in the launderette. 'Clueless' was the word that came to mind. She, and other customers, had needed to show him how to load the machines, explain about the tokens needed etc. etc.

And now he was standing outside her shop window. Business was just starting to pick up after the lunch break and via Vicenza was coming to life again. The supermarket opposite was now attracting a stream of customers and there was a short queue, mainly tourists, outside the ice-cream hatch. She watched as a small group of them stopped outside her shop window, right next to the dark, curly haired launderette operator. Consulting a map, they took a long time to make up their minds before crossing the road and heading in the direction of the church. He seemed oblivious to them and to other pedestrians who had to step off the narrow pavement into the oncoming traffic in order to get past him. Flavia wondered what he was doing there. Shouldn't he be in the launderette? Roberta never used to take a lunch break. Maybe this meant that she was back from her holiday? Or maybe, just maybe, he had come to see her? In any case, he seemed to be admiring her work. She watched his face as he gazed at the jewellery on display in her window. She decided she liked the look of him.

She nipped to the mirror to check her hair. Flavia was

blessed with long, dark hair and she looked after it well. It was lustrous. When she wore her hair up, like today, she preferred it to look casual – nothing too stylised. Effortless chic that was her mantra. Satisfied with the way she looked, she took a couple of deep breaths then flounced to the front of the shop in her boldly coloured orange dress. She opened up the door and there he stood, bathed in sunshine, facing her.

"*Ciao*, Flavia!"

"*Ciao!*" she replied, holding the door wide open. Then, smiling broadly: "Please come in."

He didn't need to be asked twice.

"How are things at the launderette? ..." she started confidently but then stumbled, embarrassed that he had remembered her name but she still couldn't remember his.

"It's Mikey!" he said, with outstretched hand, "nice to see you again."

Flavia wasn't normally big on shaking hands, but on this occasion she made an exception. She had forgotten how charming he was.

"And things at the launderette are progressing very nicely, thanks for asking. Never a dull moment!"

Wow! Great set of teeth, thought Flavia. "Is Roberta still on holiday?" she asked.

"That's right. She's not expected back for another two weeks at least."

Flavia was taken aback.

He quickly picked up on this. "Does that surprise you?"

"It's just strange that she never mentioned it to us. It's not unusual for Roberta to take weeks off. Normally she spends her holidays in the US with Dani – that's her son. He's a big baseball player. Maybe she's gone to spend some time with him, watch the World Series perhaps? But why did she go without telling anyone? That's what I don't get!"

She looked at Mikey, he was listening attentively. He told her about the text message from Roberta.

"That reminds me," added Flavia, "why has she switched her phone off? I tried to message her this morning and the line was dead."

Mikey nodded sympathetically.

Flavia was now in full flow. "And another thing, is her car still outside the launderette? I mean who leaves their car at work when they go on holiday?"

But instead of engaging with her questions, as she had hoped, Mikey changed tack.

"Look, Flavia, maybe you can help me please? Signora Montanari has done me a big favour. I haven't done a job like this for a long time and I'm loving it. Normally I'm stuck in an EasyWash office back in Catania. I want to buy a piece of jewellery for her – as a sort of thank you for helping me out."

For the second time that afternoon, Flavia was taken aback. Somehow she couldn't see Mikey in an office job. She had him down as more of a free spirit, more like herself.

Suddenly, the ring of the front door opening jolted her back to the present. She just had time to turn round and see who it was before they left again – in a rush.

Flavia moved over to the window and looked out. She immediately recognised the identity of the mystery caller. "That was my friend, Enzo – Don Enzo," she said, then returned to the counter where Mikey was still standing.

"Did you order a pizza?" he smirked.

Flavia was impressed how quickly he had made a link to the local Pizzeria, also called Don Enzo. But she wasn't quite sure if he was being serious or if this was an attempt at humour. She decided to humour him.

"Not that Don Enzo!" she smiled. "Actually, it's Don Enzo Calu. He's the parish priest."

"Sorry," said Mikey sheepishly. "Why didn't he come in?"

Flavia came straight to the point, "Probably because of you!" then winked.

Mikey seemed interested in her friend. "I think I may have seen Don Enzo before. Likes to wear brightly coloured shoes? Quite unusual for a priest?"

"That's Enzo all right. It's true that he's quite flamboyant for a priest. I guess it's part of his culture, he was brought up in Nigeria – East Nigeria. His Igbo name is Eze but he changed it to Enzo when he was ordained in Italy."

She still had Mikey's attention. "So, where did you see him before?" she asked.

"Oh, just passing by the launderette – a couple of times."

Flavia smiled. "Enzo is a great walker, walks for hours every day – says it's good for the soul!"

"Looked to me like he had things on his mind," said Mikey, looking at her more intently now.

Out of loyalty to her priest friend, Flavia didn't want to give too much away. On the other hand, however, she sensed the eagerness in Mikey's eyes and didn't want to let him down. "The truth is that Enzo hasn't got an easy job. It's no secret that the parish has lost a lot of money, in fact it's quite heavily in debt. There have been rumours going around that Enzo should have been more careful."

"Oh, in what way should he have been more careful?"

"I don't really know, Mikey. I'm not a practising Catholic, I cannot judge the guy. I like him, he's fun. And he has a heart of gold. Besides which, I have a lot of sympathy for anyone who struggles with bookkeeping. There are more important things in life than making sure the sums add up!"

Flavia could feel her heart beating faster. She was getting worked up. All that talk of keeping the books was rather close to home. Time to change the subject.

"So, Mikey, you said you were looking for a piece of jewellery ..."

"Eh, yes. I would like to buy something for Roberta. Problem is I've never met her. But you know her well. What's she like?"

Flavia wondered where to start, there were so many things she could say about her friend – all of them good. She told Mikey about Roberta's love of cats, how she always saw the best in people, loved talking to people, made people feel good about themselves.

"Does she have any enemies?" interjected Mikey.

Hell's bells, thought Flavia, that's an **odd** question. She realised that she'd never actually considered before that Roberta might have enemies. It just didn't bear thinking about. Why would anyone wish ill of the warmest, kindest, friendliest of women?

The truth was that she didn't know a huge amount about Roberta's private life. Except that she doted on her son, but everyone knew that.

"Sorry Flavia, that was a mean question," Mikey again. "It's just that no one seems to have a bad word to say about Roberta. She seems to be healthy, enjoys her work. I'm just trying to figure out what makes her tick – so I can get an idea of what kind of jewellery she might like."

Flavia's mind went into overdrive, desperate to oblige Mikey with a piece of new information about Roberta. "Hang on a minute," she blurted, "Roberta does have a health condition."

"A serious health condition?"

"Come to think of it, yes – it is serious. It can be life threatening."

"Life-threatening?"

She watched Mikey gulp.

"Yes, but as long as she takes her medicines she's fine. I just hope she's taken enough with her. Usually she needs to get an extra supply from the doctor before travelling."

"Medicines?"

"Roberta has a rare form of epilepsy," Flavia explained. "She never complains about it, and it's been a couple of years since she last had a seizure. Since then she has been using an app on her phone to remind her when to take her medicines. Oh my God!" Flavia froze for a horror stricken second. "But her phone is switched off ..." she gasped.

The words had barely left her mouth when, without any warning, Mikey raced to the door of the shop.

"Sorry, got to dash!" he shouted back, jumping out into the street, leaving the door wide open behind him and a very confused Flavia wondering what on earth was going on.

Seconds later his cheeky face appeared again momentarily, just peeking through the open door. It looked like he was literally bending over backwards to tell her something.

"Gotta make a phone call," he panted, before disappearing again.

CLANG! The sound of the shutters hitting the ground reverberated along via Verona. The street was quiet and darkness had descended. Mikey looked towards a block of flats at the bottom of the street and wondered if the noise had disturbed the residents. If so, perhaps they heard Signora Montanari closing the shutters the previous

Friday? On the other hand, they might be so used to hearing this noise around 8 pm every evening that it hadn't registered with them. Aside from the distinctive sound of the start of the TV news on Raiuno drifting out from one or two flats, the street was now quiet.

Mikey checked his phone. No new messages, thankfully. He had had a short phone call with Franco shortly after leaving the jewellery shop. Franco had seemed interested in the information about Signora Montanari's medicines, but he had kept the call short and said that they would speak further when they met later: 8.45 pm, same place as before. 8.45 pm? Mikey was glad that Franco hadn't seen the bemused look on his face when he heard that. To a Roman, 8.45 pm, 8.30 pm and 8.15 pm all had the same meaning: around 8pm. Or even just: sometime this evening. Before he had started this job, Mikey had imagined that time would be even more flexible in Sicily than it was in Rome. But *Forense*, to use the nickname that Mikey's colleagues gave to their boss (although obviously not in his presence), had a very different mindset from most Sicilians. Detail and accuracy were vitally important to the *commissario*. When he said 8.45 pm, he really did mean 8.45 pm. And woe betide anyone who didn't understand this.

Mikey had a bit of time to spare before his meeting with Franco, so – rather than crossing the street to Totti – he started to stroll up via Verona. He had been mulling over his meeting with Flavia and wondered if he should pop back, to apologise properly for his rapid exit earlier. However, the shop would be closed now; best to do this tomorrow, he thought. Looking across to the art gallery, he saw that this too was closed. Mikey would have liked to have spoken further with Signor Carusa, but it had been a busy day in the launderette. Well, sort of busy.

Especially with Lauren; that lady can really talk! He hadn't minded chatting with her, but he was hoping that she wouldn't be around tomorrow. Lauren had told him that she didn't know Roberta well. Ideally, he would prefer to spend more time with people who knew Roberta better and try to identify potential witnesses or suspects.

When he reached the top of via Verona, Mikey swithered about popping into the bar there; the lit sign "Bar Stella" and laughter inside sounded inviting. However, his interest was piqued by something that had happened that afternoon. So, instead, he turned left into via Vicenza, passing a tourist information office, until he reached Flavia's place, which was now in darkness. Looking to his right, he saw the entrance to a narrow side street, marked with a sign: via Brescia. He recognised this as the street into which Don Enzo had raced after leaving Flavia's shop. Time to investigate, he thought.

Mikey started walking up via Brescia. After a few metres, he became aware of voices ahead of him. He continued, passing some anonymous darkened buildings, before spotting lights from a building ahead on his left. A small group of young men were just coming out of the building and walking towards him. They were deep in conversation, in a language that Mikey didn't recognise. As they passed by, Mikey noted the state of their clothes; even under streetlights, he could see that their jackets were covered with dust and grime. They look like workmen, he thought.

Mikey reached the building from which the men had come; it was a church. Outside there was a sign: *SAN VALENTINO*. He smiled: he hadn't come across many churches named after the saint of love. The door was open and he looked inside. Stepping through the door, Mikey was immediately struck by the height of the ceiling; it must have been the height of a two-storey building. The soft lights on the walls revealed the outlines of a few faded frescos; otherwise, the interior was sparsely decorated. There were none of the ornate Baroque fittings that were a feature of many churches in Sicily. This was a much simpler place of worship, with a cross and a painting of the Madonna at the far end.

WOOF! Mikey turned to see a long-legged, brownish-coloured dog racing towards him from the back of the church. WOOF, WOOF! The dog put its paws on Mikey, clearly excited.

"Rocco! Down, boy! ROCCO!"

The dog turned and ran towards the man who was approaching Mikey. Mikey smiled, then held out his hand. "*Ciao!* I'm Mikey."

"Nice to meet you, Mikey. I'm Don Enzo, the priest of this parish." As they shook hands, Mikey was impressed by the priest's strong handshake. Don Enzo was a big guy: at least 1.75m tall and well-built.

"You're the guy who's running the launderette at the moment, aren't you?" asked the priest.

"That's right." Mikey was impressed; he had thought that Don Enzo hadn't spotted him when he had passed the launderette the previous day. Either that, or Flavia had told him who he was.

"I'm sorry that we didn't have a chance to speak this afternoon," continued Don Enzo. "I had gone to speak with Flavia but hadn't realised that she had company."

"No problem! Is everything OK?"

"Eh, yes, nothing really. Just the usual issues trying to maintain a building that's 700 years old whilst bringing the Word of the Lord to the people. And keeping the bishop happy too!" Don Enzo gave a half-laugh, although Mikey thought it sounded forced. "Sorry, I should have introduced you to Rocco!"

Mikey bent down and stroked the dog affectionately. "He's lovely! What's his breed?"

"He's a mongrel; I got him from the dog rescue. Rocco's my best friend! We're always together."

"Even during your services?"

Don Enzo gave a deep laugh; this one sounded real, thought Mikey. "Yes," said Don Enzo, "even then. Mind you, he can be noisy during my sermons, particularly if I go on too long. But at least that keeps the congregation awake!"

"Does Signora Montanari come to your church?" asked Mikey.

Don Enzo bent down and rubbed Rocco's head, then responded: "No, she doesn't, but I often have a word with her when I'm passing the launderette. She's a lovely lady. She often talks about her son in America. Is that where she's gone?"

Mikey paused before replying: "Maybe. All I know is that she's currently on holiday. I'm looking after the launderette for a couple of weeks, until she comes back."

"Well," said Don Enzo, "let's hope that her son finds his form again soon. He's playing baseball in the World Series. I hear that he had a poor game last night."

Mikey's ears pricked up. "Are you a fan of baseball?"

"Not really," replied the priest. "I get the sports headlines through an app on my phone. Football is my real passion. I'm a big fan of Inter: they had some great players from Nigeria in their team when I was young: Martins, West, Kanu. My first job after ordination was in Milan, and I would often go to Inter's matches when I was living there."

"Do you prefer Sicily to the north?" asked Mikey, wondering why the priest had moved away from Milan.

"In some ways, yes. I like the slower pace of life here. It's quieter, too. But trying to keep a church going – particularly one as old as this – with limited resources isn't easy."

Mikey looked down; Rocco was licking the priest's designer shoes, but the priest didn't appear to notice. Mikey was going to ask Don Enzo about the men who had left the church earlier when Rocco suddenly raced to the side of the church, barking. He stopped at what appeared to be the top of some steep steps. Don Enzo raced over and stopped the dog before it could head downstairs. "Calm down, Rocco. Calm down!"

Mikey joined them and saw that the steps led to the church's crypt. "Is there anyone down there?" he asked. Don Enzo's eyes widened and his mouth dropped: "Oh no, no-one at all. Rocco just imagines things sometimes." Then, he turned to his dog. "Come on, Rocco, I've got a nice piece of fish for you."

From down in the crypt, Mikey thought he heard a muffled sound. Was that a voice, he wondered. Just at that moment, he felt his phone vibrate. He pulled it out and groaned. The time: 8.45pm. The message: "WHERE ARE YOU?"

"It was good to meet you, Don Enzo. Sorry, but I need to dash. Be sure to pop into EasyWash next time you're passing. *Buona notte!*" With that, Mikey raced out into night-time air and sped towards Totti.

WEDNESDAY 25TH OCTOBER

CHAPTER 5

The sunrise on the Eastern side of Ortigia was spectacular. This was Flavia's favourite part of her jog around the island. Admittedly the Western side, overlooking the bay with its marina and luxury yachts was very attractive. But she preferred the freedom of the open sea, the waves, the rocks, the occasional small fishing boat and if you were lucky a glimpse of Etna in the distance. It was still a bit early for Etna today. Resplendent in fuchsia pink Lycra, Flavia climbed the sandstone steps of Forte Vigliena and paused there to put on her dark sunglasses as she looked out over the water. She was reminded of her favourite Monet painting, so strong was the sun, illuminating the heavens for miles around with bold brushstrokes of gold and red and its shimmering reflection on the sea below. She watched the silhouette of two local fishermen rowing out to sea in a tiny, wooden boat. It felt very peaceful. Just what she needed before the start of her working day.

So deep was she in peaceful contemplation that she

didn't hear anyone come up behind her. The first thing she knew was the sensation of a panting, warm tongue greedily licking her hand.

Then she heard a familiar rebuke. "Rocco!" She turned to see Don Enzo who had just reached the top of the steps, quite out of breath.

"*Buongiorno!*" beamed Flavia, as much for Rocco's benefit as for his master. She patted the dog and waited for Don Enzo to join them at the viewing platform.

"Morning Flavia," he said, wearily.

Flavia frequently met Don Enzo and Rocco, out for their first walk of the day, when she was out for her twice weekly jog around the island. In fact, that was how they had first met almost two years ago. They often stopped for a chat. She enjoyed his laid-back approach to life and his generous nature. Nothing seemed to bother him. Until recently that is …

Flavia recalled Enzo's visit to the boutique the previous afternoon. She had called him afterwards. Not for the first time, he had told her about his dilemma. And not for the first time, Flavia had felt quite helpless. She dearly wanted to help her friend but just didn't know how – apart from listening sympathetically to his story. Enzo always said, "Thanks for listening, it really helps," but Flavia was never really convinced. If it did help, then why did he keep coming back to her with the same dilemma?

How different things had been six months ago, back in April. She still had vivid memories of Enzo's enthusiasm and delight, telling her how he had befriended a group of male migrants. He had first met them at a drop-in Italian class in the modern part of Siracusa, just half an hour's walk from his church in Ortigia. Enzo had gone along as a volunteer, to help newcomers feel welcome and practise speaking Italian. As a migrant to Italy himself, he knew how important it was to make contact with local people, to help them feel part of a community and learn the local language. Many of the young men attending the drop-in had gravitated towards him and he had enjoyed spending time with them. In particular, he had established a good rapport with some of the migrants who, like himself, came from West Africa. As a compassionate man, Enzo had gone out of his way to help them feel part of the community. He involved them in church events, especially trips around the local area and found jobs for them to do around the place in exchange for food and company. That was how Flavia had met some of these men when Enzo brought them round to help decorate her flat. It was clear to her that they really looked up to the Nigerian priest. And he was only too happy to help them.

She recalled how overjoyed the guys had been at the start of summer, when the priest had managed to find them paid work with a local property developer. The prospect of employment had given them a purpose in life and a renewed sense of dignity. All was well with the world until one night a deputation of young migrant men came to their friend Enzo to complain about their working conditions: working on a construction site was hard work at the best of times, but these guys were working long days with infrequent breaks, often exposed to the extreme heat of Sicilian sun and for a pittance in pay. It had been a deep shock for Flavia to see the usually laid-back Enzo become incensed at the injustice of the situation. There was no collective bargaining agreement to protect the guys' rights to a minimum wage; no legal framework to safeguard them from exploitation. Enzo had confided in Flavia how stupid he felt that he hadn't realised this earlier. But in truth he had been so happy to find them employment it hadn't even crossed his mind to suspect foul play. Flavia had done her best to encourage Enzo not to be too hard on himself. His heart had been in the right place. But her words had been to no avail.

The migrants' situation was unacceptable to Enzo. He felt compelled to get justice for his fellow human beings. So, he had arranged to meet with their boss, the person responsible for employing them, and willingly exploiting them: property developer Alfonso Bellotto, owner of Bellotto Construction.

Shortly after that meeting, Flavia recalled a distraught Enzo telling her just how ruthless Alfonso Bellotto was prepared to be. The property tycoon had known full well that the guys had arrived by boat from Africa. As far as the government were concerned, they had come ashore illegally. And as far as he was concerned, that meant they had no status, no rights, and were therefore ripe for exploitation. It was clear to Enzo that Bellotto had agreed to take on the migrants, not as an act of charity but almost as a punishment to them and of course as a big fat favour to himself. Worst of all, the powerful property developer had threatened to have the men deported if Don Enzo or anyone else went to the police.

Her friend became preoccupied with the dilemma he faced. His conscience wouldn't allow him to ignore it. He had prayed, he had meditated, he had read the Bible. He had poured his heart out endlessly to Flavia. But none of this had helped him see a way to get justice. Then Flavia had suggested that he talk with the bishop, after all wasn't that what a bishop was there for? Wasn't a bishop supposed to be like a brother to his priests? Especially when a priest found himself in need of support?

She had been pleased when Enzo had agreed to consult the bishop. But even this turned out to be quite a palaver. Making an appointment was bad enough. It seemed to take ages before the priest was able to convince the bishop's secretary that his need to consult the bishop was genuine. Finally, he was granted a private audience with the main man – Archbishop Salvatore Argento. Then there were the preparations leading up to that meeting. Flavia remembered how Enzo had spent days rehearsing what he wanted to say, practising how he would address the archbishop and kneel to kiss his ring. Of course he had seen the bishop before on numerous occasions but always from afar it seemed, and never in a one to one meeting. This was to take place at the Archbishop's Palace in Ortigia, adjacent to the Cathedral of Siracusa no less. It was a big deal, all right.

The day of the meeting finally arrived. Enzo had looked immaculate when he set out for the Palace. Flavia eagerly awaited his return to find out how it had all gone. She really wanted to know if the bishop could help her friend. But Flavia being Flavia, she was also curious. Would the bishop be dressed in all his regalia? Would he proffer a bejewelled hand to Don Enzo? How many rings would he be wearing? And what were they like?

It was the next morning before she found out. Disappointingly there wasn't much to tell. Her friend explained that far from any pomp or ceremony, he had been ushered into a rather austere looking reception room. The archbishop had joined him there, dressed in a simple black cassock with red trim. He was wearing a big, fat gold ring on his right hand. But no sign of any jewels that Enzo could remember. Formalities dispensed with, there had been no small talk. The bishop it seemed was a busy man. He immediately got down to business, calling on the parish priest to explain what was troubling him. Once Enzo started talking, the bishop removed his heavy black rimmed glasses. He seemed to be listening and have some compassion for Don Enzo's situation. But it had not been a long meeting. In fact, Enzo had remembered verbatim what the bishop had told him. "God moves in mysterious ways," had been his opening remarks, putting his heavy framed glasses back on, which gave him an added air of authority. "Such dilemmas are sent by God to test us. There is no need to go to the police or tell anyone else. Leave this to God. Have faith Don Enzo, have faith."

If only it were that simple, Flavia mused now. She knew that her friend Enzo's faith remained severely tested. If anything, she felt that his audience with Archbishop Salvatore Argento had left the priest even more conflicted than before. After all, when he was ordained as a priest, Don Enzo had solemnly promised before God to obey his superiors. But Flavia knew otherwise. She was possibly the only person who did know that Enzo had disregarded the bishop's counsel, by choosing to confide in her and tell her the whole story. She had felt flattered that the priest had trusted her enough to do so. She felt like a surrogate mother towards him ...

The sound of Rocco's gleeful barking brought her back to Forte Vigliena and the glorious morning sky. She looked round and saw that a group of tourists had taken a liking to Rocco. Enzo, meanwhile, seemed quite happy answering their doggy questions, to all appearances he had bounced back to life again. But when the visitors went on their way and he joined Flavia again, he looked troubled. His normally radiant, open face was strained. She spotted the bags underneath his eyes.

"Had a rough night?" she innocently inquired.

"The guys came to see me again last night..."

Flavia nodded, 'the guys' was how he referred to his migrant friends. She waited for him to find the words to say what he wanted to say. She could tell from his face that there was more to this than simply a visit from the guys. What was bothering him, she wondered.

They both stood in silence for a few minutes, looking out to sea. The sea was turning blue again, mirroring the skies above. The day had well and truly broken.

"I had a surprise visitor last night!" Enzo sounded as if he had perked up again. From his tone of voice, Flavio could tell that he didn't want to talk any more about 'the guys'. She didn't force it.

"Ooh, a good surprise I hope?"

"Yes, a very good surprise! It was Mikey, the new laundry operator, the one who's substituting for Roberta. He just popped in to say hello. Nice guy!"

"Popped into the church?" Flavia did her best to sound casual. Actually, she was very curious.

"Yes! And why not? I'm always pleased to see new faces."

Flavia studied her friend's face. He did look genuinely pleased.

Then further silence between them.

Flavia was thinking. There had to be something she could do to help her friend. What would take his mind off things, whatever it was that was really bothering him and had kept him from a good night's sleep? She pondered. Then her intuition kicked in. Of course …

"You know what you need, my friend? A good night out!"

The words came out rather more suddenly than she had intended. So it came as no surprise that Enzo didn't look massively impressed by her suggestion. She took a couple of deep breaths before continuing, this time in a more controlled, less frenetic manner. "There's a gig on tomorrow evening near my parents' place, down on the beach. Should be really good – bit of reggae, bit of jazz. It's to raise funds for migrant support." Encouraged by the glimmer of interest in Enzo's eyes, she added: "You will come, won't you?"

Detecting a wry smile on her friend's face, she felt hopeful. Raising an eyebrow, he asked, "Transport?"

It was true that Flavia's parents lived about half an hour's drive round the coast from Siracusa, in Fontane Bianche. It was also true that neither she nor Enzo had a car. But she knew someone who did!

"Leave it to me!" she said. "I'll ask Mikey too, maybe he can take us all in his car?"

Wednesday started quietly at the launderette. Mikey had only had four customers by 11 o'clock. A tourist from the US, a couple of Germans who were staying in an Airbnb in via Brescia, and a student on the same course as Marco. And then Vito arrived. Now, there was someone who really caught Mikey's attention. Maybe early 50s, tanned, and very well-dressed: blue Tommy Hilfiger polo shirt and cream-coloured slacks, along with beautiful leather shoes. It's a pity that Lauren's not here, thought Mikey; she would be **very** interested in him, and that might give me more opportunity to get on with both my launderette and police duties! Anyhow, Vito and Mikey enjoyed a short chat. Vito said that he was a frequent customer and he asked kindly after Roberta. "She is such a lovely lady," he said, "I do hope she will be back soon."

"So do I," replied Mikey. "Are you from Siracusa?" Mikey had detected a Sicilian accent, but his ears weren't yet sufficiently sensitive to detect differences in accents between cities on the island.

Vito chuckled. "No, I'm originally from Catania, but I've been here for the past four years. I'm enjoying life in Ortigia: beautiful scenery, beautiful food, beautiful ladies!" As he laughed, a gold tooth on the side of Vito's mouth caught the light shining down from the ceiling of the launderette. "Yes," Mikey replied, "Ortigia has a lot going for it!"

After Vito left, Mikey mused over their encounter. Vito clearly has some money, he thought. So, why hasn't he got a washing machine? Perhaps there's no room for it where he lives? Mikey made a mental note to ask this next time Vito was in.

At midday, Mikey closed the launderette and popped into Bar Stella at the top of via Verona, for a mozzarella cheese *panino* and espresso, plus a chat with the owner, Fabio, and a couple of the customers. It seemed like a relaxed place; Mikey would definitely be back. Rather than returning directly to EasyWash, he made a detour to Flavia's boutique, to apologise for his rushed exit the previous day. However, the shop was closed and there was no sign of life, aside from what sounded like a meow. Had that come from the boutique, or from a nearby alley, he wondered? Hoping that it was the latter, Mikey decided to return later.

Between 12.30 pm and 3.30 pm, there were only three customers at the launderette, all from the UK and all based in nearby Airbnb's. After they left, Mikey swept the launderette floor and was wiping down the counter where the washing would normally be folded when he heard … a meow. He looked up.

"Good afternoon, Mikey!" The warm voice was Flavia's. She was wearing an orange and green coloured dress, with her black hair tied back. However, it wasn't only Flavia who caught Mikey's attention; it was also the small pink-trimmed transparent trolley that she was pulling behind her. Mikey had met a few customers bringing their washing to the launderette in a trolley, but

Flavia's trolley contained something very different. She reached down, opened the trolley and lifted into her arms a black cat. "I'd like to introduce you to Miles," said Flavia, softly stroking her pet.

"Miles?" Mikey looked at the cat, whose beady eyes were fixed on him.

"Yes, as in Miles Davis. I love his music – so cool! Just like little Miles here! Do you like jazz, Mikey?"

"Yes. I like all types of music." Although the only thing cool that Mikey associated with Miles the cat was the shiver now running down his spine.

"So do I! That's wonderful! Listen, are you free tomorrow evening?"

The shiver disappeared as Mikey returned his full attention to Flavia and gazed into her brown eyes. "Well, of course!" This wasn't the time to mention his regular evening catch-up with *Forense*.

"That's fantastic! You see, tomorrow evening there'll be a gig out at Fontane Bianche. Would you like to come?"

"Yes, I'd love to, thank you!" Mikey had heard of this beach resort and how it would get very busy during summer, with people escaping from the punishing temperatures inland. "I haven't been there yet. It's to the west of Siracusa, isn't it?"

"That's right, it's about 20 kilometres from here. My parents have a villa there and I often visit them at the weekend. It's a great place to go clubbing!"

"Sounds fantastic!" Siracusa had some good points in Mikey's view, but the nightlife wasn't one of them. He was still missing the vibrant scene in Rome. "It'll be good to try somewhere new!"

"You won't be disappointed! The gig will be taking place on the beach. There'll be a marquee set up with food and drinks. It should be super-relaxed, with good music, good company."

What's not to like, thought Mikey. "What time will it start?"

"Well, because the gig will be outdoors and it's getting cooler at night, it'll start at 7 o'clock."

"Ahh!" said Mikey. This was met by a muffled hiss from Miles. "The launderette's normally open until 8 o'clock."

"Do you get many customers in the evening?" asked Flavia.

Mikey was momentarily distracted by her eyelashes. "No, not many," he replied. "Perhaps I could close early, just for one evening." He briefly wondered how he would sell this idea to the *commissario*. But decided not to dwell on it.

"Wonderful! Could I ask a small favour, please?" Flavia looked appealingly into his eyes. "I don't have a car. It's not worth the cost or the hassle when you're living in Ortigia. So, when I go to Fontane Bianche at weekends, my parents normally collect me from here in their car and bring me back on Sunday. However, they've got other plans for tomorrow evening. So ... I wonder if you could give me a lift there and back, please?"

Mikey smiled. "My pleasure!" He pointed to Totti, parked as usual opposite the launderette. "That's my car. It's a bit rough around the edges, but it always does the job. That's all that matters, right? And I'm happy to stick to non-alcoholic drinks."

It was Flavia's turn to smile. "Thank you. Actually, I had another small request, please."

Miles purred. What's coming next, thought Mikey.

"You know my friend Enzo, the parish priest?"

"Yes, I visited his church last night. He was very welcoming. And he's got a lovely dog – Rocco!" That last word was met by a loud hiss from Miles.

"Sorry, Mikey. Miles can be sensitive at times." She put the cat back in the trolley, secured it and continued the conversation. "Enzo's a good friend of mine. He's having a difficult time at the moment. I think he could do with a night out."

Mikey could see now where this was heading. "Would you like me to give him a lift too?" he asked. What had seemed an excellent opportunity to spend more time in the company of an attractive woman was turning into something quite different.

"Yes, please. Let me explain. The gig's being run by a community group, to raise funds to help migrants living in the area. Enzo and I are passionate about making migrants feel welcome here and we'd like to do all we can to support this event."

As Flavia said this, Mikey thought of the lines of migrants who often queued outside the police HQ, waiting to get their documents checked. There but for the grace of God go I, he reflected, before responding. "I'd be delighted to give Don Enzo a lift too. And to support the gig!"

At that moment, a light bulb flicked on in Mikey's head. He could argue with the *commissario* that sharing a car with Don Enzo would provide an excellent opportunity to find about more about the local priest. So, having a night out in Fontane Bianche would actually count as work, rather than simply having a good time – although Mikey hoped that he could manage that too.

"Thank you, Mikey! That's so kind of you. By the way, you must drop by the boutique again! I'm sure you'll find a gift there that Roberta will like."

"Thanks," said Mikey, smiling fondly. Once they had made arrangements for the pickup, Mikey changed the subject. "Sorry again for rushing away yesterday; something came up. I'll try my best to visit tomorrow."

"That's fine, Mikey, anytime. I must go – see you soon!"

After they exchanged goodbyes, Mikey watched Flavia strolling up the street towards via Vicenza, pulling her precious cargo behind her. What a lovely woman, thought Mikey. He was already looking forward to the following evening. But, please, he thought, please don't bring the cat, Flavia! The only Miles he wanted to hear was the maestro with the trumpet.

CHAPTER 6

That same morning, just as the sun was rising, *Commissario* Spina left home to drive into work. Franco had a full day ahead of him, but felt comfortable and relaxed, skirting the coastline with his beloved car in cruise control. Across the bay the landmark pink sandstone buildings of Ortigia were just wakening up, and to his left lush green papyrus plants were growing abundantly along the banks of the Ciane river. The timeless combination of architectural beauty and natural luxuriance under cloudless blue skies induced a sense of well-being.

Franco took advantage of the relative calm to think through his priorities for the day ahead. His meeting with Officer Mikey Ricci the previous evening had highlighted a potential predicament for Signora Montanari. If her epilepsy really was as life threatening as Ricci had suggested, then she would need more medication, sooner or later. Even making allowances for Ricci's propensity for exaggeration and over dramatisation, they still needed to treat this as urgent. They could not assume that Signora Montanari had enough medication with her to cover her needs. She may, however, carry a repeat prescription with her or have it on her phone. Franco recalled his own experience with pneumonia a few years earlier. He had found it extremely helpful that his doctor had been able to provide him with a repeat prescription, which Franco had been able to use up to 10 times over a six-month period. From what he could gather about Signora Montanari she struck him as well organised. He had a hunch that she was the sort of person who would have a repeat prescription with her at all times – just in case. And she would know how to make best use of the repeat prescription service.

He reflected next on what they had been able to find out about Roberta's whereabouts. Giovanna had not found a passport in Roberta's flat. That didn't mean that it wasn't there, just that it wasn't in any of the obvious places. Inquiries with both airports had drawn a blank; Roberta's name had not appeared on any of the flight lists from Catania or Palermo over the past few days. Of course, it was possible that she had been taken from Sicily by boat. But investigating that eventuality would be well beyond the scope of Franco's team. Besides which, based on the evidence they had been able to collect, he wasn't inclined to exclude the possibility that Signora Montanari was being held somewhere in or around Sicily.

Trusting his hunch about the sort of person Roberta Montanari was, Franco's best guess was that by now she would have gone to a pharmacist with her repeat prescription or arranged for someone else to go there on her behalf. Either way, a pharmacy somewhere in Sicily would have a record of that for sure. They needed to locate that pharmacy. But where to begin?

Franco was deep in thought. But all too soon he needed

all of his wits about him, as he turned onto a busier road, joining the heavy stream of traffic inching its way towards Siracusa. This was his least favourite part of the daily commute. He hated that the slowest part of the journey was also the part that demanded his full attention. First and foremost he needed to protect himself and his beloved Alfa from other drivers, many of whom could be quite erratic at this time in the morning, not to mention the ubiquitous electric scooters that appeared from nowhere and darted around all over the place. He slammed on the horn in frustration at some pedestrians straying aimlessly over the road in front of him – gormless visitors, he hissed, the tension building up in his shoulders.

When he entered the police headquarters ten minutes later, he passed Pappalardo at the front desk without exchanging as much as a 'good morning'. The officer seemed fully engrossed in something – Franco doubted it was work related but felt he had already wasted enough time that morning to stop and find out. He continued down the corridor to his office, where he removed his jacket and carefully hung it up on the back of his office door. Then, whilst his computer was booting up for the day, he proceeded to the kitchen to make himself a coffee. He instantly felt better after his first gulp of the black stuff.

Back in his office, he had started perusing his emails when an intermittent buzzing noise caught his attention. His work phone was vibrating. It was a notification that something had come through on his second SIM. He didn't recognise the number on the screen, but he had a strong hunch about the sender when he saw it was a WhatsApp message from out of town. Picking up his coffee mug for a final mouthful with one hand, with the other he swiped the screen on his phone. Looking down he saw that he had been sent an image. He put down his mug and gave the screen his full attention.

On the screen was the photo of a woman seated on a wooden chair. Franco looked closely, yes, it was Signora Montanari all right. Her face was pale and gave very little away. Her expression was neither happy nor sad. But at least she was alive. In her hands she was holding up to the camera the front page of a newspaper. Franco immediately recognised *La Sicilia*, a daily newspaper for the island of Sicily. Underneath the photo he read a short message: D GOT THIS PHOTO LAST NIGHT. It was from Tommaso all right.

Franco zoomed in on the paper. It was dated the previous day – Tuesday 24 October. On closer inspection of the newspaper heading, he discovered a further helpful detail. The edition of *La Sicilia* that Signora Montanari had in her hands was for the province of Siracusa. It was the local edition of the paper. In all likelihood she was being kept on Franco's patch, somewhere within the province of Siracusa. That narrowed down their search quite considerably. Franco leapt out of his seat and punched the air, before racing out of his office.

He slowed down a bit when he reached the front of the building and strode purposefully towards the front desk. The duty officer jumped to attention.

Franco got straight to the point. "Listen carefully, Pappalardo, I've got an important job for you. I want you to draw up a list of all the pharmacies in Siracusa province."

"Sorry, *dottore*, did you say pharmacies?"

"Yes, that's right – where people go to buy their prescriptions. Where medicine is dispensed." Franco let out a small sigh of exasperation and took a deep breath before continuing. "This is very important, Pappalardo. It could be a matter of life or death. I need a name, address and contact number for each of the pharmacies. Have you got that?"

Pappalardo repeated the instructions to himself as he wrote them down; Franco crossed his fingers that the officer was writing it all down correctly. He waited a moment, before speaking again. "And another thing, I need to have a separate list of those for each municipality in the province."

"All 21 of them, including Siracusa city?"

"Yes, Pappalardo. Especially Siracusa city. The information shouldn't be difficult to find. I'll need everything on my desk in two hours' time, earlier if possible. That's an order!"

Franco strode back to his office, pausing only briefly to summon Giovanna to his office.

Minutes later, Franco and his deputy sat facing each other, the police chief behind his desk. He felt back in control again and resumed his usual calm, business-like demeanour. Wasting no time, he explained to Giovanna what was now known about Roberta Montanari's whereabouts. Giovanna quickly grasped the significance of the latest photo and newspaper clues. For now, Franco was satisfied that he didn't need to spend more time discussing that particular aspect of the investigation. Instead, he focused attention on the matter of Roberta's health.

"I've got an important job for you, Gio. Signora Montanari has an epileptic condition – could be life threatening. She has a repeat prescription for anti-epileptic drugs, which she relies on to keep the condition under control."

Giovanna looked as if she had something to say.

Unusually for Franco, he stopped what he had to say. "Go on," he instructed Giovanna.

"I know something about AEDs, boss …"

"AEDs?"

"Sorry, that's anti-epileptic drugs. I used to live with someone who had been taking AEDs for years. It's the main medicine to stop epileptic seizures happening. Really strong drugs, they work by changing the levels of chemicals …"

"Yes, yes, I've got the message, Gio."

To Franco's surprise, Giovanna continued talking.

"The thing is, boss, even with the strongest drugs, a seizure still can be triggered. There are different factors that might do that, including stress or lack of sleep."

Franco immediately grasped the implications of what Giovanna had just said and turned his attention back to the photo of Signora Montanari that Tommaso had sent through earlier that morning. On closer inspection, he could detect signs of tension in the pale, drawn face and in the hunched shoulders, also signs of anxiety behind the lifeless eyes. In fact, everything pointed to someone under stress. He had seen enough. Time was of the essence.

He looked over to his deputy and nodded.

"OK, here's what I want you to do, Gio. I want you to check with pharmacies in the province, is there any record that Signora Montanari has used her repeat prescription in the past few days?"

"Are we looking at any particular area boss?"

"I suggest you start with Siracusa city and then work outwards. Get some of the others to help you with phone calls, this is urgent. Pappalardo is putting together a list of all the pharmacies according to municipality."

"Gee boss! You do realise this might take hours? There's probably thirty plus pharmacies in the city alone."

Franco knew that Giovanna was right. But without knowledge of Roberta's precise whereabouts, how could they narrow the search? They had to give this line of enquiry a try at least.

"OK, I'll tell you what, Gio. Begin with those pharmacies that were open last Sunday – the duty pharmacies. That should narrow it down quite a bit."

"Makes sense as well, boss – if she was abducted on the Friday after work, chances are she'd make it through the Saturday but by Sunday she ...."

"... may have been desperate. Yes, that's exactly the point, Gio!"

He picked up the phone and instructed Pappalardo to restrict the pharmacy search to only those pharmacies which had been open the previous Sunday, adding that the complete list needed to be on Giovanna's desk within the hour. Then, turning to his deputy he said: "That's settled then, start with the duty pharmacists in Siracusa city then move out to the other municipalities in the province. Report back to me as soon as you find anything. That's ..."

"Got it, boss!" smiled Giovanna and headed for the door.

Franco, meanwhile, made himself another coffee. He needed to be super focused for a meeting with his senior colleagues at 9 o'clock.

It was midday before he finally left that meeting, feeling mentally drained and frustrated. Instead of getting on with police business he had just spent three hours going through the latest statistical report for the provisional division. He needed to clear his mind. Grabbing his jacket from his office, he decided to get some fresh air. He'd only got as far as the corridor leading to the front desk when Giovanna called out from her open office door. "Boss! Boss! We've got it!"

Franco stopped in his tracks. A very excited looking

Giovanna headed towards him waving a piece of paper. "You've found the pharmacy?" guessed Franco. Giovanna beamed, a huge grin on her face. "Let's take this outside," was Franco's abrupt reply.

The pair of them walked down the corridor, past the front desk out into the beating sun. Thankfully there was a slight breeze, which Franco took a few seconds to savour before putting on his dark glasses. Turning to face his deputy he said, "OK, tell me what you've found out."

"Well, boss, we found out that Roberta's prescription was used on Sunday morning and signed for by a Bruno Mangiafico."

"Mangiafico! Of course! I knew I recognised that name when you mentioned it the other day. Bruno Mangiafico was put inside a couple of years ago for aggravated burglary – a nasty piece of work. Has a record of robbery, armed robbery, arson, you name it."

"So, that means we'll have his DNA in the national forensic … "

"… DNA database!" Franco was energised by the news, this finally felt like a breakthrough. "Let's get Rome to send his DNA down to us, so we can compare it with the sample of blood collected from the lane next to the launderette."

"Bit of a coincidence that Roberta's neighbour is also a Mangiafico!"

"Check that out, Gio – could well be a sister or cousin." Franco reflected on the information his deputy had told him, something was missing. "You still haven't told me which pharmacy was used," he said.

Giovanna consulted the piece of paper she was holding. "It was in the city, boss. Farmacia Romana in Corso Garibaldi."

It was indeed good news that the pharmacy was

located in the city, even more local than Franco had first thought. However, he didn't recognise the street name.

"Near to where they're building all those new houses," Giovanna helped him out.

"Great work, Gio," said Franco, removing his glasses to look her in the eye

But Giovanna hadn't finished yet. There was more to come as she reported back on her surveillance of Roberta's flat. She had not seen anyone enter or leave Roberta's flat but had observed Rosa dressed to the nines, leave the complex in a taxi the previous afternoon. This hadn't really come as a surprise to Giovanna, because, as she reminded her boss, Rosa had previously been photographed at a posh campaign dinner on the arm of Bellotto. Franco rolled his eyes when he heard this; he had no time for society tittle tattle. He preferred to get his news from the TV or radio, but when he did read a newspaper, he always made a point of bypassing the society pages.

"Continue with the surveillance, Gio," he responded bluntly, putting his sunglasses back on. "And be on the lookout for any signs of anyone else entering or leaving Rosa's flat." Irrespective of the Bruno Mangiafico development and any possible link between him and Rosa, Franco was still not convinced that Rosa knew nothing of Roberta's abduction.

"And circulate the photograph of Bruno Mangiafico among the officers. We need to be vigilant of his whereabouts."

"Yes, boss, I'll tell them to be on the lookout and to keep us posted of any sightings. After all, Bruno could lead us to Roberta."

"That's exactly the point! But whatever happens, Gio, there must be absolutely no word about Signora Montanari's disappearance to the rest of the squad. That's an order!"

Confident that he could reply on Giovanna to create a believable pretext for the interest in Mangiafico, Franco turned to head back into the police station.

"Time for lunch," he said.

Lunch seemed like a long time ago now. Franco was ready to call it a day and head home. The previous two evenings he had stayed on late so that he could meet up with Ricci face to face, after the launderette had closed. But not tonight. It had felt like a long, slow afternoon. He really didn't feel inclined to hang on another two hours just so that he could see Ricci. So, he decided to go home 'early' and made arrangements for Ricci to phone him later that evening with an update.

As usual, *Commissario* Spina didn't leave his office until he had organised his desk for the following day. He went through the same ritual every time, clearing his desk of anything that didn't belong there and checking that everything else was lined up exactly where he wanted it to be: pen pot, calendar, photo of his daughter and clean coffee mug. He treated it as a kind of wind down time, an opportunity to reflect briefly on that day. In his mind they were no longer dealing with the case of a disappearance, Roberta Montanari had been abducted and was being held somewhere on his patch.

His ten years based in Siracusa, four of them as Head of Criminal Investigations, had taught him that a systematic approach to solving crime was what paid off in the longer term. This suited his temperament and penchant for detail. Maybe that was why he had been so successful – even if his superiors didn't always fully appreciate his achievements. But with the Roberta Montanari case there was the added pressure of needing to solve the crime within an uncertain and tight time frame. Potentially the World Series would be over in two days from now, but possibly it might run for another five days. Either way, time was short and added to which, the time frame was outside Franco's control. He felt uncomfortable acknowledging this, so didn't dwell on it.

Before leaving the office, his thoughts turned briefly to the day's achievements. Admittedly there had been no further leads or breakthroughs during the afternoon. But it was still a relief to know that Signora Montanari's repeat prescription had been used. He reassured himself that she had the medicine she needed to control her condition and trusted that she would not miss a dose. That small breakthrough had been largely down to Giovanna. Again, he reflected on how fortunate he was in having such an efficient deputy. And then there was Ricci. Who knew what the police officer would have to report back later that evening? A faint smile crossed Franco's lips.

Walking across the car park towards his reserved parking space, he felt much calmer than he had felt when he first arrived that morning. He used his remote control to open the car boot where he deposited his small rucksack and picked up a small bottle of water, his third that day. It would be empty by the time he had driven the short journey home. Before sitting in the car, he removed his jacket and carefully hung it up on a hook behind the driver's seat. Then, once seated behind the wheel, he checked his smartwatch for any recent notifications. AHA! There was a WhatsApp voice note on his personal phone – from Amelia.

"Ciao papà! It's me. Need to speak with you about the weekend. Give me a ring back please. Love you."

Hearing his beloved daughter's voice again, lit up his serious face. The anticipation of speaking with her helped to dissolve some of the day's tensions. Wanting to enjoy that feeling of anticipation, he would wait until he was home before ringing her back. He relaxed his tight shoulders and looked forward to his drive home.

It suited father and daughter to keep in regular contact via WhatsApp – it was convenient. Franco used his personal phone for this, relying on his smartwatch to notify him when messages came in. Amelia was under strict instructions only to use Franco's work number in case of emergency. Thankfully, she had never needed to use it.

Despite this convenient arrangement, to Franco's mind, messaging was not the same as speaking. They hadn't actually spoken with each other for a couple of weeks now. There was nothing unusual in that. They tended to speak regularly, but not that frequently. Every two or three weeks was about the norm. So, he wondered, switching on the ignition, what was on this weekend that she needed to talk with him about?

The clock on his dashboard showed 18.40, he should be home by 19.00. The last of the setting sun accompanied him for the first part of his journey; by the time he had turned onto the country road that led to the small headland where he lived, it had disappeared completely. The sea, lapping up against the rocky shore, looked very dark now with the occasional flash of white broken up by the movement of the water. Just three more nights like this before the time change at the weekend. Come Sunday, his entire journey home would be in the dark but at least he would still be able to enjoy the sun when he set off for work at 7am.

It was precisely 18.59 when he looked at his smartwatch before activating the push button control to lock the garage door. His precious sports car safely ensconced for the night, Franco went indoors. He would phone Amelia from the lounge on his personal phone. But first he parked his work phone for the time being, on a ledge in the entrance hall and carefully hung up his jacket. Then, using a remote, he switched on the wall lights in the lounge and closed the shutters, which overlooked the sea. From there he went into the adjoining small kitchen and opened himself a bottle of ice-cold beer. The first couple of swigs went down very easily, very easily indeed. The cool amber brew pepped up his taste buds and a sense of wellbeing infused his weary body. He enjoyed another couple of swigs before returning to the lounge, where he used another remote to make himself comfortable on the leather sofa. He was ready now to call his daughter.

"*Ciao*, sweetheart!"

"*Ciao*, papà!"

Amelia sounded upbeat. Franco was looking forward to their conversation. She had had a good day so far. School had been OK, she had her favourite lesson – Italian literature. At 1.30pm, after school, she had taken a bus into Catania city centre with a group of friends, where they had bought pizza and hung out in a café. She had stayed there for most of the afternoon until her guitar lesson at 4pm. Franco let her speak, captivated by her zest for life. He wondered what he would say if she asked him about his day. But she didn't. So, he changed the subject.

"So, what's on this weekend that you need to speak with me about?"

There was a slight hesitancy as she seemed to clear her throat.

"The thing is, papà, Amnesty Italia are holding a rally on Saturday in Siracusa."

"Y – e – s," said Franco, bracing himself for what was to follow.

"I thought it would be a great chance to see you again. I could come down Friday night on the coach, so we'd have more time together. What do you –"

"WOW, WOW, WOW!" interrupted Franco. "Hold on a minute. You have school on Saturday!"

"Sure, but I don't think the teachers mind as long as I catch up with the work. Besides, the rally itself will be an education. They held one last weekend in Catania and it was amazing! Honestly, I met so many interesting people from different parts of Sicily who had come to Catania to support Amnesty. There were fantastic speakers – really impassioned. And –"

"Are you telling me you missed school last Saturday as well?"

"No, papà! A group of us went to the rally in the afternoon, after school. Which reminds me, would it be OK if I brought a few of my friends along on Friday to sleep at yours? They can camp out in my bedroom and the lounge. Please papà! It's only for one night."

He could tell from her voice how much this mattered to his daughter and he started to soften. She was 18 after all. Old enough to take responsibility for her studies and make her own decisions about how to spend her time. He felt flattered that she had chosen to come down on the Friday evening. There were plenty of coaches travelling from Catania to Siracusa on Saturday mornings, which she could have chosen instead. Besides which, it would be good for him to spend time with his daughter and he had no other plans for Friday evening. He just wasn't quite comfortable with the thought of Amelia's friends coming as well. It wasn't so much that he had any reason to distrust them in any way. He trusted his daughter's judgement in her choice of friends. What was making him feel anxious was the thought of his home being thrown into disarray, chaos or worse.

As if she could read his mind, Amelia continued, "Don't worry, papà. I promise we won't make a mess, we'll all help to tidy up before we leave. And they'll even pay you for giving them a bed for the night."

Franco came straight to the point. "How many friends are we talking about?"

"Just three or four, five tops. The girls can share my room, and the guys can have the lounge floor – they've all got sleeping bags."

"OK five tops, no more than five!" ordered Franco, relenting to her youthful exuberance.

"*GRAZIE!*" Amelia screamed with delight. "*Grazie mille!* That's such great news! Once we're on the coach Friday evening, I'll let you know how many we are. Oh, and I'll let you know what time we'll be getting in, as well!"

Before finishing their conversation, Franco added in a more measured tone, "And tell your friends, I don't want any payment. They are welcome anytime."

It was a more composed Amelia who replied this time. "*Grazie, papà.* You really are the best. I love you."

"I love you too, sweetheart." Franco smiled, contentedly.

THURSDAY 26TH OCTOBER

CHAPTER 7

Here she comes again, thought Mikey. He watched her striding down via Verona, with a bright lemon-decorated shopping bag over her shoulder and a large brown-coloured umbrella that was protecting her coiffured blond hair from a brief shower of rain. "Hiya Mikey!" Lauren called out. "How are ya doing?"

Standing in the door of the launderette, wondering whether Thursday would be any busier than Wednesday, Mikey smiled and waved. "I'm fine, thanks. How are you?"

"Great! Shame about the rain, but the sun's due out later. If it's warm enough around midday, I'll head to Cala Rossa – I might have a dip!"

Mikey nodded. Shortly after his move to Sicily at the start of September, he had walked around Ortigia, taking a multitude of photos. Along the way, he had been struck by the hordes of people lying on the small shingle beach at Cala Rossa, on the south-east of the island. Even now, as October drew to a close, Mikey knew that many residents were still keen to get their fix of late autumn sun.

"That sounds good," replied Mikey. "Are you going to the market first?"

Lauren flung back her head and laughed. "Of course! I'd never miss that! I'm going to get some fresh fish and vegetables; I'm thinking up rustling up a seafood salad for when I get back from the beach. Say, you wouldn't have time to pop by for a meal? It must be a long day for you here, all by yourself." She raised her eyebrows, slowly.

Mikey smiled once more. "Sorry, I can only take a short break during the day. Maybe another time?"

Lauren's face creased into a half-smile. "Sure, Mikey. You're always welcome. I'd like to find out a **lot** more about you! Anyway, I must dash. *Buona giornata!*"

"*Ciao!*" Mikey watched Lauren heading down the street, holding her umbrella tightly as the shower got heavier. He enjoyed chatting with her, but today – Thursday – his focus had to be on the case. *Forense* had been insistent on that when they had spoken the previous evening.

His boss had been quite critical of Mikey during the phone call, asking why he wasn't making more progress. Mikey had thought this was rather harsh; after all, he had a launderette to run! Besides which, he had already passed on information to the *commissario* about the schedule of matches in the World Series and about Roberta's epilepsy. What more progress was *Forense* expecting?

Mikey had also told the *commissario* about his conversation the previous evening with Signor Carusa, the owner of the art gallery. Carusa had been very polite with Mikey and even given him a short tour of the gallery. However, he had seemed preoccupied and had dashed out into the street at one point to take a call. Despite protestations to the contrary, Mikey thought that Signor Carusa looked strained. On hearing this, *Forense's* response had been "Keep an eye on Carusa!" To be honest, Mikey had been hoping for more of a reaction and at the time had felt somewhat aggrieved. But as he recalled the phone call now, he accepted that showing any appreciation, beyond a curt 'thanks' was simply not *Forense's* style.

"*Buongiorno.*" A gruff voice brought Mikey back to the present. He recognised the man stubbing out his cigarette just outside the launderette; it was the guy who had been waiting for him to open up on his first morning there.

"*Buongiorno!* Can I help?" Mikey's attentive smile was met by a shrug and an almost imperceptible "No" as the man shuffled over to a washing machine and proceeded to pull out bedding from a plastic bag, before stuffing it into the machine. Mikey was immediately struck by the stink of cigarette smoke, even though he was standing several metres away. Unlike many of his friends, Mikey didn't smoke and although he had often visited smoky homes, he couldn't begin to imagine what this guy's house was like. The man put his coins in the machine, pushed the start button, then wandered over to a seat just outside the launderette, where he lit another cigarette and opened the latest copy of *La Sicilia*.

Best to give 'Mr Grumpy' a wide berth, thought Mikey, as he stepped into via Verona and looked up the street towards the junction with via Vicenza. He smiled as something much more pleasant came to mind; his conversation with Flavia the previous afternoon and her invitation to attend a gig in Fontane Bianche on Thursday evening, together with Don Enzo. How kind of her! On the other hand, this had been a bone of contention during his catch-up with Franco the previous evening. "Closing the launderette early?" Franco had queried. "For a night out? Where? And with a priest??" However, Mikey had stood his ground and, after a few minutes of tense conversation, Franco had given his OK – provided that Mikey rang him shortly before he left the launderette to discuss how the day had gone and messaged him when he got back to Siracusa with any further updates. "Of course, *dottore*," Mikey had said: "you have my word."

He was still looking up via Verona, turning over the previous day's events in his head, when a familiar face appeared from around the corner. "*Ciao*, Mikey!" Marco sauntered down the street, smiling cheek-to-cheek. "Did you hear the news?"

"Yes," said Mikey. He had checked his phone first thing that morning and had been dismayed to see that the Bats had beaten the Kats the previous evening. Consequently, the Bats were now one step closer to clinching the World Series, which – as Tommaso had explained to the *commissario* a few days earlier – would place Roberta's life in acute danger. But Mikey couldn't reveal his true emotions to Marco. "A great win for the Bats!" he said, with a broad smile.

"It certainly was," replied Marco, coughing briefly as he passed 'Mr Grumpy' smoking outside, before stepping into the launderette. "Come on, let's watch the highlights."

Marco brought out his phone and once again he and Mikey were transported across the world, virtually at least. This time there was no rain falling on the baseball field. Indeed, from the way that many of the fans were dressed, it appeared to be a warm evening. Not surprising for California, Mikey thought. As in the previous match in Kentucky, the home fans were screaming their support at full belt.

"So," said Marco, "the Bats had a different starting pitcher for this game. His name is Ramos, he's very good, but he's not quite at the same level as Dani in my view. That's him there!"

Marco pointed at the screen and Mikey watched as Ramos pitched the ball, a Kats player swung the bat with all his might – and missed. Then, the same sequence again. And again. "Great pitching!" exclaimed Marco, as the batsman lowered his head and slowly departed the field, with the Bats fans shouting and waving in the background.

The highlights continued in much the same fashion. A few of the Kats players managed to hit the ball, but in most instances the ball was caught by a fielder or the batsman failed to get to first base. Ramos conceded just one home run. Meanwhile, the Bats seemed to score at will when they were batting. Each of their runs was greeted with a whoop by Marco. At the same time, Mikey spotted 'Mr Grumpy' stand up and walk down the street, away from the launderette. Clearly, he wasn't a fan of baseball, or of Marco's reaction to the game, or both.

"Here we are at the start of the 7th innings," said Marco. He pointed at the screen, which displayed the score: Bats 5, Kats 1. "Ramos has had a great game, but it's time for Dani to take over as relief pitcher." Mikey watched as Dani walked out on to the field, looking a bit tense – almost as though his mind was elsewhere. Dani took a deep breath, glared at the Kats batsman, then hurled the ball towards him.

CRACK! The sound of the bat hitting the ball engulfed the launderette. The batsman stood motionless as the ball flew high into the air, then was caught – by a spectator in the stand on the far side of the ground. The stadium fell quiet, as the batsman jogged around the bases to claim a home run.

"HMMM!" Marco grimaced, then continued, "At least there weren't any other Kats on the bases; otherwise, we would have conceded more than one run."

The 7th innings continued in a similarly subdued manner for the Bats, with another couple of runs conceded and no more scored by themselves. With the score reading Bats 5, Kats 4 at the start of the 8th innings, it was now Dani's turn to depart. "It's not unusual to switch relief pitchers during a game," said Marco. "It just wasn't Dani's day." With that, the pattern of the match swung once more; the Kats managed no more runs, while the Bats scored a couple of runs in the 9th and final innings, to win by 7 runs to 4.

Marco muted the cheers of the Bats fans as he closed the video. "The Bats are 2-1 up in the World Series. We just need a couple more wins! And we've got two more home games coming up, tonight and tomorrow night in Bakerside. That'll do it, I'm sure. I can't wait!" Marco gave Mikey a friendly slap on the back. "Fantastic," responded Mikey, doing his best to sound enthusiastic. "So, what are you doing the rest of today?"

"We're going on a trip!" said Marco. "Not that far, just to Villa Santa Panagia, in the northern part of the city. There's a new housing development being built there. The architect for the project has kindly offered to show students from the faculty around there. Unfortunately, part of the area has been closed off to us for safety reasons. That's because some of the new homes have cellars and they'll need extra work. It's a pity; we've seen the plans for these homes and the designs for the cellars are very innovative. On the other hand, the homes we'll be looking at have a new type of solar panel; I'm keen to see how they're installing this! It should be a good afternoon."

"I hope you'll enjoy it!" Mikey wasn't interested in the intricacies of architectural design, but he appreciated Marco's passion for his subject. "Who's building these homes?" he asked. Mikey didn't have plans to stay in Sicily for the long-term, but – just in case he did want to buy a house here – it wouldn't do any harm to find out more about the local housing market.

Marco laughed. "The same guy who builds all the new homes around here! Look, there he is!" He pointed across the street.

Mikey was perplexed. Marco seemed to be pointing at 'Mr Grumpy', who was now walking back to EasyWash to retrieve his bedding, currently on its final spin in the washing machine. "Do you mean him?" asked Mikey.

"No!" Marco roared. "Definitely not! I'm talking about the guy on the poster. Signor Bellotto!"

Mikey looked at the smiling face on the election poster across the street. He then watched in amusement as 'Mr Grumpy' took a final puff on his cigarette and stubbed it out carefully and firmly on the first 'o' in the name 'Bellotto' printed on the poster. Mikey turned to Marco. "I don't think he'll be buying one of Bellotto's new homes! Have a good afternoon!"

Flavia did her best to keep up with Enzo as the pair of them legged it along the esplanade at Fontane Bianche. That wasn't easy in high heels, dodging the rapidly spreading puddles of rain. Ahead of them they could see Mikey, leading the way back to his car. This was more than a passing shower, it was more like a deluge. But despite the weather and the havoc it was wreaking on her Liberty print dress and matching sandals, Flavia had really enjoyed the night out. It was just a pity that they had to head home already, it was still only 9pm.

She had noticed some of the party goers abandoning the gig about half an hour earlier, as soon as the wind started getting up. But she had dismissed the idea of leaving at that stage because it felt like they'd only just arrived. Besides which, she, Enzo and Mikey were too busy having a good time, swaying and swinging along to the music. It had given her such a lift to literally let her hair down and shake her long, dark locks in time to the music, it had felt like she was shaking all her troubles away. Enzo had stood out in his traditional African shirt, but it was his hip action that had attracted a small crowd of admiring onlookers. And then there was Mikey: lots of arm movements and wrist actions – an animated dancer. Mikey's samba was a classic! Flavia liked the contrasting dancing styles: the cool and the enthusiastic.

Mikey was already sitting at the wheel of his car. When Flavia and Enzo approached, dripping wet, he opened the passenger door of his Cinquecento for them. Flavia pulled back her hair and wrung out the worst of the water from it, before climbing into the back. On the drive out she had sat next to Mikey and given him directions how to get there. But there was no need for a navigator on the way back – they just needed to follow the line of traffic heading towards Siracusa. This arrangement meant that Enzo would have more room in the front for his large frame. And more importantly, from Flavia's point of view, it would be easier for Enzo and Mikey to chat to each other. Left to their own devices, or maybe with just a little prompting on her part, Flavia was intrigued to find out what they would talk about and how they would engage with each other. On the drive out, all three of them had exchanged banter, looking forward to the night out and relaxing in each other's company. Mikey had fitted in really well; it felt as if the three of them had quickly formed a bond of friendship. But now that the gig was behind them, she really wanted to see if her friend would open up to Mikey about his dilemma with the migrants. Would he come clean about what was on his mind, she wondered. And how would Mikey deal with that? Deep down she hoped that perhaps Mikey would be able to offer some helpful advice to Enzo, the sort of advice that she herself had so far struggled to find. She put herself in Enzo's position: cocooned in Mikey's car, protected from the rain and dark outside, among friends. Perfect conditions for a heart to heart chat, thought Flavia, as she sat back in her seat behind the driver. She wiped her steamy window, through the rain pelted glass she was unable to make out anything but headlights and more rain. It seemed like hundreds of vehicles were attempting to leave the car park. She heard Mikey sigh.

"Glad I'm not out there!" she exclaimed, catching Mikey's eye in the mirror. She winked, and thought she detected a smile on his face.

"It's the musicians I feel sorry for," said Enzo. "They were just getting into their stride. I hope they got all their gear packed away ok."

All three of them agreed that the band had put on a great show. Then Mikey asked, "Did they give the concert for free?"

Flavia sat back and let her friend explain that all the proceeds from the gig, including the band's fee, were going towards a charity called Amnesty Italia. The money raised would be spent on food, clothing and other support for migrants, especially those who had no work or were homeless.

Mikey seemed interested. By the time they joined the highway to Siracusa, he and Enzo were deep in discussion about the plight of migrants and the response of the Italian government. Flavia left them to it. Much to her relief, both men were passionate in condemning current immigration policy.

The road was a bit quieter now, much of the traffic had turned in the opposite direction once they reached the highway. Meanwhile the rain had eased off a bit and there was a lull in the conversation. All three of them seemed deep in thought. Flavia wondered what Enzo was thinking. To her relief, she didn't have to wait long to find out.

"It's really not easy being a migrant in Sicily at the moment ..." he said, facing straight ahead. Flavia watched as Mikey turned his head briefly to look at Enzo. This seemed to encourage the priest to continue with his story. He told Mikey about how he had got to know some of the migrants at a drop-in Italian class and had managed to find work for some of them with a construction company. Then he went on to explain how he had found out that the guys were being exploited by their boss, Bellotto.

Mikey seemed to recognise the name. "Is that the same Bellotto who is standing for election? The one whose face is plastered on billboards all over Siracusa?" he asked.

Enzo nodded. "That's him all right."

Mikey's response was the same as Flavia's had been. "Why don't you report this to the police?"

She leant forward and said, "Enzo can't do that, Mikey. You see, Bellotto knows that the guys came here by an unauthorised route. If there is any word of contacting the police, that bastard will see to it that they are all deported."

"Flavia's right," said the priest. "I'm afraid that involving the police is too big a risk."

Mikey thought about this for a second. Flavia watched him stroke his moustache. Then, catching Flavia's eye in the rear-view mirror, he tentatively asked, "Supposing there was a way to inform the police without Bellotto knowing about it?"

"I'm not sure about that, Mikey," she replied. "Who can we trust in the police? And how easy would it be for a police officer to investigate without letting on to anyone else? Who would be willing to take that risk? Especially at the moment, when Bellotto might be our next mayor. There's a lot at stake here."

"Sure, but maybe it's worth a try?" Mikey came back, holding Flavia's gaze in the mirror.

Flavia didn't really know what to make of his reply. Had he even heard a word she'd said?

Meanwhile, Enzo, who had gone very quiet, broke the silence.

"There's more," he announced. His voice had a dramatic ring to it. Flavia was all ears.

He turned round to face Flavia and then back again to face Mikey. "Can I trust you both? I haven't mentioned this to anyone."

"Of course, you can trust us, Enzo," Flavia jumped in. But Mikey seemed preoccupied, manoeuvring a tricky junction. He said nothing.

"Remember, Flavia, when we bumped into each other yesterday morning at Forte Vigliena? I think I may have mentioned to you that the guys had paid me a visit the previous evening. Well, the reason for their visit was to tell me about their latest concerns."

Flavia had known all along that something was up. She could tell when she met her friend at Forte Vigliena that something was troubling him. "Go on," she said.

"They told me there's something fishy going on in one of the houses out at Villa Santa Panagia, near where they are working. They've seen two big men going in and out these past few days. Always the same two men, but never together, with bags and stuff."

"Is there somebody in the house they are visiting?" asked Flavia.

"No, not visiting. These houses are still being built there's nobody living there yet, no electricity, no water. But there's something going on in there. One of the guys said he'd heard shouting and screaming."

"Are those the new houses at Villa Santa Panagia? I was speaking with someone about those today." Mikey suddenly chipped in.

Enzo nodded. "That's right, it's a new housing development in the north of the city. What did you hear about them?"

"Oh, only that they are built to a very interesting design specification, especially the ones with cellars. The houses of the future, I heard," replied Mikey. "Something about a new solar panel system."

"What do the guys think is going on?" Flavia asked, keen to return to the matter in hand.

"That dear Flavia, is the million-dollar question!" declared Enzo. "Who knows what's going on? For all we know, there may be human trafficking of some sort or other going on."

"You mean, people are being kept in the house against their will?"

"I'm sorry to say this, Flavia, but I wouldn't put anything past Alfonso Bellotto."

Crikey, she thought, unsure how much of this to believe. If it was true, then Enzo really did need to talk to the police. Except he couldn't. That could jeopardise things for the migrants. Bellotto could turn nasty very quickly, seek retaliation.

"The thing is," Enzo continued, "I just don't know who

to turn to. As part of my ordination as a priest, I promised to obey my superiors. But I'm reluctant to go the bishop again. You see, the last time I asked for his help, I didn't feel entirely satisfied with the advice he gave me. It felt like he was sitting on the fence and was expecting me to do the same. So, I did some investigating …"

"And what did you find out?" asked Mikey.

"Salvatore Argento, Archbishop of Siracusa, and Signor Alfonso Bellotto are first cousins!" announced Enzo, looking first to Flavia and then back to Mikey.

Flavia's eyes opened wide in disbelief. The thought of so much power in one family was abhorrent to her. She had grown up during Berlusconi's heyday, and still associated power with corruption. They already suspected Bellotto of abusing his power, she would not be at all surprised if his bishop cousin was equally guilty of fraudulent behaviour. It made her blood boil to think of this. What chance did migrant workers stand?

Then, recovering her composure, she reminded herself that Don the priest had just taken a huge risk by confiding in herself and Mikey. She knew of course that he had absolutely nothing to fear from her. But did he know that? And what about Mikey? He had heard every word. She looked in the mirror, Mikey had a determined look on his face. He looked like a man on a mission.

"You did the right thing in telling us, Enzo. Didn't he, Mikey?" Flavia waited for Mikey to respond.

"Sure. We're your friends, Enzo," Mikey offered. He sounded genuine enough, but he didn't elaborate.

"I just wish we knew a way to help you and your friends," thought Flavia out loud. "There must be something we can do …"

Inside she had a niggling feeling there was still something that Enzo was not telling them. There was something else bothering him.

But this line of thought was soon interrupted when Mikey asked, "Will you be taking Rocco out tonight – in this rain?"

She watched Enzo turn towards Mikey and smile. There was definitely a good vibe between the two of them. But before the priest could reply to the question, Mikey continued, "He's a great dog is Rocco! He got a bit frisky on Tuesday night! I was glad I wasn't down in that crypt. You don't suppose there was anyone down there, do you?"

Enzo didn't reply to Mikey's question. Instead he suddenly jerked his head around almost 180 degrees to face the passenger side window. Flavia took it all in, conscious that there was nothing to see from the side window – just darkness. Why didn't Enzo like that question, she wondered.

They continued the journey in silence for a few more minutes, by which stage they had reached the outskirts of Siracusa and were heading now towards Ortigia. Flavia was deep in thought.

Then from out of nowhere, Enzo exclaimed, "What about Amnesty Italia? Maybe they can help the guys?"

Flavia sat up. "Of course!" she responded. "Why didn't I think of that? That is precisely what Amnesty are there for, to offer help and legal advice to refugees and asylum seekers."

"Oh, that's the group who organised the gig tonight!" Mikey seemed to have finally grasped what it was all about. Flavia caught his eye in the rear mirror and smiled. He was growing on her.

Enzo meanwhile posed another question. "I wonder if they run an advocacy service for migrants?"

"That I don't know. But I'll tell you what I do know,

Enzo," said Flavia, feeling fired up now. "There's going to be an Amnesty Italia rally in Siracusa this weekend! Why don't you and I go along there together and speak to them?"

Meanwhile, Franco was sitting comfortably at home. He put on his wire-framed reading glasses, so that he could concentrate on the grid displayed on his phone. Could it be a 4 here, he thought. Or is it a 7? He considered different options for a few seconds, then pressed the number 7 on his phone keypad. Franco smiled; he felt confident that he would solve this Sudoku puzzle.

He had many apps on his personal phone; apps that collected information on the fuel efficiency of his car, on the amount of electricity he used in his home, and so on. Apps that were very useful in his day-to-day life. But this particular app – Killer Sudoku – was the one that gave him most pleasure. Most evenings, he delighted in pitting his brain against the people (or perhaps the machine) that devised the toughest Sudoku games imaginable. He wasn't always successful, but he was proud with his success rate of 53% displayed at the top of the screen. According to the app, Franco was ranked in the top 15% among regular users of the app. His goal now was to get into the top 10%.

Sitting on his sofa, Franco looked up and surveyed his lounge. Earlier that evening, he had collected potentially breakable items placed around the room and put them in cupboards. He knew that the visitors due tomorrow shouldn't cause any bother, but accidents can happen, can't they? And he certainly wasn't prepared to lose the blue Murano glass jug that he had received for topping his class at the Police Academy in Catania, more than 20 years ago. So, the lounge – which had always been neat and tidy

– was now looking distinctly spartan. Even the framed photo of Amelia, taken when she started secondary school, had been moved from the table beside the sofa into Franco's bedroom.

Franco looked back at his phone. He needed to work out where to put the number 4 in the square in the centre of the grid. Four, he mused. An important number: the number of games needed to win the World Series. Perhaps the 4 should go between the numbers 2 and 3 already placed in this square? As he pondered this, Franco recalled his phone conversation with Ricci earlier that evening. He didn't have much to report; in fact, he seemed to be in a hurry. Probably something to do with that night out he had planned in Fontane Bianche. Franco hadn't been convinced by Ricci's claims the previous day that spending more time with the parish priest could provide leads for the case, but on the other hand it shouldn't do any harm. However, one thing that Ricci said had really hit home with Franco: that the Bats had now won two games and – if they won tonight – they would have three victories under their belt. Meaning that another win on Friday night would take them to the magic number: four. In which case, the Bats would have won the World Series. But what would that mean for Roberta Montanari?

Franco stood up, walked to the kitchen and poured himself a glass from the water dispenser next to the sink. The cold water instantly cleared his mind of the Sudoku; instead, concerns about the case rushed to the forefront of his thoughts. Yes, they had a lead – potentially a very important lead. They knew that Bruno Mangiafico had collected Signora Montanari's prescription a few days earlier and Giovanna had confirmed that Bruno was the brother of Roberta's neighbour, Rosa Mangiafico. However, Giovanna's surveillance of Rosa had so far failed to discover anything new. Rosa's trips to a supermarket, to the market in Ortigia and to a smart boutique had seemed innocuous. Furthermore, there had been no reported sightings of Bruno since his visit to the pharmacy the previous Sunday, when he had collected Signora Montanari's medication. Officers had been keeping a discreet eye on his last known address, a small flat in the north of the city, but there was no sign of life there.

If there was an upside to all of this, it was that there had been no further photos sent through by Tommaso. If the kidnappers were really threatening to harm Roberta Montanari, then Franco would expect them to contact Dani again. So, if they hadn't messaged him, then maybe the situation hadn't worsened. However, if the kidnappers had issued a very strong threat – even to kill Signora Montanari – then Dani might have decided it was too dangerous to share this information with his father.

Franco opened a kitchen cupboard and took out a bar of chocolate. Not any chocolate, but Modica chocolate. Real chocolate, in the view of Franco and of most Sicilians. Brought to the town of Modica several centuries earlier by the Spanish, during their rule of Sicily, this very dark chocolate with its grainy texture and aromatic flavour was now a favourite of both locals and visitors to the island. A piece of this chocolate would really help me concentrate on the Sudoku, thought Franco. But, looking up at the digital clock on the wall, he saw that it was nearly 22.00. He wouldn't normally eat at this time and – with cocoa this strong – he might find it difficult to sleep. Best to leave this for now, he thought, putting the bar back in the cupboard.

Franco had walked back into the lounge and just sat down when he heard a ring tone. It wasn't from his personal phone, lying on the coffee table in front of him. Rather, it was the ordered tones of Bach's Prelude in C Major coming from his work phone, lying on the ledge in his hallway. Franco strode through and dutifully collected his phone, before returning to the lounge and sitting back down on the sofa. He looked quizzically at the name on the display: RICCI. Why on Earth is he ringing me now, thought Franco. Hadn't we agreed that Ricci would message me when he returned to Siracusa?

He pressed the green phone button, then barked, "What have you got for me?"

"*Dottore*, I've got something really important! Really, really important!" Franco was struck by the speed of Ricci's delivery; the words came flying out of the speaker, as though they were racing each other to see which would reach Franco's ear first. Franco had experienced Ricci get excited before, but not as much as this.

"Yes," he replied, slowly.

Franco listened carefully as Ricci recounted his conversation with Don Enzo earlier that evening, during the trip back to Siracusa from Fontane Bianche. Initially he couldn't understand why Ricci had got so worked up about this; something about migrants working on a building site who were being exploited by their boss. The situation didn't sound good, but surely it didn't warrant a call at this time of night. Then Ricci mentioned the name of the construction company that the migrants were working for.

"Bellotto!" responded Franco, his ears pricking up. "Are you sure?"

"Absolutely!" said Ricci. "In fact, Don Enzo raised this matter with the bishop, who wasn't inclined to pursue it further. He later discovered that the bishop, that's Archbishop Argento, and Alfonso Bellotto are cousins!"

"I see," said Franco. He had no love for Bellotto or what he stood for. But pursuing an investigation against him – either on a criminal or solely financial basis – would be fraught with risks; Bellotto had very good connections and any case would need to be iron-tight. If a criminal investigation were initiated and Franco carried it out successfully, then it could give his career a much-needed fillip. But the consequences for him if it went wrong were too awful to contemplate. Best to pass this on to the financial police, he thought.

"This is useful, Ricci," continued Franco. "But why are ringing me now? Couldn't this wait until tomorrow?"

"No, *dottore*! There's more!" Ricci blurted out what Don Enzo had told him about suspicious activity in one of the houses that was being built by Bellotto Construction. Two men going in and out of a house that had no electricity or water. Reports of shouts and screams from there. By now, Franco was listening intently, slowly rubbing his beard as he did so.

"Where is this house?" asked Franco.

"It's in Villa Santa Panagia," Ricci responded. "In fact, I was speaking this morning with Marco, the architecture student who's a big fan of the Bakerside Bats. He's the guy who's been telling me everything about the World Series. Well, he and other students were going to Villa Santa Panagia this afternoon, to look round the houses that Bellotto Construction are building there. Except that they couldn't visit the new homes with special cellars. My bet is that the house that Don Enzo's friends are talking about is one of those with a –"

"Cellar!" Franco's voice reverberated around his lounge. Of course, he thought, it all fits!

"Oh," said Ricci, with a puzzled tone. "Is there something else?"

Franco realised that he hadn't told Ricci about the link between Alfonso Bellotto and Rosa Mangiafico – or, for that matter, that the person who had collected Roberta's prescription was related to Rosa. There hadn't been any need: Ricci's job was to keep an eye on people using the launderette.

"Yes, I'll tell you later," replied Franco. "Before that, I want you to track down the parish priest's friends and bring them to the police station first thing tomorrow. I need to speak with them asap. That's an order!"

Franco heard a long "AAAAH" from the phone, then he spoke again. "I said, that's an order!!"

"I don't think that's a good idea, *dottore*." Ricci's voice was quiet but firm. He went on to explain that the migrant workers didn't wish to report Bellotto's exploitation of them to the police, for fear of being deported. So, if they had any inkling that the police wanted to bring them in for questioning, they would quickly make themselves scarce. As Ricci said this, Franco looked to his side, through the door to his bedroom, to where he could see the recently moved photo of Amelia. He thought about her impassioned support for Amnesty Italia and for people whose circumstances left them at the mercy of unscrupulous individuals such as Bellotto. Maybe there's another way to do this, he thought.

"OK," said Franco. "I see what you're saying. What do you propose we do?"

"I think we should move very carefully," responded Ricci. "Don Enzo is planning to raise the workers' case with Amnesty Italia on Saturday; there's going to be a rally in Siracusa."

Franco gave a half-laugh. "Yes, I know! However, we can't wait that long. If Dani's team win tonight, then we might have only 24 hours to find Roberta."

"Exactly. Here's my suggestion ... I seem to have Don Enzo's confidence now. He took a big risk this evening in telling me about the migrants and what they had seen. As far as I can tell, he doesn't suspect that I'm a police detective. Also, the migrants are willing to confide in the priest. So, I'll suggest to Don Enzo that the two of us meet with the workers tomorrow and find out more about this house in Villa Santa Panagia."

"But why would they agree to meet with you?" asked Franco. "You're just a guy who works at a launderette. Why should they tell you what they've seen?"

"I'd tell them the truth," said Ricci. Franco took a deep breath; an extremely deep breath. But just before he could explode, Ricci continued.

"Not the whole truth, obviously. Just part of it. That I was concerned for Signora Montinari who normally works at the launderette; that I thought she might have been taken against her will. And that, as a colleague, I wanted to investigate a possible lead in tracing her – but without involving the police. Furthermore, I'd tell the migrants that if the police did get involved subsequently, then I wouldn't reveal my meeting with them. Instead, I would say that I visited Villa Santa Panagia following a conversation with an architecture student and happened to notice something strange there."

"Do you think they'll buy it?" Franco was sceptical.

"I think there's a good chance they will," responded Ricci. "Clearly I would need to ask them and Don Enzo not to reveal this to anyone else. However, provided I can gain their trust, I think it's possible."

Franco paused briefly as he rubbed his goatee beard once more. "Ricci," he said, "this is what you're going to do: contact the parish priest and set up the meeting for tomorrow. Don't worry about closing the launderette;

people can cope for a few hours without it. Find out what these workers have seen and tell me straight afterwards if it's worth pursuing this. I want to hear back from you by 5pm tomorrow; 5pm at the latest! And let me know asap if the meeting's not going to happen! If necessary, I'll bring the priest and his friends in for questioning."

"I'm sure I can convince Don Enzo to arrange the meeting. *Buona notte, dottore.*"

"*Ciao*, Ricci. Speak tomorrow." Franco ended the call and sat back on the sofa, reflecting on what Ricci had just told him. There was a lot at play here: Signora Montanari's safety, the career of one of the city's most high-profile citizens – and Franco's own career. Plus, the future of migrants wishing to start a new life in Italy. But Franco felt exhilarated; solving cases like this was what he lived for.

He knew what he needed now. He went to the kitchen, collected the bar of Modica chocolate, sat back down on the sofa and bit into a piece of the bar; so good! So much so that Franco decided to eat the rest of the chocolate bar. No matter that he might find it difficult to sleep tonight; he had so much to think about. What would Ricci find out? Who to pick for surveillance of the house? What more could they discover about the development at Villa Santa Panagia? But before all of that, Franco picked up his own phone and returned to the Sudoku. Of course, he thought, it's obvious! He put the number 4 between the 2 and the 3 – then smiled.

FRIDAY 27TH OCTOBER

CHAPTER 8

Flavia stood on the pavement outside her boutique on Friday morning, sipping on a cup of sweet, milky coffee. Soon it would be time to raise the shutters and open shop. The weather had calmed down since the previous evening and the roads and pavements were already dry again. In the warm morning sun, everything looked shiny and new.

However, Flavia herself was feeling neither shiny nor new. She hadn't slept well and was suffering the after-effects of missing out on her usual eight hours sleep. The ring tone on her phone had woken her with a start at 7 o'clock that morning. As it did every morning. But this morning it had still felt like the middle of the night when she stretched out to take the call. She struggled a bit with time management at the best of times, hence the morning call from her mother, checking that Flavia was up, but also for a chat. The two of them spoke several times a day, every day. But this morning Flavia had not been in the mood for a long conversation. Doing her best to sound bright and breezy, she briefly assured her mother that they had all had a great time at the gig the previous evening, despite the weather. Then abruptly she made some excuse about needing to jump in the shower, before promising to phone her mother later with all the details of the night out at Fontane Bianche.

The truth was that Flavia hadn't wanted to worry her mother. Signora Vitale didn't need to know about the recurring thoughts of migrants that had kept her daughter awake most of the night. Nor that she had been sick at the thought of that beast of a man, Bellotto, exploiting those vulnerable men. Anxious for their wellbeing and the wellbeing of her friend Enzo, Flavia had tossed and turned for hours on end. At some stage she had got up to make herself a milky drink. That was when she had discovered that she wasn't the only insomniac in the flat. Miles had sprung up from his basket and meowed at her feet when she'd switched on the kitchen light.

Sitting down in her favourite, battered old easy chair with Miles on her lap, she had soothed herself, gently stroking his soft fur. She had calmed herself by telling Miles that she and Enzo would go to the Amnesty rally on Saturday and they would seek advice there. After all, what else could they do, she had reasoned. Then she and Miles had sat contentedly together, the occasional purr from Miles punctuating the silence that ensued. Flavia couldn't remember how long they had sat like that.

The next thing she remembered was reflecting on the car journey back from Fontane Bianche. Something Mikey had said had struck a chord. They had been talking about possibly going to the police. "Maybe it's worth a try," he had said. Again, sharing her thoughts with Miles, Flavia had spent a long time trying to figure out what Mikey had meant by that. What was he trying to suggest, she had wondered. He had certainly seemed interested in the plight of the migrants and had strong feelings about current government immigration policy. He was definitely on their side, Flavia had felt sure of that. And if it was true that people were being kept against their will at Villa Santa Panagia, then Enzo really would need to talk with the police. She had ended up convincing herself that Mikey had a point, they could at least try to find a way of informing the police without Bellotto finding out about it. Maybe, just maybe, Mikey could help … That was when she had hatched a plan. And then finally fallen fast asleep.

It was nearly 10 o'clock now. Having opened the shutters, Flavia paused to stretch her aching back. An easy chair was fine for chilling but not for a good night's sleep. She took a drink of her takeaway coffee and glanced into the window of her shop. Reflected in the glass, she spotted the familiar figure of the parish priest, walking towards her with the ever-faithful Rocco at his side. Turning quickly round to face him, she almost choked on her coffee. "Enzo! Enzo!" she spluttered, "we need to talk. I've had an idea!"

It didn't take much to persuade Enzo. He seemed to like her suggestion very much and was more than willing to give it a go. Just ten minutes later she watched as he strode down via Vicenza, heading for the launderette. "Good luck!" she called out after him.

That afternoon, Mikey was afoot. He had closed up the launderette for the day and had set off at 3.30pm, together with his new friend, Enzo, and Rocco. As they were leaving via Veneto, Signor Carusa had called across to Mikey. Something about wanting to have a word with him. However, Mikey had given his apologies; this would need to wait for another time.

Now they were crossing the bridge from Ortigia over into the main part of Siracusa. Mikey checked his phone: 15:40. Good, we should get there shortly after 4pm, he thought, whilst he quickly looked at the message notifications on the phone.

Suddenly he gasped.

"*Scusi!*" The woman who had just bumped into Mikey took a step back, then smiled at him. He noticed her American accent and her red 'I love Sicily' baseball cap.

"No problem!" he replied, in English. "Have a good day!" he said as she walked on and re-joined the group of tourists walking across into Ortigia.

Mikey spotted another tour group coming towards him. Glancing to his left, he saw a massive cruise ship moored in the Porto Grande. He remembered visiting Siracusa on a cruise ship the previous year and taking the same route into Ortigia that the tourists were following now. He had good memories of that trip. But musing on them would need to wait for another day.

WOOF! Rocco's bark unnerved a few of the tourists, who pressed themselves against the steel railing on the side of the bridge whilst the parish priest and his dog passed by in single file, followed by Mikey.

"Quiet, Rocco!" Enzo spoke softly as he calmed his dog. "Sorry," he said in English to the tourists. "He gets very excited." Fortunately, the tourists were understanding; a couple of them patted Rocco affectionately and one man took a photo of the dog on his phone. Stopping briefly, Mikey surveyed the visitors from the New World; many of them were wearing designer trainers and the logos of Tommy Hilfiger, Donna Karan and such-like were prominent on their tops and jackets.

Rocco, Enzo and Mikey crossed the bridge and walked through the modern part of the city, heading in the direction of the venue for the migrant drop-in. Mikey had offered to give them a lift in Totti, but the priest had preferred to walk. At least this gave the two of them more time to chat. An opportunity to find out more about each other, and for Mikey to learn more about the drop-in.

"Does this drop-in take place every day?" asked Mikey.

"Yes, every day from Monday to Friday," responded the parish priest. "From 4pm through to 7pm. I can't make it every day, but I try to get there two or three times a week."

"And how many people normally attend?"

"It varies. Some of the guys work most afternoons, so – on Mondays or Tuesdays, for example – there might be fewer than 10. But building work ends early on Friday, so I hope there'll be 20-25 today. Maybe more."

They were now well off the tourist track. Indeed, Mikey realised that they weren't far from where he was living. However, he hadn't previously been in the street that they had just entered. Passing a series of anonymous apartment blocks, Mikey saw a couple of boys wearing blue Siracusa Calcio tops in the middle of the street, kicking a football to each other. Good skill, he thought, as one of the boys deftly brought the ball under control; maybe he'll be good enough to get a trial with AS Roma one day?

BEEP! It was Enzo's phone. He opened it and smiled. "A WhatsApp from Flavia!" he said. Then showed Mikey the message: *GOOD LUCK!* with a smiley face.

"That's really nice of her," said Mikey.

"Yes," replied Enzo, putting the phone away. "Flavia's a really good friend. I'm glad she suggested that you come with me to the drop-in today, Mikey."

"Yeah, great idea." In fact, Mikey had been delighted when the parish priest had visited him at the launderette that morning and told him about Flavia's suggestion. As a consequence of this, he would be able to attend the drop-in and meet the migrants without needing to reveal Roberta's disappearance to either Enzo or Flavia.

And there had been more good news earlier that day, when Mikey had checked *La Gazzetta dello Sport*'s website and discovered that the Kats had beaten the Bats in the previous night's match. The Bats had chosen not to use Dani, even as a relief pitcher; sounds as though his performances in the past two matches had influenced that decision, thought Mikey. The score in the World Series was now 2-2, meaning that the championship wouldn't be decided until Sunday night at the earliest. So, the police now had at least two more days to find and free Roberta Montanari.

Mikey was looking forward to speaking with the priest's friends and hearing more about what was happening at Villa Santa Panagia. Before then, though …

"Have you known Flavia long?" he asked.

Enzo nodded. "A couple of years. We first met when I was walking round Ortigia early one morning, shortly after she opened her shop. We seemed to hit it off straight away and we try to chat at least once a day. It's good to have someone outside of the church with whom I can speak. Someone I can be open with."

"She seems like a very caring person," responded Mikey. "Does she talk much about herself?"

"Oh yes! Flavia loves to talk. She's passionate about her business and the jewellery she produces. And she's close to her parents."

"Is there anyone special in her life?" Mikey tried to sound nonchalant.

His friend laughed. "Yes, there is – Miles!" Rocco started barking. "Easy boy!" continued the parish priest, stroking his dog. "I actually like Miles, but Miles and

Rocco don't get on. Flavia and I try to keep them apart as far as possible."

"To be honest, Enzo, I would much rather spend time with Rocco than with Miles!"

"Miles is cool when you get to know him, Mikey. But to get back to your question, Flavia has spoken in the past about boyfriends, but I don't think there's anyone at present." Mikey noticed Enzo raise an eyebrow, very slightly, as he said this. A few seconds later, the priest pointed to a single storey building at the end of the street. "Here we are!"

Approaching the open door of the building, Mikey could hear the sounds of a guitar being played. Rocco raced ahead of both of them, yapping excitedly as he did so. "*Ciao*, Rocco!" Mikey heard friendly voices greeting the dog, just before he stepped through the door himself.

Mikey was now in a large space, the size of a café. Enzo had explained to him earlier that the building had previously been a bar. It had closed a couple of years earlier and then been bought by a community group that supports migrants. The bar counter was still there, but with no alcohol on the shelves behind it. Instead, there appeared to be various types of coffee and tea. A few men were standing at the bar, chatting. In the far corner of the room, Mikey saw a young man playing the guitar, with others sat nearby, nodding their heads in rhythm with the tune and smiling. Standing next to a table nearby, a man, woman and child – perhaps part of the same family – were examining the many loaves of bread and bags with fruit and vegetables that had been laid out. Meanwhile, at other tables spread throughout the room, people were talking; some in Italian, some in languages that Mikey didn't understand. Surveying the room, he guessed that there were around 20 people in total. Aside from a couple of others, he was the only white person there.

Enzo walked towards two young men who were patting Rocco and offering him biscuits. "Please don't do that," he said, "Rocco gets plenty to eat as it is!" The men laughed, then each in turn shook Enzo's hand vigorously. "This is my friend, Mikey," continued the parish priest. "Pleasure to meet you!" they said as then they shook Mikey's hand. He was impressed by the warmth in their voices.

The four of them moved over to the bar and ordered various teas and coffees. Enzo recommended a herbal tea to Mikey; not his usual tipple, but he was willing to give it a go. Mikey offered to pay, but was politely refused; here, drinks were free to all. They sat down at a table and indulged in small talk for a few minutes, discussing football and their favourite players. Mikey was surprised when the others said that they didn't know Totti; surely it wasn't that long since he retired, thought Mikey. Their favourite was Mbappé. "He's a good player," said Mikey. "But he's still got a lot to prove, in my view."

Suddenly, Enzo raised his hand and started waving. Mikey turned around and saw a couple of young men entering the room. He wasn't sure if he had seen them before. However, their dust-engrained jackets were similar to those worn by the men he had noticed leaving San Valentino church on Tuesday evening. Mikey followed Enzo's lead, standing up and walking towards the men, then shaking their hands as Enzo introduced everyone.

"Come, let's sit down." Enzo motioned towards to an unoccupied table towards the back of the bar. "We can have a private talk there."

The four sat down and the parish priest explained that Mikey was a friend who wanted to help. The two young men initially said nothing, then looked at each other and started speaking in what Mikey guessed was their own language. One of the guys, with a massive chest and arms like tree trunks, spoke animatedly and at length; the other guy, who was slimmer with a goatee beard, was less demonstrative and said little. Although he couldn't understand the conversation, Mikey had the impression the big guy was trying to convince the slim guy to engage with the parish priest's friend.

After a couple of minutes, the big guy turned to Mikey and spoke to him in faltering English. "You won't tell the police about us, will you?"

Mikey maintained his poker-face expression. "You're in no danger, you have my word."

"You can trust Mikey," added Enzo, placing his hand on Mikey's shoulder.

The big guy nodded to his friend, then turned back to Mikey. "This is just between us, OK?"

"OK," replied Mikey.

Before saying anymore, the big guy looked around to check that they weren't being overheard. He then took his time to explain how he, his friend and several other migrants had taken up jobs at a building site on the edge of the city, following Enzo's representations to the head of the construction company; how promises of good wages and good working conditions had proved to be lies; and how they had been threatened with the authorities and deportation if they contacted the police. Mikey said little but nodded occasionally to show he understood what was being said. He sensed the depth of feeling in what he heard.

"Don Enzo knows all of this," said the big guy. "I wouldn't have told anyone else."

He stopped and turned to the priest. "Have you told

your friend what happened this week?"

"It's better if you say," said Enzo.

"OK," said the big guy. He then related how he and his friend had – over the course of the past few days – seen a couple of men going in and out of one of the apartment blocks that was still under construction. They had never seen the two men together; one would turn up in a van, go into the building, then shortly afterwards the other would come out, get into the same van and drive off.

"Have you ever been in that building?" asked Mikey.

"No!" roared the big guy. "We've been told to stay away! They say that the buildings in that street are dangerous, because they've got cellars. Dangerous? Nonsense! What about the unsafe scaffolding that we use every day? That's dangerous!"

Rocco, who had been dozing after enjoying a good snack of biscuits, suddenly woke up and barked. "Easy!" said Enzo, looking first at his dog, then at the big guy. "Easy!" he repeated.

"No," continued the big guy, "we haven't been in there. There's no electricity there, no water. But then yesterday …" He hesitated, then continued, in a quiet voice, "Yesterday we were passing the end of the street and we heard voices. They seemed to be coming from inside that building."

"What did you hear?" asked Mikey.

"We couldn't make out what was being said. There seemed to be a couple of screams; perhaps a woman or a child's voice. Then there was some shouting; sounded like a man. Then it was quiet."

Mikey rubbed his moustache, slowly. "What do you think might be going on?"

"No idea. But whatever it is, it's not good." The big guy sat back in his chair. "My friend here has something for you to see." He nodded to the slim guy, who took out his phone, briefly scrolled through it, then placed the phone on the table.

The big guy pointed at the photo on the phone. "This is the street," he said.

Mikey looked at what appeared to be two partly constructed three-storey buildings on either side of a dirt track leading to wasteland. The big guy magnified the photo. "This is the building here." He then zoomed the photo out. "Here's the van these guys are using. We took this photo today." Mikey saw a white van parked at the end of the track. The registration plate wasn't legible. Nevertheless, this was a highly useful piece of information.

"Could I have a copy of this photo, please?" asked Mikey. The two guys spoke briefly in their own language, then the big guy responded. "My friend doesn't want to give you his phone number, but he's willing to send the photo to Don Enzo and he can send it to you."

"Perfect!" Mikey smiled. As the slim guy tapped on his phone, Mikey continued. "Where on the building site is this street?"

"The street doesn't have a name yet. However, it's on the left off the avenue when you come through the main gate. You can't miss it!"

PING! Mikey checked his phone; the photo had just arrived from Enzo. He then checked the time displayed at the top of the phone: 16:55. Just five minutes to go until the *commissario's* deadline.

"You've been extremely helpful, thank you so much! I will do my very best to help and I'll keep Enzo informed." Mikey stood up, shook everyone's hands and said his goodbyes. Eager to make a call, he was secretly delighted when the parish priest said that he would need to stay on at the drop-in. Stepping outside, Mikey checked he was out of sight, then punched the air in delight. He pulled out his phone, scrolled through his contacts and pressed the phone symbol under the name: *FORENSE*.

Franco Spina was reflecting on the call he had just received from Mikey Ricci following the drop-in and the new information received. There was a lot to think about and he didn't want to get things wrong. Walking over to the window of his office, he looked out in the direction of Etna, seeking inspiration. But there was no sign of the volcano today and certainly not at this hour. It was already 5.20pm, the sun was retiring for the day. In an hour's time it would be dark outside.

Returning to his desk, he opened his emergency supplies of Modica chocolate. Not that today was an emergency, of course, but Franco knew that a sneaky square or two of the dark stuff would help him to calm down and concentrate. He got stuck into a bar of his favourite flavour, Sicilian citrus, his nostrils dilating at the intense scent of toasted cocoa mingled with lemon zest. Munching away, he took stock of what was now known about Roberta Montanari's likely whereabouts. He studied the photo that Ricci had just forwarded to him. It had been taken by Ricci's informants, a group of guys who were currently working on the Villa Santa Panagia building site. The photo showed the building, or the shell of a building, where it was claimed a person or persons was being held against their will.

Franco noted that this building was located in what looked like a cul-de-sac that ended in wasteland. The building itself also appeared to back onto wasteland. He reckoned it had been designed to house six apartments, two on each floor, with a communal basement. It reminded him of apartment blocks he had seen elsewhere in the city, nothing too large but built in close proximity to each other in order to create a sense of community.

By the looks of things, this particular apartment block was situated on the edge of the Villa Santa Panagia estate. But to be sure, he would need to see a plan of the estate. That could quickly be arranged. But first he called Giovanna to his office, before searching the council website. Fortunately, he was familiar with the website and knew exactly what he was looking for. By the time Giovanna tapped on his door a plan of the Villa Santa Panagia building site was opening up on his large computer screen.

Beckoning his deputy to take a seat near his desk, Franco swiftly returned what was left of the Modica chocolate to his emergency supplies drawer. He briefly filled Giovanna in on Ricci's call. Together, they then looked at the plan of the building site. The whole site was surrounded by a fence. Outside the perimeter fence was nothing but wasteland. The site entrance was on a fairly busy road, linking suburbs in the north of the city with the southern part of mainland Siracusa.

The main road leading into the estate extended from the site entrance at one end to a vast expanse of wasteland at the other. Along one side of the road were plans for three buildings. Leading off the main road, Franco quickly located a solitary cul-de-sac with plans for two further, similarly sized buildings. The buildings were directly opposite each other

Basta! Franco thought to himself. He had made his mind up. Turning away from the screen to face Giovanna, he said, "I need you to get out there before darkness falls."

"To Villa Santa Panagia?"

"Take one of the unmarked cars and park on the street

outside the site. The last thing we want is to raise any suspicion."

"OK, boss. I guess you want me to –"

"Suss out the perimeter of the site." Franco interjected, pointing to the plan, "The main gate will surely be locked at this time, go round the outside – target the wasteland at the end of this cul-de-sac."

"What about –"

"CCTV?" Franco was one step ahead. "That's precisely the point, Gio. And it's another reason to avoid the main gate. Look out for any cameras. You're wearing dark clothes, that's a good start but be vigilant."

He stopped to check his smartwatch. "OK, it's 5.40pm now. You should get there in five minutes. If you leave now, that should give you about half an hour of daylight."

Giovanna was already on her feet.

"Call me when you get there, I want to be kept informed."

Giovanna gave him a thumbs up.

Franco knew he would not have to wait long before hearing from Giovanna. So, when his smartwatch alerted him to a call twenty minutes later, he was ready for it. Except, the call that came through was not on his work phone.

"*Ciao* papà!"

"Amelia!"

With the turn of events following Ricci's call, Franco had momentarily forgotten that his daughter and her friends were coming to Siracusa that evening and he had promised to put them up.

"Where are you? Are you on the bus?"

"Sorry papà, change of plan!"

"But you are still coming, aren't you?"

"Sure! Wouldn't miss the rally for anything! But we

can't make it tonight. You see –"

"So, does that mean you'll be coming down tomorrow morning instead?"

"Yip! Coming down tomorrow morning and I'll be staying over tomorrow night – just me."

"Great!" Franco responded, genuinely delighted that he would now be able to spend more time with Amelia on her own. And secretly pleased that this freed him up to spend more time on the case, especially at this crucial stage.

"Let's talk more tomorrow. Let me know when you get here," Franco continued, his mind already refocused on the evening ahead and the call from Giovanna.

Placing the phone back in his pocket, he heaved a sigh of relief. He just had time to bring up again on his computer screen the plan of Villa Santa Panagia. Paper copies of the site plan would be needed. He sent the link with printing instructions through to the front desk, then studied the plan anew in readiness for Giovanna's call.

A few minutes later, he had a paper copy of the plan in front of him and was following it as he listened to Giovanna's update. She had had little difficulty in locating the cul-de-sac from the wasteland adjacent to the site. But pointed out it was little more than a dirt track. Just after 6 pm, an unmarked van had turned up at the site entrance. There was no other vehicular traffic around at that time and the gate was closed. Clearly the van driver had means of unlocking the gate. Giovanna had watched the van turn into the cul-de-sac and pull up at the end of the track. A bulky looking man got out, bearing a supermarket carrier bag, and entered a building, that backs onto wasteland.

Franco was all ears. "Go on, Gio!" he urged.

"About ten minutes later, another person of slighter build left the same premises alone and proceeded to reverse the van out of the cul-de-sac, down the main makeshift road to the site entrance. The driver opened the gate, and drove out onto the street, before returning on foot to secure the gate."

"And in which direction did the van leave?"

"Oh no doubt about that, boss. It was heading south into town and at speed."

All the while, Franco had been following what Giovanna said on the map in front of him. He had heard every word, and now he wanted to speak. But Giovanna hadn't finished.

"Just a minute, boss. You did tell me to suss out the perimeter! And that's exactly what I did!" she exclaimed. Franco could visualise a defiant impish look on her face.

"Go on," he said.

"Well, here's where things get very interesting," enthused his deputy. "You see, the surrounding fence is pretty tatty. I found a weak spot, where we could easily climb through unnoticed. And …" she paused for effect, much to Franco's irritation.

"It's very close to the end of the cul-de-sac! Not only that, boss, there are two buildings in the cul-de-sac. One where the action is going on, and another one directly opposite, on the other side of the dirt track. Both of them back onto wasteland."

Franco opened his drawer again and brought out the Modica. Then, perching himself on his desk, he conceded, "Good work, Gio." Munching away contentedly, Franco thought through the implications of what Giovanna had found out, especially in light of the baseball developments that Ricci had told him. The result of the latest baseball match meant that the championship wouldn't be decided until Sunday night at the earliest. It was still only Friday. They had time. And with his daughter not expected now until the next day, Franco had the opportunity.

Franco's mind was made up. He jumped down from his desk, announcing to his deputy, "We'll stake out!".

"We'll stake out, boss?" asked a puzzled Giovanna.

"That's right, Gio. I'm going to set up 24-hour surveillance of the property in Villa Santa Panagia. The second building in the cul-de-sac, the one directly opposite the property we are interested in, will be our stakeout house. We will base ourselves there. You and I will do the first shift – this evening, starting at 8pm." There was no questioning Franco's authority. He was a man on a mission. And he felt fired up. But he was also smart enough to realise that he needed to take his deputy with him. He couldn't do this without her.

"Is there anything else I should know, Gio?" he asked.

There was a pause.

"Oh, I almost forgot!" exclaimed his deputy. He heard her leafing through her notepad.

But Franco was one step ahead of her. "Not the registration number of the white van, by any chance?" he quizzed with a wry smile on his face.

"Spot on, boss!" Giovanna sounded pleased, reading out from her notepad the number she had written down.

"Excellent work, Gio. I'll get that checked out. Grab something to eat if you need to and meet me outside in the car park in an hour's time."

SATURDAY 28TH OCTOBER

CHAPTER 9

The voice of Lady Gaga drifted out into via Veneto, accompanied by a pounding disco soundtrack. On hearing his ringtone, Mikey – who had been standing out in the street – turned and walked back into the launderette. Picking up his mobile phone from the table where customers would fold their newly dried clothes, two things on the phone's screen caught his eye. Firstly, the day and time: Saturday, 08.15. Secondly, the name of the caller: *FORENSE*.

On pressing the answer button, Lady Gaga's voice went silent. "*Pronto!*" said Mikey, feeling energised after his early morning espresso at Antonino's bar.

"Any news, Ricci?"

Mikey had guessed that Franco would get straight to the point. They hadn't spoken since Mikey's phone call the previous evening, when he had relayed the details of his visit to the migrant drop-in.

"Nothing here," he said. "I re-opened the launderette

about half an hour ago and it's been very quiet so far. But there has been news from America."

"The baseball?" Franco sounded interested, although Mikey also detected an element of tiredness in *Forense's* voice.

"Yes, that's right. I've watched some highlights from last night's match. It wasn't good for Dani – but it might be good for his mother."

Mikey relayed what he had seen on his phone whilst in Antonino's bar earlier. He had been so engaged by the latest game between the Bats and the Kats that he had accepted the offer of a second espresso, rather than scoot off as on previous mornings. In short, it had been a very bad night for the Bats and for Dani in particular. The young man had been selected as starting pitcher by his team, clearly hoping for a return to winning ways after leaving him out for the previous match. However, the video highlights showed the Kats' batters scoring a succession of home runs off Dani's pitching. A few days earlier, Marco had expressed his shock to Mikey when Dani was taken off in the 4th innings in the second game of the World Series. However, in this latest game, Dani was substituted at the end of the 3rd innings, at which point the Bats were losing 5:0!

"What was Dani's reaction?" asked Franco.

"He was in tears, *dottore*. He looked absolutely broken."

A long hmmm came down the phone line, then Franco continued: "From what you're seeing in the sports press, is anyone suggesting that Dani's trying to play badly deliberately?"

"No, *dottore*. People are saying that Dani is a great talent but he's still young, this is his first World Series. He's not used to dealing with this level of pressure."

"Except that it's not just the pressure of playing baseball at its highest level that Dani's having to cope with …"

"Indeed," said Mikey, before his boss could continue. "I guess that Dani had been told by the mobsters holding his mother not to make it obvious that he was playing poorly on purpose. But he must be thinking a million different things at the moment. There's no way he can focus."

Mikey went on to explain that the Bats had made a mini-comeback after Dani's departure. However, they still lost the game 4:7.

"So, Ricci," said Franco, "there've been five games now and the Kats lead by three games to two? Meaning they need to win just one of the two remaining games to become champions, right?"

"Spot on, *dottore*!" Mikey was impressed by how quickly and accurately Franco had worked this out, given everything else that he was dealing with. "The Bats need to win both these games. But the Kats have home advantage for both of them. The first of those is tomorrow night. The Kats are favourites now to win the World Series – you wouldn't get much money if you bet on them today."

Franco sighed: "Hopefully a Kats win will mean that Signora Montanari won't come to any harm. But for sure her captors are going to be totally cock-a-hoop! It looks as if all the crooks who knew about the plan before the World Series started and who bet on the Kats when they were rank outsiders will be set up for life!"

Mikey heard very clearly the frustration in Franco's voice. "Yes," he said, deciding that it was time to change the subject. "How's the investigation going?"

"It's going well." Franco sounded more relaxed as he

explained how he and Giovanna had staked out the building at Villa Santa Panagia that Mikey had heard about the previous day. "For the most part it was pretty quiet. We could hear traffic on the main road nearby, but there was no noise from the building site. However, we did see some activity a couple of times during the night."

"What happened?"

"Remember the white van in the photo you sent us yesterday? It arrived on site around midnight and was driven up to the building, the small apartment block, you mentioned. Giovanna and I were watching from the building opposite, just about 10 metres away – across the dirt track. We saw someone get out of the van and walk into the block opposite us. In the dart it was difficult to get a good view, but Giovanna thought it might be the same man who had left the site in the same van around 6 pm yesterday. After a few minutes, someone came out of the same building – male, large – got into the van and drove off. Giovanna's pretty sure it was the same person who had arrived there six hours earlier."

"Sounds as though the two of them are sharing shifts," said Mikey.

"Exactly!" Any trace of tiredness had vanished now from Franco's voice. "The van returned at 6 am this morning and what looked to be the same two guys switched places again. They seem to be working on a 6-hour on, 6-hour off basis."

"How long was your shift, *dottore*?"

"12 hours! Gio and I have just finished; Pappalardo and Tacchini have taken over. I'm on my way home now. We'll need to follow up other lines of enquiry, but I've got a feeling we're on the right track thanks to the information you collected. Good work, Ricci."

Mikey was taken aback. Although his boss hadn't been

fulsome in his praise, Mikey felt a sense of pride, nonetheless.

"Thank you, *dottore*! Be sure to get some sleep now."

"Will do. But remember to keep a look out for other possible leads, Ricci! There might be something we've missed."

"Of course, *dottore*."

With that, the line went dead. Mikey was accustomed by now to Franco's abruptness and wasn't surprised by the absence of any greeting at the end of conversations.

Mikey put the phone in his pocket and wandered out into the street. Glancing up and down via Veneto, he wondered if he would have a chance to take part in the stake-out at Villa Santa Panagia. Franco had acknowledged his help in locating the property. But did *Commissario* Spina value Mikey sufficiently to bring him into his inner circle, alongside Giovanna Campisi? Participating in the stake-out and maybe even arresting the kidnappers would be a fillip for Mikey's career. There was no doubt about that.

He looked across the street to Totti. There weren't many cars parked there on this Saturday morning and finding a space had been easy. Gazing at his beloved Cinquecento, Mikey smiled; he and Totti had been together for a long time, zooming around Rome, and driving to and from his parents' home in the countryside outside the capital. Good days, he thought. He had never viewed his move to Sicily as being permanent; rather, he had hoped that it would help him advance his career in the police. But for now, he felt marooned in the launderette in Ortigia, away from the main action in the north of the city. Had this really been a step up for him or was it a step sideways – or even backwards? In which case, wouldn't he be best returning to the city and the area he knew best and loved?

Well, he pondered, perhaps there might be one reason for staying in Siracusa. A picture of Flavia, with her long dark hair and bedecked in her gorgeous handmade jewellery, came into his mind. Here's someone who knows how to enjoy life, thought Mikey. He really would like to get to know her better. Perhaps he could pop by her shop later? But wasn't this the day of the Amnesty Italia rally? In which case, Flavia wouldn't be around?

Mikey turned and walked towards the launderette entrance to check details of the rally on his phone. Before he reached there, his attention was captured by an animated conversation taking place outside Bar Stella at the top of the street. Two men were gesticulating and pointing at the front of a newspaper. One of them was clearly Signor Carusa, dressed elegantly as always; however, Mikey didn't recognise the middle-aged man who was holding up the newspaper. On the other hand, from its distinctive pink colour, Mikey knew instantly that the newspaper was *La Gazzetta dello Sport*, Italy's most famous sport daily. He was intrigued; what could be in the paper that would engage the two men in this way? Then the middle-aged man took what seemed to be an envelope out of his jacket pocket and passed it to Signor Carusa. Suddenly, both men were smiling, laughing and shaking hands vigorously as they said their goodbyes.

Mikey watched Signor Carusa's friend walk down via Veneto towards him. As he approached, Mikey realised that he had seen this man before; he had been a customer at the launderette the previous Tuesday, taking a keen interest in Mikey's conversation with Marco about baseball. The man smiled at Mikey as he passed by, his copy of *La Gazzetta dello Sport* under his arm. Mikey couldn't miss the photo splashed over the front page of the newspaper: it was a picture of a disconsolate Dani.

"Well, how did it go?" Flavia came bouncing up to Enzo, who was waiting for her at the Temple of Apollo. The pair had arranged to meet at the ancient temple and walk together to the assembly point for today's march which was the Foro Siracusano, a Roman ruin located in the park on Corso Umberto, one of Siracusa's busiest streets.

She felt excited about the day ahead and looked a vision of joy in her lime green palazzo pants, topped with a vivid pink and yellow floral blouse with matching baker boy cap. She had chosen to accessorise this with some items from her latest range of ethnic jewellery, featuring large hoop earrings and boldly coloured bangles. But sadly for Flavia, her friend did not appear to have noticed her.

By the looks of things, he was miles away. Rocco, on the other hand, came bounding up to greet her, tail wagging furiously. Nonchalantly ignoring the onlookers who had turned to see what all the fuss was about, Flavia sat down on a bench near the priest and did her best to placate the dog. By the time Rocco's breathing had returned to normal, Enzo had finally noticed what was going on.

"*Ciao*, Flavia," he said.

Flavia smiled. "*Ciao*! You looked like you were miles away!"

"Just going through what I'm going to say later at the rally. Amnesty Italia have asked me to say a few words about my own experience as a migrant living in this country."

Flavia sensed a little apprehension in his voice, but she knew he had nothing to worry about. Everyone loved the parish priest. Even on Sundays, when sometimes his sermons went on a bit, his parishioners stuck with him and always thanked him at the end of the service for his uplifting words. Actually, on reflection, this maybe wasn't quite true of all the congregation. Flavia knew that a small number often sneaked outside for a cigarette when it came to sermon time. But Enzo being Enzo, he probably knew that already.

"You'll be brilliant!" she enthused. "Shall we?" she asked, offering him her arm. And with that the pair of them left Ortigia, with Rocco in tow, and headed over the bridge into Siracusa. Flavia waited until they had crossed the bridge but then could wait no longer. "So, how did it go with Mikey?" she burst out. "Did he meet any of the guys at the drop-in?"

"Oh yes!" replied Enzo. "Sorry, I forgot to tell you. It all went very well. Mikey asked some questions and took away some photos of the building site – as evidence, I guess."

"So, is he going to take those photos to the police?" she persisted.

"Maybe. I haven't heard from him again, since the drop-in."

Mmm, mused Flavia, why would Mikey collect 'evidence' if he **wasn't** going to show it to the police? Again she recalled the conversation in the car on their way back from Fontane Bianche, and the determined look on Mikey's face that night. It was he who had raised the possibility of informing the police about Bellotto's wrongdoings but without Bellotto knowing about it. She was now more intrigued than ever to find out more about Mikey and what he was up to.

As they made their way up the Corso Umberto, and got closer to the park, Flavia was relieved that she had spoken to Enzo when she did. More and more people were filling the pavement now, all heading in the same direction. Many of them looked much younger than Flavia and Enzo, some as young as 15 or 16, talking loudly and enthusiastically to each other. Flavia was loving the positive energy. Lots of people were wearing brightly coloured clothes; some also had brightly coloured hair and faces.

She felt quite at one with what was going on around her.

When they reached the park, uniformed police had closed the road near the entrance to the park and were busy diverting traffic. But judging by the honking of horns and vociferous protestations, not everyone was in agreement with the diversion.

Inside the park a large crowd was congregating near the ruined Foro Siracusano. A young woman with carrot red hair and tatty purple dungarees was addressing the crowd through a loudspeaker. Demonstrators were being instructed to walk no more than three abreast when they joined the march and made their way along the streets of Siracusa to Piazza Santa Lucia where the rally would take place. "I guess that's you, me and Rocco!" Flavia announced to her friend. "Come on let's join the happy throng!"

They ended up marching behind a large, handmade banner, held aloft by a group of young women who, judging from their clothing and skin colour, looked like they might come from a different corner of the globe. The scene made Flavia smile, sending loving energy to the women. At the age of 32, she was excited to be taking part in her first ever demonstration. Better late than never, she thought. And she could think of no more deserving cause. Every now and again she stopped to take in the slogans written on banners coming behind them: *NO ONE IS*

ILLEGAL, NO BORDERS, SOLIDARITY WITH OUR MIGRANT FRIENDS and, Flavia's favourite, *OUR COUNTRY IS YOUR COUNTRY.*

The woman in purple dungarees walked alongside the march with her loudspeaker. Every now and then she led the demonstrators in venting their feelings. The rallying call of 'justice, freedom, compassion' echoed through the narrow streets of Siracusa as the demonstration wound its way up past the Greek Arsenal, along the straight street where the old railway line had once been. En route, the rancour of protestors was most vociferous and most noticeable whenever they passed or caught sight of one of Bellotto's election billboards. Some of the protestors spat on the big man's beaming image, others wrote *FASCISTA* across his large forehead and some even attempted to gouge out his eyes with stones or anything else they could find lying around. Flavia observed that these actions met with a mixed reaction from local bystanders who were looking on. It saddened her to think that amongst the Siracusa public, there was support for Bellotto and his anti-immigration stance.

It was almost midday when Flavia and Enzo arrived at their destination. Away from the traffic, trees and benches lined the large piazza which was dominated on one side by the Basilica dedicated to Siracusa's patron saint, Santa Lucia, and which gave the square its name, Piazza Santa Lucia. Various organisations had set up stalls in the shade of the trees. And in the centre of the square a small stage had been erected. Flavia spotted a few musicians limbering up nearby; then she was drawn to the smell of food wafting through the air. Volunteers were in the process of transporting large pots of food across the square to a row of tables on the far side. By the time all the demonstrators had arrived the piazza had transformed into a vibrant mass of humanity under blue skies and brilliant sunshine. Flavia reckoned there must be at least 200 people there, representing many different backgrounds, ages and ethnicities.

The woman in the purple dungarees jumped onto the stage, loudspeaker in hand. After welcoming everyone to the event, in different languages, she reminded them of what had brought them together. The words 'justice', 'compassion' and 'freedom' brought a particular cheer from the crowd. But it was mention of 'handing over to our speakers' that struck a particular chord with Flavia. This was the priest's cue to move down to the stage. Before doing so, he handed her Rocco's lead. "Good luck, my friend!" she just managed to get the words out before the tall, imposing figure of Don Enzo disappeared into the crowd, his cassock flapping behind him.

His speech went down a storm. As usual, he didn't rush what he had to say. He greeted the crowd in his native language before continuing in Italian, talking about growing up in Eastern Nigeria and his family who still lived there. He told the crowd about coming to Italy for the first time and how different he had felt, like an outsider. How learning to speak Italian had helped him a lot. He mentioned joining a seminary in Milan and experiencing prejudice for the first time. How his faith had given him the strength not to give up. Then he changed tack and referred to migrant friends who had recently come to Italy. He talked about exploitation, blackmail and abuse. His final message was one of love and compassion. "It is vital to embrace difference," he implored the crowd, with great aplomb. Flavia was brimming with pride and admiration for her friend, the parish priest. So much so, that in the excitement of putting her hands in the air to applaud him, the dog's lead slipped through her fingers.

In an instant Rocco had bolted, bounding through the crowd, furiously wagging his tail and barking with delight.

A panic-stricken Flavia ran headlong into the crowd, shouting: "Rocco! Rocco!" at the top of her voice. She didn't get very far before running into a small group of young people. "Slow down, sister," one of them smiled at her. "What's the matter?"

"Have you seen a dog pass this way?" she gasped.

"A dog, you say?"

"Actually, he's not my dog. He belongs to Enzo, Don Enzo – the priest, who just gave the speech."

Mention of Don Enzo made an impression on them. Now they knew who the dog belonged to, Flavia sensed their eagerness to help. "Come on guys, let's find this dog," said the group leader. And the others followed. Together with Flavia they scoured the crowd, until finally she heard a loud, familiar laugh coming from the trees on the periphery of the square. She knew that could only be one person. "This way," she instructed her small group of helpers. Following her ear, she caught sight of Rocco's lead lying under one of the trees. And on the end of the lead was Rocco himself, sprawled out in the shade, lapping up the attention of a young woman who was sitting cross-legged beside him. Standing next to both of them was the reassuring figure of Don Enzo. "Flavia!" he called, without the slightest trace of recrimination in his voice.

Later, after they had both got something to eat, they found a quiet spot to sit down with Rocco. By this stage, the speeches had finished and the group of young men had disappeared to watch the musical acts who were now on stage. Flavia was keen to browse the different stands, especially the Amnesty Italia one, and to find out more about available support and legal aid for migrant workers. After all, that had been their primary reason for wanting to come to the rally. She sensed that Enzo wasn't quite ready yet to leave the shaded bench where they were sitting. For some reason he seemed to be procrastinating. Did he have something on his mind, she wondered. But time was moving on. If they didn't do something soon, they'd miss the opportunity.

Flavia stood up. "Tell you what, Enzo – why don't you sit here with Rocco and I can go and ask the Amnesty people about advocacy work?" He thought this was a good idea. Flavia left her friend to his thoughts and went over to the Amnesty stand. Half an hour later she made her way back to the bench with a handful of leaflets, satisfied that Amnesty would be able to help the guys from the building site.

Sitting down next to her friend, she started to explain about irregular contracts that don't conform to Italian law and about underpaid workers or workers not contracted for all the hours they actually work. This was precisely the sort of malpractice that Amnesty were seeking to make public. She showed him some of the flyers she had picked up, which gave contact details of an Amnesty advocacy service. This involved volunteers working alongside and speaking up for migrants who were prepared to whistle-blow.

Flavia paused for breath and looked over at Enzo, fully expecting him to share in her enthusiasm. Instead she saw agony written all over his face.

Clasping and twisting his hands together, he took a deep breath. In a voice that sounded much lower than the one that had inspired the crowd earlier, he said, "Flavia, there's something I want to tell you."

There was no doubt about it, this was serious.

"Of course, Enzo. Go on, I'm all ears."

He took his time before responding. "You see, it's not only our migrant friends that Alfonso Bellotto has been exploiting and blackmailing. He's also been blackmailing me."

Flavia had known all along that there was more to her friend's low moods than he had been letting on. Nevertheless, she gulped in horror on hearing this revelation. "But why? How? How can he do that?" she spluttered.

Enzo paused, then continued. "The bottom line is this: if Bellotto finds out that I have any intention of going to the police or doing anything at all that might help bring him to justice, he will see to it that I am defrocked."

"So, for example, if you were to contact Amnesty Italia to support the guys in speaking out?" asked Flavia.

"Absolutely. First of all, that would mean curtains for them. Bellotto would disclose them as illegal migrants and see to it that they are deported – in the blink of an eye. But it would also be curtains for me. His big, fat cousin, the bishop, would see to that. Meanwhile Bellotto would be hailed a hero by the national government and by members of his party, not to mention their large following here in Sicily."

"But I don't understand," protested Flavia. "That's totally corrupt. How can such an unscrupulous brute be allowed to get away with that? Why is he allowed to stand for election as mayor of our beautiful city? And what about his big, fat cousin?"

Enzo didn't respond. But Flavia wasn't ready to give up. Driven by an intense curiosity and a genuine concern for her friend, a man for whom she had nothing but the utmost respect and affection, she tried again. "What about the bishop, Enzo? Is he also involved in the blackmail? I mean, the treatment of those poor guys on the building site is bad enough – no, it's worse that than that, it's downright evil." She paused briefly before coming to the nub of what she wanted to say. "But why would anyone want to blackmail **you**, Enzo? I don't get it. You're a priest! You're a good man! I just cannot believe that anyone would want to blackmail you. Why?"

Enzo remained silent. Reaching over he placed his hand on her shoulder.

Once she had calmed down a bit, Flavia reflected on what she had just heard. She had known for some time that Bellotto was exploiting the guys on the building site and using the threat of deportation as a form of blackmail. But what did Alfonso Bellotto know about the parish priest that he was using to blackmail him? Enzo hadn't said.

CHAPTER 10

CHING, CHING! Mikey had grown accustomed to the sound of falling coins in the change machine on the launderette wall. This sound, along with the whirl of the washing machines and dryers, had filled much of Mikey's Saturday afternoon, so far. Indeed, since around 9am, things had been pretty much full-on at the launderette. In addition to tourists staying at Airbnb's, there were many more locals doing their washing today. Including 'Mr Grumpy', who had brought his bedding in. The sheets looked to be well worn, but Mikey could see that they were made of good quality cotton. "You don't find sheets like these, nowadays!" he had said jovially.

However, 'Mr Grumpy's' sullen, "No!" brought their brief exchange to an abrupt conclusion.

In contrast, most of the other customers had been in a good mood, happy to tell Mikey about their plans for the rest of Saturday and for Sunday. A few were planning trips around the area, but much of the discussion revolved around food – what people had bought from the market, what they would be eating for lunch tomorrow, which restaurants they were planning to go to, etc. All of which was very pleasant for Mikey, but it wasn't helping with the investigation into Roberta's disappearance. A few times during the morning, Mikey had glanced across the street in the direction of the art gallery, wondering whether he might be able to speak with Signor Carusa. Mikey was still intrigued by the conversation outside Bar Stella that he had witnessed earlier that morning. Why had Signor Carusa been so happy? However, Carusa had been on the phone every time that Mikey had looked across. Mikey hadn't heard what the gallery owner was saying, but he had seemed very animated, laughing loudly several times. Since lunchtime, the gallery had been closed, with no indication as to when it would reopen.

Speaking of lunch, Mikey had been really enjoying his breaks at Bar Stella over the past few days. Today he had chosen an *arancino alla Norma*, with aubergine – absolutely delicious. Fabio, the owner of the bar, had told Mikey that this version of the celebrated Sicilian street food was a speciality of Catania, the birthplace of the composer, Bellini. Mikey wasn't a fan of opera, but the *Norma* he was eating seemed like a fine tribute to the composer's masterpiece. Appropriately for this type of food, Mikey had decided to sit outside the bar and enjoy the midday sun. An opportunity to people-watch. He spotted several customers from the launderette pass by, including Vito, who waved briefly at Mikey before heading into the bar. The sound of Vito and Fabio laughing soon wafted out into the street. These two appear to get on well, best buddies by the sound of it, thought Mikey. In fact, everyone seems happy today. Well, everyone except 'Mr

Grumpy'.

Back in the launderette, the old clock on the wall had just passed 4pm when Mikey heard a familiar voice. "*Ciao, Mikey!*" Lauren appeared at the entrance, wearing a mint-green cardigan over a white top and vivid green slacks. "How are things?" she asked.

Lauren told Mikey that she had been walking around the outside of Ortigia, soaking up the sun. "You wouldn't believe the number of people sunbathing at Cala Rossa – there isn't a spare space! It's the same at Forte Vigliena. It's always busier at the weekend, that's why I prefer to sunbathe during the week."

"I must do the same sometime," responded Mikey. "But I'll be busy here for the next few days, if not longer."

"Ah, Mikey, you're so devoted to your work! You should treat yourself. Say, why don't you join me for an *aperitivo* this evening, after you've finished? There's a lovely wine bar I know not far from the cathedral."

This suggestion made Mikey feel rather uncomfortable, but he chose to keep his feelings to himself. "Thanks Lauren. That's a good idea." he replied. "But I'm planning to head back to my apartment after work and have a quiet evening. I have to be here again early tomorrow morning."

Lauren gave Mikey a quizzical look. "That's a pity," she said. "I really would enjoy company this evening."

Then a name dropped into Mikey's mind. "Actually, do you know Vito? He's a customer here. Very smartly dressed. I'm sure he would be good company for you."

Lauren threw back her head and laughed. "Ha! Vito, yes, I know him alright! He certainly does like his clothes – almost as much as he likes himself. We met in the bar at the top of the street about a year ago and we went out a few times. He must have thought that I'd be a good catch

– but I wriggled free! To be honest, Mikey, he's not my type. He's too wrapped up in his own business."

At that moment, Mikey's phone vibrated in his back pocket. Taking it out, he saw that he had received a WhatsApp message. It was from Marco. The opening words caught his eye:

HEY, WATCH OUT!

Mikey pressed on the message and read the rest of the text:

BIG TROUBLE NEAR PIAZZA SANTA LUCIA! HOPE YOU GET HOME OK.

Mikey clicked on a link below the message. This opened a video, which transported him to a place just a couple of kilometres from the launderette, in a totally different environment.

The shaky pictures showed a group of young men racing across Piazza Santa Lucia, wielding batons, and causing the participants at the rally to race away in all directions. Some of these men were attacking the stalls lined along the side of the piazza, others were climbing onto a stage and tearing down the Amnesty Italia banners. Shouts and screams filled the air, along with what appeared to be police sirens. Mikey was appalled. The normally tranquil district in which he lived had been transformed into a riot zone.

Lauren moved to Mikey's side and gasped as she watched the frightening scenes unfold. "This is awful! That's Piazza Santa Lucia! What the hell's going on?" she said.

Mikey's thoughts immediately turned to Flavia and Enzo. "Excuse me a moment, Lauren. I know some people who may be there. I want to check how they are." With that, Mikey closed the video, walked out into the street and made a call.

After three rings, there was a click as the phone was answered. "Mikey?" The voice sounded tired.

"Enzo!" exclaimed Mikey. "Are you OK?"

"Yes, Mikey. It's total chaos in Piazza Santa Lucia, but we managed to get away. We're back at the Greek Arsenal now, it's quieter here."

Mikey breathed a sigh of relief. "What on earth happened?"

"There had been no trouble at all at the rally, up until about 30 minutes ago. Then two or three vans pulled up and about 20 youths got out, all waving batons. This was entirely premeditated. They were looking for trouble and intent on causing fear and destruction!"

"What about the police?"

"There were a few police officers at the rally, but they were totally outnumbered by the thugs. We passed some police cars and vans heading towards the piazza shortly after we left. Since then, there's been tear gas drifting along the streets in the area."

Mikey was shaken. He felt for his fellow officers dealing with this riot, but he knew there was nothing he could do about that. "Is Flavia OK?" he asked.

"Yes, Mikey. She's with me. She's trying to calm Rocco down. He was racing around in all directions when the violence started, barking his head off. He's still agitated, but a lot better now."

"Is that Mikey?" Mikey heard Flavia's voice in the background. "Tell him we're fine. Rocco ... good boy, good boy, Rocco!"

Mikey breathed more easily. "That's a relief, Enzo. Is there anything I can do?"

"No, Mikey, we'll be OK. We're walking back to Ortigia now. I'm hoping to have a quiet evening. I've got a sermon to prepare for tomorrow!"

"Take good care! If you or Flavia need anything, please let me know." After saying goodbye, Mikey walked slowly back to the launderette, still processing the events of the afternoon. When he had left Rome, he had never imagined that the normally quiet city to which he moved could be the scene of riots. What's going on, he wondered. Who's behind such violence and hatred?

Franco didn't need an alarm to wake him up that afternoon. He had been lying awake for about an hour when his mobile pinged, letting him know he had a news alert. Instantly recognising the sound, he fumbled for his phone in the darkened room before stumbling out of bed. Opening the shutters, he shielded his eyes against the intensity of the afternoon sun, before returning into the room to read the headline: Trouble at close of Amnesty Rally in Siracusa. Franco scanned the accompanying video footage. It didn't look good. Uniformed police were attempting to break up groups of youths brandishing batons, some of whom were violently tearing down some of the stands, others appeared to be attacking anyone who stood in their way, in the background he spotted a group of skinheads ominously brandishing a National Front banner.

Franco had seen enough. As a detective, public disorder wasn't his priority. But as a father, his first instinct was to contact Amelia. Hopefully no harm had come to her. He needed to get her out of that mess and safely back home, as soon as possible. He put his phone on speaker mode and placed it on the bedside table. Pulling on his trousers, he waited for Amelia to pick up. But there was no reply. Without further ado, he hurried out of the house, bellowing the words "I'm on my way!" in a voice note to his daughter's phone. Seconds later he was at the wheel of his Alfa Romeo, tearing down the country road, clouds of dust billowing in his wake as he headed for Siracusa.

He managed to reach Piazza Santa Lucia in record time, thanks largely to the blue light he attached to his car as he approached the city. The flashing lights certainly helped to clear the way for him, as he accelerated through the busy streets. By the time he arrived at the site of the rally, he was relieved to see that the police had dispersed most of the crowd and arrested some of the troublemakers. Getting out of his car, he wandered over towards a group of young people who were helping to tidy up the debris. He spotted Amelia right away, her wild mane of auburn hair had been a bit of a giveaway. As soon as she caught sight of him, she came running over and threw her arms around him, holding tight. How small she felt as she snuggled into his strong, firm body. Franco smiled. Still not too old for a hug, he thought. For the first time in a long time, he felt needed. It was a good feeling.

Later that evening, a sense of calm had descended again, at least in Franco's home. He was sitting in the lounge with a small bottle of chilled beer, reminiscing on the past few hours. The journey home with Amelia had been more leisurely than the drive out. She had insisted that he remove the blue light from his car. "No way, papà," she had said, and of course, she was right. Franco smiled at the memory. He wondered what she was up to now in the kitchen. When she had offered to prepare dinner for both of them, she had made it clear that he was banned from the kitchen until she was ready to serve. Again, she had stood her ground. Left to his own devices, Franco would have been happy with his usual Pasta alla Norma and had been quite prepared to cook that for his daughter. After all, Pasta alla Norma was what he ate most Saturday nights: roasted aubergine in tomato sauce with pasta and ricotta cheese. "Come on, papà!" she had insisted, "Pasta Norma's a bit dull, don't you think? How about I make us both a lovely North African dish instead? It'll be a change! You'll love it!" He smiled to himself and took another swig of beer. It seemed only yesterday that he had taken her to school, taught her how to ride a bike ...

Minutes late, father and daughter were sitting together at the kitchen table. Pride of place had been given to a large bowl of what looked like a colourful salad, topped with roasted aubergine. "*Buon appetito!*" enthused Amelia, tucking in.

Franco was a bit more circumspect. "So, what have we got here? Roasted aubergine?"

But Amelia was too busy eating to go into details. "It's called fattoush," she said. "Try it, papà! It's all good. I promise you there's nothing here that will do you any harm!" she said with a wink. Sure enough, once Franco got started, he found the dish astonishingly tasty. And he started to relax.

They were both on their second helpings, before the conversation turned to Amnesty Italia and the rally. They talked about the troublemakers and discussed how best to deal with them. By this stage, Franco had been informed that the thugs had all been rounded up. He was all for punishing them, they deserved to be punished for the damage and hurt they had caused. "Lock them up!" he had suggested. But Amelia argued this wasn't a solution. The problem of racial hatred would still be there, maybe even worse. Hate crime, violence, abuse would continue. Education was needed, she had argued, to challenge prejudice and to change people's attitudes and thinking. In time, even the most recalcitrant National Front members could be saved.

Franco couldn't bring himself to challenge his daughter's well-meaning and heartfelt view of the world. Besides which, he didn't want to change the relaxed mood. Enjoying spending quality time together was a luxury and he wanted to savour every second of it. So, he chose not to go into issues of who had been responsible for the rioting that afternoon. It was clear that the plight of migrants was a subject very close to Amelia's heart. But heated discussion of who was behind the thuggery and how to deal with society's ills could wait for another day.

Throughout the evening, he kept his work phone on the table where he could see it and took advantage of any lulls in the conversation to keep an eye on incoming messages. If there were any developments in the case, the team knew to message him directly. He had left very explicit orders to that effect. So far, there had been nothing that required his urgent attention and he was able to enjoy the evening with his daughter.

"So, how did you first get into Amnesty Italia and the work of supporting migrants?" he wondered aloud.

"It all started at school, papà. We have hundreds of migrant kids at my school, every day there are new arrivals from various countries like Libya, Senegal, Eritrea, Ethiopia, Afghanistan, Ivory Coast –"

"Are they in your classes? How do they manage with the language?" interrupted Franco, taken aback at the large numbers involved.

He listened intently as Amelia explained how new arrivals were supported at school. He learned about special classes to bring everyone up to a basic level of survival Italian. And about integrating new arrivals into the mainstream of the school. She explained that the student who came top in a recent maths exam was native

Eritrean, and how other migrant kids were excelling in science, music, sports and art.

"They're human beings, papà – just like us. Some are brainy, some are sporty, some are arty. My best friend at school is Fatemeh, she taught me how to make fattoush – it's a recipe from her country, Syria."

"Great recipe!" quipped Franco. "I guess she learnt it from her mother?"

As soon as he'd asked the question, he noticed the change of expression on Amelia's face and realised he'd jumped in.

"Fatemeh left Syria when she was eight years old. She lost both her parents in the conflict there, when their home was bombed. Friends of the family helped to smuggle her out of the country and brought her here to safety."

Neither Franco nor Amelia spoke for some time.

It was Amelia who broke the silence. "Actually, Fatemeh is probably one of the luckier ones. She lives with a loving foster family. She has many friends, gets on well at school and wants to become an engineer. But most of the new arrivals at school have miserable lives. Not that they complain, they never complain but I don't know how they manage sometimes. Where do they get that resilience from? Some of them have seen horrendous things back home and have risked their lives to escape from torture, war and violence and to find a better life."

"What sort of life do they have in Catania?" asked Franco, now genuinely curious.

"Well, they have to manage on very little money, so depend a lot on the charity of others. But there are lots of organisations offering support and help, there's a whole army of volunteers in Catania. Fatemeh and I help out once a week at a Jesuit run service for refugees."

"Jesuit?"

"Don't worry, papà! It's not about religion, it's an after-school club. We help primary school kids with their homework. They struggle sometimes with reading and writing in Italian, and many of them have no one at home to help them. We meet at a sort of drop-in centre that's used by the refugee service."

"What else happens at the centre?"

"There's lots of teams of volunteers who help in different ways – for example, legal aid, medical assistance, help finding work, Italian classes. And there are lots of clubs at the centre – the sewing club is really popular – it's run by a couple of refugee women who teach others how use electric sewing machines so they can make clothes. The centre receives donations of cloth and the machines were also donated. It's all free but it means so much to the migrant communities."

Franco sensed that Amelia was just getting into her stride. Over the next hour, she argued passionately in favour of sanctuary for all those who had risked everything in order to start a new life in Sicily. She fervently condemned the indifference, prejudice and malice of those who should know better. Franco was spellbound, and not a little envious of his daughter's political nous. But what left the deepest impression on him was her strong sense of social justice and her compassion for those less fortunate than herself.

By 11 o'clock, an exhausted Amelia had gone to bed, leaving Franco the opportunity to look more closely at the phone messages he'd only glanced at in the course of the day. There was a lot for him to process.

Pappalardo and Tacchini who had taken over the surveillance shift that morning had reported a similar pattern to what he and Giovanna had seen overnight. The same white van would turn up outside the house at regular intervals of six hours. Each time, the driver would leave the van and disappear into the house, swopping places with an accomplice. Other news from the office was that the van spotted on site had been traced to one Bruno Mangiafico, the same person who had collected the prescription for Roberta Montanari. Franco was excited by this connection. Surely this was no coincidence? Scrolling back to the start of the day, he recalled his chat with Mikey Ricci that morning and the news from the World Series. According to the best of seven ruling, the Kats only needed to win one more game to win the series. The next game was on Sunday evening (US time) or early Monday morning (Italian time) and the Kats had home advantage. What might this mean for Dani Montanari?

Franco was mulling over all of this, when, shortly after midnight, a message came in. It was from Giovanna, currently back on stakeout duties at Villa Santa Panagia. He read:

TROUBLE AT THE HOUSE. SCREAMS AND SHOUTS FOR HELP FROM INSIDE. WOMAN'S VOICE. TIME TO MOVE IN?

Giovanna had a valid point, thought Franco. He tapped his fingers on the arm rest of his chair, thinking through possible implications of moving in **now** to rescue the woman in the house. Such a move could only be done by bringing in more police, uniformed police, which meant that Franco might not be in charge of that operation. This mattered to Franco because uppermost in his mind was the increasing likelihood that the woman in the house was in fact Signora Montanari. Moving in now would inevitably draw the attention of those behind her abduction and they could escape justice. Franco's mind was made up. In light of the intelligence gained earlier that evening, his preference was to postpone the raid until it could be conducted on his terms. Nevertheless, a woman's life might be in danger and he couldn't ignore that risk. He messaged back to Giovanna:

HOLD ON! LET'S TALK TOMORROW. ANY MORE TROUBLE GET BACK ASAP!

SUNDAY 29TH OCTOBER

CHAPTER 11

Flavia had had a troubled night. Tossing and turning in her bed, she couldn't stop thinking about the rally. She and Enzo had been sitting on the bench together shortly before the hooligans had arrived and the rally had come to a very abrupt, ugly finish. It had not been a happy ending. Poor Rocco had nearly gone berserk when the fighting started. She and Enzo had decided to head back to Ortigia before the trouble escalated out of control and the police arrived. Later at home, she had been horrified at the scenes of senseless violence and destruction broadcast on the local TV news. Overnight, going over the day's events, she wondered who was behind this. Who was perpetrating such blatant hatred towards people seeking sanctuary in Sicily? Was there a link here to what their migrant friends had been telling them about the building site and how they were being exploited by Bellotto, cousin of the bishop. How could it be possible for a man of God to be of the same blood as such a racist bully? Flavia struggled to process these conflicting ideas. Thoughts of the riot and who had instigated it were scary enough, but it was thoughts of her friend Enzo and what he had told her that kept turning over in her mind. She felt very concerned for his welfare. As his friend, and as an Italian citizen, her instinct was to protect him as best she could. Of course, she understood that maybe he didn't feel able to share with her any details about the blackmail. But there must be something she could do to safeguard him from possible abuse and violence. Those hooligans had meant business. The more she thought about it, the more alarming the prospect of blackmail became in her mind. It all seemed very serious. Very serious indeed.

By first light she was still wide awake. Picking up her phone, she didn't want to believe her eyes at first – surely it couldn't be only 06.30. There must be some mistake. Slowly it occurred to her that there was no mistake. She let out a long, loud groan. How could she have forgotten! All week radio, television and social media had been continually reminding everyone to put their clocks back this weekend – it was the end of daylight-saving time. But far from enjoying the extra hour in bed, a restless Flavia was desperate to get up and find something to do that would take her mind off her concerns and anxieties. Four tee shirts and a pair of jeans later, she had given up on the ironing as a bad job. Instead she put her mind to cleaning out Miles' cat litter tray. To be fair, that had been moderately successful and at least Miles appreciated it, rubbing his cheeks against her bare legs. But to be honest, it hadn't really made her feel any better. Even sitting in her favourite chair with her favourite feline on her lap had failed to change Flavia's mood. She was still feeling anxious.

She checked the time on her phone again: still only 8

o'clock on Sunday morning. This was a big day for Enzo, the Sunday before All Saints Day. He had told her that the bishop, or to give him his full title, Archbishop Salvatore Argento, would be attending Mass that morning at San Valentino, Don Enzo's parish church. She knew her friend would be feeling under scrutiny. She racked her brain, there must be something she could do to help him. But probably not on her own ... She recalled the phone call from Mikey, when she and Enzo had been making their way back home to Ortigia after the rally. Clearly concerned for their well-being, he had phoned to check up on them. She smiled, it had been sweet of him to do that. And then it slowly came back to her what Mikey had said to Enzo, "if you or Flavia need anything let me know." She reflected on his offer of help for a moment or two. Finally, and in the end quite out of the blue, all her hours of soul searching came to fruition. "Of course!" she shrieked. That was it! Solidarity – that was what was called for. And she knew exactly how to go about that.

Her eureka moment scared the living daylights out of Miles, who leapt off her lap and took refuge under the table. Flavia meanwhile wasted no time in jumping into the shower and emerged minutes later feeling like new. Next on her list, was a cup of good coffee. She flicked on her trusted coffee machine and was soon savouring the mouthfeel of her favourite smooth, mellow blend. Sipping her coffee, it was time to decide what best to wear to mass. She finally settled on a classic black, knee-length dress which she chose to accessorise with matching bangles and beads in strong shades of red, orange and yellow – all from her own collection. Satisfied with the look, she completed the outfit with scarlet red lipstick and killer black heels. Then, grabbing her bag, she pulled the door of her flat behind her. She didn't have far to walk but rather than risk damaging her heels on the uneven pavements, she climbed instead onto her electric powered scooter, gracefully gliding through the quiet Sunday morning streets of Ortigia. She was a woman on a mission.

By 9.15am she was sitting at a table outside the launderette. The place didn't look busy. As far as she could see there were just a couple of tourists inside, folding away their washing in a large laundry bag. The machines all seemed to be sitting empty. She heard Mikey wish the couple a 'good day'. This was Flavia's cue. Stepping purposefully inside the launderette, she closed the front door behind her and turned the 'open' sign to 'closed'. Mikey looked slightly taken aback. Was he surprised to see her? Was he in awe of the way she looked? Or maybe he simply wasn't expecting her to behave in that way? Flavia didn't have time to dwell on that.

She took a deep breath. "*Ciao* Mikey!" she said. "Look, I need your help."

"*Ciao* Flavia! You're looking very smart. Have you recovered from your ordeal yesterday? It must have been very frightening ..."

Hoping that she wouldn't need to remind him of his offer of help, Flavia remained focused on the purpose of her visit. "Mikey, I need your help."

Mikey immediately offered her a seat and promptly sat down next to her. "I'm all ears," he said, looking her in the eye. This was exactly the response she needed and wanted. It felt safe to speak and Flavia didn't hold back. She told him all about her conversation with Enzo at the rally. Mikey listened, letting her speak. When she got to the bit about the priest being blackmailed, he finally asked a question. "So, are you telling me that someone is threatening Enzo in some way?"

"Yes, but it's not just 'someone'." She looked Mikey

straight in the eye. "Enzo told me that he is being blackmailed by Alfonso Bellotto."

"The guy who is building the new development at Villa Santa Panagia? The same one who is standing for mayor?" asked Mikey, aghast.

He looked as shocked as Flavia had felt when she had first heard the news. It made her feel a bit less anxious, knowing that Mikey shared her concerns. And this encouraged her to tell him more.

"There's more, Archbishop Salvatore Argento, the bishop, is also involved somehow. Enzo didn't go into details but Bellotto and the bishop are first cousins. If word gets out that the parish priest has been helping the migrants bring Bellotto to justice, then the bishop will see to it that Don Enzo is defrocked."

By this stage, she could tell that Mikey was hanging on her every word. Leaning over ever closer towards her, she became aware of his breath against her cheek and an aroma of strong coffee. Fortunately, she was spared embarrassment when Mikey returned to a bolt upright position and started stroking his moustache. "Maybe the bishop knows something we don't know?" he suggested. "Something about Enzo that would be good reason to defrock him …"

Before Mikey had the chance to start rambling on, Flavia decided to take the plunge. She had come to ask for help and now was her chance. "Why don't we both go to Mass this morning at San Valentino?"

Mikey raised his eyebrows in response. She smiled and gently explained that by attending the church, Mikey and herself would be showing solidarity with Don Enzo. This being the Sunday before All Saints Day, Archbishop Argento and his entourage would be at the service, and possibly other dignitaries as well. Enzo would be feeling under scrutiny. It might help his morale to see at least two friendly faces in the congregation.

Mikey thought about this before responding. "Well, I suppose I could close the launderette for a couple of hours. As you can see, I'm not exactly rushed off my feet this morning." Then added, with a twinkle in his eye, "Of course, I'll do that. It will be my pleasure to help you."

Hopefully Mikey realises it's not **me** who needs the help, thought Flavia, smiling back at him. "Just one thing," she said, "I hope you don't mind sitting on the back of my scooter!"

Franco glanced up as he sat at his desk, then blinked in disbelief as he looked at the clock on the wall: 10.15 am. Really? Surely he hadn't been in the office for the past two hours?

Then he sat back in his leather-upholstered chair and sighed. Of course, the clock hadn't been put back since daylight saving ended on Saturday night! The clock was high up on the wall and he didn't fancy the idea of standing on his very comfortable chair to change it. He'd mention this to the estates staff next time he had a chance – but not now.

So, it was 9.15am, not 10.15am; Franco was reassured to know that he hadn't been wasting his time this Sunday morning. He hadn't had a great night's sleep, following the late-night communication with Giovanna about the stakeout at Villa Santa Panagia. But he had been relieved not to get any further news from her overnight. Indeed, there had been no more messages by the time he got up at 7.30am. After an espresso, he had knocked lightly on the door of Amelia's room, but – having heard nothing – he decided not to wake her. Amelia had told Franco the previous night that she would get a bus to the coach station on Sunday morning, rather than ask him for a lift into Siracusa. So, he had been delighted to receive a voice note from his daughter shortly before the confusion with the clock, saying that she was now in town, waiting for the coach to Catania. Hearing her voice, he reflected on their long conversation the previous evening and felt reassured by her strong sense of direction and principled approach in helping those in need. He had responded in kind on WhatsApp, pressing the microphone sign he left a short message. "Good to hear that you're on your way home. Great chat last night – really proud of you! *Ciao, amore.*"

A sharp, double knock on the door interrupted Franco's musing. "Come in!" he barked. He was pleased to see Giovanna enter his office. "Have a seat! Have a seat!" he said. Then, noticing how she was out of breath, he added in a softer tone of voice, "Coffee?"

"No, thanks," replied Giovanna, pulling a water bottle out of the sports bag she had been carrying and taking a swig from it. "I'll be trying to get some sleep shortly. I'll stick with the water for now!"

"Have you come directly from the stakeout house?" asked Franco.

"No, I drove home first, then ran here. It's only a couple of kilometres, but I really needed some exercise. I hardly moved all night!"

"Understood," said Franco. "So, tell me again what happened last night, Gio."

Giovanna reached into her sports bag and brought out a small notebook. "It was difficult to make notes in the dark, but I was able to jot down a few points. The shouts from the house started at 12.13am. Just before then, I had spotted one of the two men who've been going in and out of the building. He was standing outside at the door of the building and looking out towards the main entrance. As soon as the shouting started, he went back into the house. About a minute after that, I heard a couple of screams, then silence."

"You think it was a woman's voice?"

"Yes, I'm 99% sure of that."

"Just to check, Gio. You mentioned 12.13am. Was this based on the old time, before the clocks went back?"

Giovanna smiled. "Absolutely! In fact, my guess is this is why the guy had come out of the house. He would have been thinking that he would finish his shift at midnight. As it turned out, the other guy didn't turn up until 1am – old time."

Franco pointed to the clock on the wall. "It's still the old time here! Fortunately, my phone updated itself automatically!"

"So did my phone! But not until 2am old time, when it switched itself to 1am."

"Exactly! This means that the changeover should have taken place at midnight – old time."

Giovanna nodded. "When his accomplice turned up at 1am, I heard raised voices coming from the property – male voices. My guess is that the guy who had been on duty had been unhappy with his colleague for turning up late."

"Understandably. That said, with the extra hour, one of them was bound to have an extended shift."

"And not just them!" said Giovanna, with a hint of a smile.

Franco was momentarily silent, then moaned quietly before responding. "Sorry, Gio, I should have realised that you would have a longer shift last night."

"No problem, boss. As it turned out, things were quiet after that changeover. The next one took place at 6am – new time. It was much the same as the usual."

"OK, that's really helpful, Gio. I want to show you something." Franco picked up his phone from his otherwise-empty desk and opened WhatsApp. "When I was driving in this morning, I received a call from Tommaso Montanari. Dani had rung him a couple of hours earlier."

"What did he say?"

"Dani had just received another photo from the kidnappers. He sent it to his father, who forwarded it to me." With that, Franco handed the phone to his deputy.

Giovanna looked at the photo displayed on the phone. "That's Roberta! Is that a copy of La Sicilia that she' holding up?"

"If you zoom in, you'll see that it's Saturday's edition."

"Yes," replied Giovanna, squinting as she enlarged the photo. "I remember seeing that picture of Alfonso Bellotto on the front of yesterday's paper. He had been at an election rally next to the Temple of Apollo." She continued to scan the photo. "What's that on Roberta's forehead? It looks like –"

"Bruising," said Franco. "As though she's hit her head, or –"

"Someone hit her," continued Giovanna. "What was Dani's reaction to this?"

"His father said he was very confused. The captors had sent a message along with the photo, telling Dani to keep on playing like he had been, and everything would be OK for Signora Montanari. However, Dani had seen the bruising and wasn't convinced that the captors would release his mother unharmed. He's really not sure what to do."

"What do you think, boss?"

Before responding, Franco wondered briefly whether to raid the lower drawer in his desk, the one where he kept an emergency supply of Modica chocolate. But he decided against prevaricating.

"I've been thinking about this a lot since Tommaso's message came through. My first thought was to wait until after the next baseball game, which will be taking place overnight our time. But now I'm not so sure we can wait that long. From what you've told me about the shouts and screams last night and assuming that Signora Montanari is in the house, then she may well have been trying to attract attention, thinking that her captors had left her alone in the house –"

"But one of them attacked her when he returned?"

Franco nodded, noting that his deputy was picking up one of his habits. "Exactly! In my opinion, the photo was taken shortly after she was attacked. I don't think it was pre-planned, but the captors may have wanted to send a message to Dani that they were serious."

"True," replied Giovanna, "but there's still nothing to suggest that they can be trusted to release Signora Montanari alive and well."

"That's my view, too, Gio." Franco could wait no longer; he opened the drawer and took out a bar of his favourite chocolate, offering a piece to Giovanna.

"No, boss, I'll be heading home after this. I'm dying for a few hours' sleep. Chocolate will keep me awake!"

Franco leaned forward. "Gio, we'll both need this later. We're going to pounce this evening, after sunfall, and release whoever's in the house!"

Giovanna took a deep breath, then responded. "I think that's a good decision, boss. How many of us do you need?"

Over the following half hour, Franco and Giovanna discussed plans for the raid on the property at Villa Santa Panagia: who would go, who would guard outside, the route into the house, and so on. Franco was pleased that Giovanna, like himself, was happy to talk about the fine details of the operation. Then, as they looked again at the photo sent through by Tommaso, Giovanna pointed at the picture on the front of the newspaper that Signora Montanari was holding.

"What about Bellotto?" asked Giovanna. "He owns the land at Villa Santa Panagia. Do you think he'll be paying much attention to what's going on at the house?"

Franco shrugged. "I'm not sure he'll have time for that. He'll be busy campaigning, ahead of the mayoral election. Even today, on a Sunday. Or rather, especially on a Sunday!"

Having closed up the launderette, Mikey climbed onto the back of Flavia's red scooter. As he did so, he thought back to an earlier trip as a passenger on a scooter, also on a Sunday and again with a female driver. On that occasion, his then-boss, Antonella, had zipped through the streets of Rome on her Vespa and then headed out to the port of Civitavecchia, so that Mikey could catch a cruise ship that was about to leave. That was the start of an amazing week that turned out to be the highlight of his police career; so far, anyhow. Today's journey, thought Mikey, would be much shorter, on a different type of scooter, and didn't promise the same impact. That said, he had been struck by Flavia's concern for her friend Enzo and wanted to help in any way he could. Plus, as Flavia started up the scooter and sped up via Veneto, Mikey reflected that the sight of the long flowing dark hair immediately in front of him – Flavia hadn't bothered with a helmet – was very nice indeed. He smiled to himself. He couldn't imagine *Forense* giving him a lift on a scooter, far less in the Alfa Romeo that was his pride and joy.

Approaching the top of the street, Mikey saw a familiar figure sauntering around the corner, bedecked in a bright orange dress. "*Ciao*, Lauren!" he shouted. Mikey saw Lauren looking side to side with a puzzled expression, before she spotted him. "*Ciao*, Mikey!" she replied. As Lauren waved, Mikey saw that she was now half-smiling, with a knowing look. A second later, Lauren was left behind as the scooter turned sharply into via Vicenza, passed Flavia's boutique, then swung into via Brescia.

"Was that a friend?" shouted Flavia, turning her head towards her passenger. "A customer," replied Mikey, very definitely.

Travelling along via Brescia, they passed several elderly people in their sober Sunday best, walking slowly in the same direction. Possibly regular worshippers at San Valentino, thought Mikey. But as they approached the church, he spotted a different demographic amongst the people mingling nearby. Mostly middle-aged. Trendier dressers. Lots of dark glasses. All-in-all, a well-heeled bunch.

Approaching the entrance to the church, Mikey could see Don Enzo standing outside, greeting people as they entered. Suddenly, the scooter veered to the left, then came to an abrupt stop just a foot or so from the wall of the church. Mikey instinctively put his hand on the wall to stop himself falling over. Meanwhile, Flavia – who had kept her left hand on the handle of the scooter – started shouting and waving her right arm wildly. "What are you doing? You could have killed us!"

Regaining his balance, Mikey saw that Flavia was directing her ire at a huge black Porsche Cayenne that had just pulled up in front of the entrance to San Valentino. The vehicle seemed, in Mikey's eyes, to be the size of two or possibly three Tottis, so it was just as well they hadn't collided with it. "Take it easy," said Mikey, putting his hand on Flavia's shoulder. "There's no damage done. You did really well to avoid him!"

Flavia turned towards him, but said nothing, her eyes seemingly on fire. Then she turned her attention back to the car, as a short, rotund man dressed in a dark suit and shades got out of the driving seat, walked slowly all the way around the Porsche, then opened the passenger door on the side nearest the church. Mikey caught his breath as he recognised the man stepping down from the car. The man on the election poster that Marco had pointed to a few days earlier. The man who was allegedly blackmailing Don Enzo. Signor Alfonso Bellotto.

At first sight, Bellotto didn't look as impressive as he did in the election poster. Quite chubby, a bit like his driver. Perhaps too fond of *cannoli*? thought Mikey. His face was contorted in a scowl, rather than beaming as in his election photo. But then the smile appeared as shouts of "Bellotto, Bellotto!" rang out in Piazza San Valentino. Mikey turned and saw some of the middle-aged men and women he had spotted early, calling out their hero's name. Beside them, a couple of photographers were eagerly snapping away, whilst a reporter – standing with her back to the church – was talking excitedly into a news camera that was capturing the scene. Bellotto stopped briefly to wave to his fans and even blew a kiss to them.

"PIG!" Flavia's outburst was drowned out by applause as Bellotto strolled towards the entrance of the church. Behind him, Mikey saw a large woman – possibly in her late 30s – with masses of curly hair and wearing a half-length fur coat descend from the Cayenne and tiptoe along behind her beau, apparently struggling to keep her balance in her narrow red stiletto shoes. What an interesting couple, thought Mikey.

Don Enzo held out his hand as Bellotto approached. However, before they had a chance to shake hands, a man dressed from head to toe in purple robes came out of the church and embraced the property tycoon, who reciprocated enthusiastically. This drew more cheers from the group in the square, who now numbered around 20-25. The two men chatted briefly, then went inside the church, ignoring Don Enzo totally.

"That's the archbishop, I guess", said Mikey.

"Of course!" responded Flavia. "The two of them are as bad as each other – they're evil!" Mikey squeezed her shoulder and realised that she was shaking with anger.

"I know," he said. "Come on, let's go and see Enzo."

As they approached the priest, many of the people in the square were entering the church. Some shook his hand, others nodded towards him as they went past. Mikey and Flavia both embraced their friend in a big hug. Enzo said little but gave them a brief smile. It was enough to show that he appreciated his friends' moral support.

Entering the church, Mikey and Flavia found some seats towards the back. From there, Mikey could make out Bellotto's tanned bald pate, right at the front at the congregation. Most of his supporters were sat in the rows just behind him. Every so often, one of them would approach, embrace him and have a short chat. A couple of times, Bellotto's squeaky laugh rang all around the stone-walled church, causing Mikey to wince. Just as well Rocco's not here, thought Mikey, he'd howl the place down if he heard this!

Mikey turned his attention to the three men seated near the altar, facing the worshippers. He had a better opportunity now to study Archbishop Argento. Plump in the face, with a slight resemblance to Bellotto around the eyes, he had the air of someone who greatly enjoyed his food. The finery of his purple hat and robes, along with the gold crucifix around his neck and the large, ornate rings on his fingers, contrasted with the austere surroundings inside San Valentino. The archbishop sat on a high throne-like chair, with what seemed to be jewels encrusted into the handles, while on either side – on lower, plain chairs – sat two other clerics. Both were a bit thinner than the archbishop and their white attire, whilst smart, was not as striking as Argento's.

"Who are they?" whispered Mikey, pointing at the men next to the archbishop. "His flunkies, I guess," replied Flavia, in a dismissive tone. "Look!" she said, suddenly becoming animated. "Enzo's coming in now. We're about to start!"

The chatter died down as the parish priest called the congregation to prayer, before leading the singing of the first hymn. A reading and another hymn followed, before Don Enzo walked to the lectern, under the watchful eye of his superior. "Come on, Enzo," whispered Flavia. "You can do it!" Mikey squeezed her hand as she spoke, but she seemed oblivious to this.

The topic of the priest's sermon was justice. He spoke about justice taking different forms and quoted extensively from the Bible to back up his points. Indeed, he spoke a lot. An awful lot.

After what appeared to be a quarter of an hour or so, Mikey could see a few heads dropping down in the congregation, nodding off under the monotony of the priest's delivery. Indeed, even the archbishop's eyes occasionally closed briefly, then flicked wide open as he struggled to stay awake. Meanwhile, he noticed a few of Bellotto's friends wandering towards the side door of the church, pulling out packs of cigarettes as they did so. Mikey swithered: should he stay and support Enzo and

Flavia? Or should he follow his policeman's instinct?

"Excuse me," he whispered into Flavia ear, "I'll be right back." "Don't be long," she replied curtly.

Within a few seconds, Mikey had stepped into Piazza San Valentino. No sooner had he done so than he bumped, literally, into a man wearing an elegant cream suit, who had been walking past the church. "Signor Carusa!" exclaimed Mikey. "Sorry, I didn't see you."

"*Buongiorno Mikey!*" The owner of the art gallery sounded upbeat. "My fault, I'm in a bit of a rush."

"Are you going to Mass?" asked Mikey.

"No," replied Signor Carusa, "I'm going to my daughter's apartment, in Siracusa. We'll then be coming back to Ortigia, for lunch. I've had some good news and I want to celebrate with her!"

"What's the good news?"

"Mikey, do you remember your visit to the gallery last week? I pointed out a pair of paintings of Ortigia at sunset; one of them showed the silhouettes of the buildings above the sea walls, the other captured the view out to sea with water lapping over the rocks. I really rate the painter, Salvatore, a young guy from Siracusa, but he's not well known."

"Ah," said Mikey. "Yes, you talked a lot about those paintings. I liked them."

"Well, I'm pleased to say that I've found a buyer for both of the paintings! I'm delighted they're being sold as a pair, they'll look lovely hanging next to each other. It took a bit of negotiation, but I think the fee we agreed was reasonable. Obviously, Salvatore will get most of this, but I'll receive a cut for having exhibited the paintings. This'll help with the costs of heating and lighting in the art gallery during the winter. I have to admit, Mikey, it's been difficult recently."

"That's excellent," said Mikey with a broad smile. "Who's bought the paintings?"

"Actually, it's one of your customers at the launderette!" Signor Carusa laughed, while Mikey's expression turned to one of perplexment. Who could this be? Lauren? Surely not 'Mr Grumpy'? Then something clicked in Mikey's brain.

"Ah, I saw you yesterday morning with one of my clients! You were standing together outside Bar Stella, at the top of via Veneto."

"That's right!" Signor Carusa was beaming now. "That was Signor Lentini, a lovely man. Like me, he's a fan of Catania! Our team had a great win on Friday night."

Another click in Mikey's head. "Yes, Catania beat Palermo 2-0, didn't they!" Mikey felt totally at ease talking about football, rather than baseball.

"It was a fantastic game. Signor Lentini showed me the report of the game in *La Gazzetta dello Sport*. All our players had top ratings! Anyhow, I must rush now. Signor Lentini gave me a generous deposit yesterday; he'll be paying the remainder of the fee tomorrow, when he collects the paintings. My daughter and I will definitely be raising a glass to celebrate over lunch!"

Signor Carusa said goodbye and hurried down via Brescia, while Mikey thought about their conversation. Maybe there wasn't anything suspicious at the art gallery after all …

A peel of laughter about 10 metres away caught Mikey's attention. He saw several of the men he had followed out of the church, standing next to Bellotto's huge car, chatting and smoking. He also spotted Bellotto's chauffeur there. Rather than approach them, Mikey turned away, pulled out his phone and pretended to check his emails whilst keeping his ears open.

He couldn't make out everything that was being said, but some phrases were clear. For example: "It's a sure bet, you won't lose!" "You always say that, what about last year's cup final? I lost a packet then!" "Don't worry, there's always tomorrow!" Repeated laughs rang out in the piazza.

After a few minutes, Mikey could hear footsteps getting closer. He turned to see most of the group heading back to the church's side door. "See you all this evening," said one of the men, smiling. Two people were left: Bellotto's chauffeur and a white-haired man, with his back to Mikey. This man turned around, then waved his hand. "*Ciao*, Mikey!" he called out.

Of course, thought Mikey, it's Vito! "*Ciao*," said Mikey, walking towards the ever-elegantly dressed man. "How are you?" he asked, as he shook Vito's hand.

"Very well, Mikey. Very well indeed!" As Vito laughed, Mikey was conscious once again of his customer's prominent gold tooth.

"Mikey, can I introduce you to Silvio?" said Vito as he turned towards the chauffeur. "Pleased to meet you," said Mikey holding out his hand. However, Silvio declined the offer and continued to drag on his cigar. In contrast to the happy faces he had seen earlier, Silvio appeared reluctant to betray his emotions. A bit of a poker face, thought Mikey.

"Silvio, Mikey here runs the launderette in via Verona," said Vito, who then turned back to Mikey before continuing. "Silvio and I go back a long way. We're both originally from Catania. Silvio used to work for me."

"Was he your chauffeur?" asked Mikey, spotting a slight smile cross the chauffeur's face.

"Not exactly," responded Vito. "But I know I can rely on him. And he has good contacts. We were talking earlier about the lovely Rosa, Signora Mangiafico. She's an interesting lady, I'd really like to meet her." Vito turned to address his friend. "Silvio, do you think you could arrange that?" Silvio said nothing but nodded gently.

Rosa and Vito? Not an obvious pairing, thought Mikey, although probably not as odd a couple as Rosa and Bellotto. His musings were interrupted as Vito continued, "Incidentally, Mikey, you told me the other day that you're a big fan of AS Roma?"

"That's right," replied Mikey. "I haven't been to their matches for the past couple of months, but I watch them on TV whenever I can. Also, my pals in Rome give me regular updates on how the team's doing."

"That's ideal, Mikey!" exclaimed Vito. "You know that *Roma* have a big Europa League match coming up next Thursday. Some of my friends would be very keen to chat with you ahead of the game. They would be interested to hear your thoughts on which of the *Roma* players would be most likely to score. Which of them might provide assists for goals. Even which of them are most likely to be yellow-carded! It's not just the results that count, Mikey. Nowadays, there are so many aspects of sports that can be …" Vito waved his hand, without finishing the sentence.

"Profitable?" said Mikey, aware of where this conversation was going.

Vito raised his eyebrows. "That's one way of putting it. I prefer to view it as making the most out of sporting events, wherever they take place." Vito glanced at Silvio, who took a long drag on his cigar, but said nothing. "You know Bar Stella, don't you, Mikey? Why don't we meet there after you finish at the launderette next Thursday evening? The owner of the bar, Fabio, is **very** accommodating. We can have a good chat there ahead of the match."

Mikey smiled. "Sounds great! I look forward to seeing you and your friends then." Then, pulling out his phone and holding it in front of his face, he quickly pressed a couple of buttons, before exclaiming, "Oh dear! I've just missed a call! Excuse me, but I'll need to ring back straightaway, it could be important. *Ciao*, Vito! Nice to meet you, Silvio!"

With that, Mikey hurried towards the top of via Brescia, out of earshot of Vito and Silvio, and proceeded to make a call. The phone rang for about 15 seconds before being answered.

"*Dottore*," said Mikey. "I think I may be on to something. I've been keeping an eye on Bellotto and his entourage and I've just spoken with a guy called Vito – I have a strong suspicion that he's running a gambling ring. Here's a photo I just took of him."

Mikey pressed some buttons on his phone, before placing it back to his ear. After a few seconds he heard a long groan from the other end of the line, followed by Franco's voice:

"Well, well, well! It's the crook with the gold tooth! Watch out, Ricci. Vito Lupo is a **very** dangerous man."

CHAPTER 12

Franco was standing at the waterfront, watching. Raging swirls of wave battered their way through the rocks, before crashing against the promenade wall. WHOOSH! He stepped back to avoid getting soaked, allowing the occasional, wet tourist to pass by. There had been no sight of Mount Etna all day today, even the habitual blue Siracusan skies were covered over. On days like this, Franco turned to the sea for inspiration. He had left police headquarters and driven the short distance to where he now stood. He needed to clear his head, to sort out in his own mind events of the past few hours and calculate the next move in his quest to bring Signora Montanari to safety.

He had a lot to think about. It had been a busy morning, starting with the photograph that had come through on WhatsApp – evidence that Roberta Montanari was still alive. Or at least she had still been alive when the photo was taken. The strain of a full week in captivity showed on her face; the eyes that once had twinkled now looked flat and empty, the ready smile had disappeared, usurped by a tense looking jaw line. And then there were the bruises on her forehead. Franco went through the chronology of events one more time. Dani Montanari had received the photo late last night, Italian time. That would have been soon after the altercation out at Villa Santa Panagia, which Giovanna had reported. The altercation had involved a woman, shouting and screaming for help. Franco's chat with Giovanna had left him in no doubt about the seriousness of the incident and the need to act. In all probability, he reasoned, the woman that Giovanna had heard was Roberta. And even if it wasn't, Franco knew that they needed to pounce. It was the right thing to do. There was a woman out at Villa Santa Panagia who needed their help. And she needed it soon.

He thought back to the mid-morning phone call from Mikey Ricci. What was it Ricci had said? "I think I might be on to something." He wasn't wrong there, thought Franco, smiling now at the incongruence of Ricci and understatement. Franco had been all ears, listening to Ricci's update.

But it had been the photo that Ricci shared that had really piqued Franco's interest. The man with the gold tooth – it had to be Vito Lupo. Franco knew only too well that Lupo came over as a bit of a charmer and wealthy with it. Always smiling, he was very popular with the ladies. So maybe, it was no surprise that he seemed to have taken a shine to Bellotto's latest fancy woman, Rosa Mangiafico. Then there was the fact that Lupo was no stranger to the launderette where Ricci was based. Franco was intrigued by all of this. What was behind Lupo's interest in Bellotto's girlfriend? Why would a man of Lupo's means be frequenting a launderette? And why this launderette – the very launderette from where Roberta Montanari had disappeared? Amongst all this uncertainty, however, one unquestionable truth stood out in Franco's mind. Lupo was a dangerous man, very dangerous indeed.

Indeed, Vittorio Matteo Lupo, Vito to his friends, was no stranger to the police. Franco had first come across Lupo in Catania, in his early days as a police cadet. The instructors at the Police Academy there would use Vittorio Matteo Lupo and his people as a case study illustrating the challenges of tackling organised crime in the city. Even then Lupo had presented well, always well turned out in hand tailored suits and silk ties. He ran a very lucrative second-hand car business in the city, the success of which was down to a mix of personal charm and business acumen. But behind the respectable public veneer, lurked a cruel and heartless thug. Behind the façade of the car business, Lupo ran a gambling and money lending racket. It was rumoured that he employed upwards of twenty henchmen to carry out his dirty business. Franco still recalled with horror the photos he had seen of Lupo's victims, the unfortunates who had been beaten up and left to die just because they didn't pay up or had tried to go to the police. Franco had not been joking when he had told Ricci that Lupo was a very dangerous man. But what was Lupo doing now, down here in Siracusa?

The sound of screaming seagulls pierced Franco's consciousness, abruptly bringing him back to the waterfront. He watched the birds squabbling over a morsel of food they had found on the rocks. It was a familiar occurrence and one to which he could easily predict the outcome. He turned his attention instead to the stones on the ground around him. Without thinking about it, he bent down and picked up a largish, flat pebble.

Franco's thoughts turned to Bellotto. The police had known for years about Bellotto's links to an illegal gambling syndicate. But they had never been able to prove any wrong-doing. On the contrary, there were rumours that some cops were regular gamblers, benefitting from the syndicate in exchange for tipping off the big man and his pals about police interest in their illegal activity. Franco himself had come close to making an arrest on a couple of occasions but much to his chagrin had never managed to press any charges.

It had been a matter of professional pride to Franco that since his arrival in Siracusa ten years ago, he had never been even remotely tempted to turn a blind eye to this gambling syndicate and the corruption that went with it. In truth the rumours of police corruption had irked him beyond words. So much so that he had tended not to socialise with his colleagues. They, for their part, couldn't understand his inability to leave the job at the office, and he, in turn, failed to comprehend how any self-respecting police officer could joke about bribery and corruption, behaving as if the Bellottos of this world did not exist. Franco knew that if he could finally nail Bellotto once and for all, then his own long standing, unpopular views would be vindicated.

He looked down at the stone he was holding. Then angled it carefully in his right hand and skimmed it across the waves. He watched until it eventually disappeared beneath the water and smiled.

Bellotto's appearance at Mass today was easy to explain. It seemed obvious to Franco, that the big man would want to be photographed at Mass alongside the bishop in all his finery. For sure he would be lapping up all the attention he could get. This was nothing more than a massive publicity stunt for his election campaign.

After the call from Ricci, Franco had done some investigative work of his own. Reading and re-reading reports that had recently been filed of strange goings on out at Villa Santa Panagia had been instructive. Everything pointed to Bellotto's involvement in the disappearance of Signora Montanari. But proving Bellotto's involvement was another matter. Actual evidence remained elusive. At the same time, a sneaking suspicion was starting to form in the police chief's mind that Lupo might also be involved. It was true that they didn't have much to go on at this stage, but *Commissario* Spina was not someone who believed in coincidence. He smelt a rat.

Franco deeply despised Bellotto as he despised all fat cats who made themselves rich at the expense of others, especially those who were struggling. Up until now, he had always included in that category the poor, the unemployed and addicts. His chat with Amelia had helped him see that illegal immigrants were also just as vulnerable. He picked up another stone and, with all his might, flung it across the sea. He watched and counted as it bounced off the surface of the water nine times before disappearing out of sight. His resolve to rescue Signora Montanari and to catch the thugs holding her in captivity was stronger than ever. But it was the prospect of nailing Alfonso Bellotto for his role in the abduction that really fired him up.

He watched as another wave crashed mercilessly against the promenade wall. Franco found it strangely comforting to know that millennia of pounding waves had erased the once sharp edges on the rocks below. In time, no doubt, the holding wall itself would also be wiped out, such was the power of the sea. In that moment, he knew that this was his opportunity to rid Siracusa of at least one of its vilest and most despicable inhabitants. And he was going to grab that opportunity, confident in the knowledge that if anyone could do it – he could, with the help of his trusted deputy.

Feeling ready for one final espresso, before he met up with Giovanna, he looked again at his watch – 15.00. Thank God, Amelia had offered to make her own way down to the coach station that morning. She'd be back in Catania by now, no doubt regaling her mother with tales of the weekend. Franco smiled. But not for long. The first few drops of rain landed on his smart cashmere jumper. He raced back to his Alfa Romeo and seconds later sped off in the direction of town and his favourite bar.

Meanwhile over in Ortigia, Flavia had waited for the rain to ease off before venturing out again. She had changed her footwear from the morning, smart heels were OK for church but when it came to walking down the cobbled streets of Ortigia, only sneakers would do. Of course, Flavia being Flavia hers were no ordinary sneakers. Brilliant white with a flash of gold, they showed off her perfectly neat ankles and bronzed legs. Sauntering down via Vicenza, on her way to Bar Stella, she hadn't met a soul. But it was still only 4pm. Still rather early for most locals to stir after a large Sunday lunch and no doubt the overcast weather had also played a role.

She was soon sitting under the canopy outside Bar Stella with a cup of coffee, enjoying the only sun of the day, which was just managing to break through the clouds and light up the sky. Closing her eyes she cast her mind back to the Mass at San Valentino earlier that day. As a person of no faith, Flavia was not a regular church goer. Over the years, she had only ever been to a handful of Don

Enzo's services and those had included one marriage, one christening and two funerals. So today had been her first experience of Don Enzo leading regular, Sunday worship. She had found the whole experience quite fascinating. Not so much the service itself, if she was honest, but observing what was going on. And there had been a lot for her to take in. For instance, she still wasn't quite sure why Mikey had needed to pop outside midway through the sermon. He hadn't been the only one to do so. She had noticed a slow trickle of men, mainly those sitting on Bellotto's side of the church, using a side door to go in and out of the church during most of the service. This had happened at intervals of about 15 minutes. Fortunately, the parish priest had carried on regardless, unfazed by all this activity.

And then there was the way that Mikey had rushed away at the end, without so much as a friendly embrace. Maybe she had been wrong about him after all. Of course it had been kind of him to leave the launderette and agree to attend Mass with her. But he hadn't really shown much interest in the reason they were there – to support their friend, Enzo.

It had not escaped Flavia's attention how Bellotto had deliberately ignored Enzo at the church door, making a beeline instead for his big fat cousin, the bishop. She had found it loathsome how the two of them had made a big deal of posing for the cameras before entering the church together. During the service, after Mikey had left her, Don Enzo had led the congregation in prayer. Flavia had taken advantage of this opportunity to scan the congregation. Around Bellotto, there seemed to be a flurry of activity with heads turning in different directions, looking at phones. Then there had been a brief period of commotion as one of the men got up and left by the side door. At the end of the prayer, there had definitely been eye contact between Bellotto and his purple clad cousin. The bishop appeared to direct a knowing look in his cousin's direction with a very subtle nod of his heavily adorned head. Flavia was convinced there was something going on. But she was still puzzled as to what it might be ... If only Mikey had been in less of a rush, they could have talked about what was really going on.

Lifting her espresso cup to her lips for one final sip, she paused with the cup mid-air. A familiar voice coming from the bar inside stopped her in her tracks. At least it seemed to be coming from the bar, but that didn't make sense. What would the parish priest be doing in the bar on a Sunday afternoon? And who was he talking to?

Then a second man raised his voice, silencing Enzo. The tone was unambiguously threatening. What on earth is going on in there? she wondered. She listened hard but it was difficult to make out what they were saying, apart from the odd word or two. She heard '*scusi*' several times and a sort of whimpering sound. But was that Rocco or Enzo?

That did it. Flavia had to find out what was going on. Putting her cup back down on the table, she picked up her bag and stepped into the bar. But when she looked round the room there was no sign of her friend Enzo. In fact, apart from Fabio there were just a few women in the bar enjoying an *aperitivo*. Flavia decided they were French tourists.

"*Ciao* Fabio!" she approached the bar owner. "Has Don Enzo been in today?"

"You kidding me? The priest never comes here, least of all on a Sunday!"

Flavia wasn't convinced. But then, why would Fabio lie to her? It was turning out to be a very strange day. She ordered herself an *aperitivo* and returned to her table outside.

The voices she had heard earlier were less audible now and sounded more muffled. By the time she had finished her martini, the street was a bit busier. The only voices Flavia could hear were those of Fabio and his customers. She had seen them go into the bar but hadn't recognised any of them. She looked at her phone, it was almost 5 o'clock. She resolved to phone Enzo later that evening.

Then, just as she was about to leave, she heard a male voice speaking loudly with Fabio. Seconds later, she caught sight of a well-dressed man leaving the bar, stepping confidently out into the street, his gold filling glistening in the disappearing sun. That's strange, thought Flavia, recognising Vito. Where did he come from? He definitely hadn't been in the bar earlier.

By 5pm Franco and Giovanna had left the police headquarters in an unmarked police car, with Franco at the wheel. En route they remained in radio contact with colleagues in a small fleet of marked cars who had left shortly before them. Following Franco's orders, the police cars took up position in some of the small side streets close to Villa Santa Panagia, well hidden from the main road. These uniformed colleagues were providing backup for Franco and Giovanna who would be going into the building site on foot.

Franco parked outside the perimeter fence surrounding Villa Santa Panagia and switched off the engine.

"All set, Gio?"
"All set, boss."
"Top priority?"
"Get the woman out alive."

Franco noted that Giovanna had referred to 'the woman'. Nice one, Gio, he thought, but what he said was, "That's right. We assume, and really hope that the woman is Roberta Montanari, but we cannot be certain at this stage. OK, next priority?"

"Next priority is to confiscate the phones of her captors. We will need those to help us find out who the captors are in contact with and working for."

"And let's try not to get shot in the process!" he said, with a hint of irony.

Turning his head to look at his deputy, Franco noticed that she had tied back her thick dark hair. She looked strong and determined, even in this light.

"Have you ever shot anyone before, Gio?"

"Never. How about you, boss?" She looked over in his direction.

Franco nodded. It had taken him a long time to accept that sometimes, shooting was a necessary part of the job. The lesser of two evils.

Giovanna broke the silence, "Was it self-defence?"

"No, not self-defence. Defending a colleague who would have been shot dead otherwise. She was a really good cop. Was taken hostage by a lunatic drugs courier up in Catania, in a disused warehouse."

Franco stopped there. Now was not the time to go back over old memories.

He had seen the clock on the dashboard, it was 17.07.

"Time to go!" he announced and with that he flung open the driver's door.

The two of them crept out of the car and headed for the perimeter fence. A few hundred metres from the road, they snuck onto the building site through a gap in the fence. In the fading light, their dark tracksuits and sports shoes helped them blend in well with the wasteland surroundings. They soon arrived at the stakeout house, just as darkness was beginning to fall.

Once safely ensconced there, they had no difficulty making out a faint light emanating from the basement of the house directly opposite. Franco looked at his smartwatch – 17.10. Giovanna was looking at him expectantly. He shook his head, 5.20pm would be time enough. If the captors stuck to their usual routine, they would be swapping over at 6pm. He and Giovanna would lie in wait for another ten minutes, give the darkness more time to descend. He held up ten fingers. Giovanna nodded.

They waited in silence. Both of them were familiar with what to do in this sort of situation. They had rehearsed the police raid procedure so often that it was almost second nature to them. And that was just as well because on the rare occasions where Franco had needed to lead an armed raid, there had been no time to think about it. It was reassuring to know that, on this occasion, uniformed police were on hand as backup. But Franco, being Franco, would only contact them if absolutely necessary. Plan A was to do the job of rescuing the woman without drawing attention to themselves. Franco, being Franco, was also a stickler for detail, he used the waiting time now to run through in his own mind the precise procedure that he and Giovanna had agreed on. He would lead. The first step would involve the short passage across the dirt track road to the house. Giovanna was under strict instructions not to proceed without his signal. Franco would advance with his pistol loaded and held aloft, safety catch on. When he reached the house, he would flip the safety off and wait for Giovanna to join him there. Once over there, they would need to have their wits about them as they proceeded into the house together in search of the captive woman. That was the unknown. Franco briefly checked that his pistol was loaded and the safety catch on. He checked the time again – 17.19. He used the remaining minute to take some deep breaths. Then he felt ready.

They needed to act swiftly. And that they did. The front door had not been locked, so Franco had not needed to use the skeleton key that he had brought along, just in case. Within three minutes, he and Giovanna found themselves in the entrance lobby of the house. He briefly paused to catch his breath. The dark air felt dry against his throat. The smell of wood shavings filled his senses. Vague noises were coming from below. Stealthily they explored the floor space around the lobby area until they found the door to a staircase leading down to the basement. Franco took the lead, holding back for just a couple of seconds to check that his deputy was behind him. Having established eye contact, they exchanged nods, then carefully made their way down the steps. They blended in well with their surroundings. Their soft sports shoes absorbed any noise as they went downstairs, diminishing any potential echo. Franco silently counted the 20 steps that took them down into the basement.

They stood at the bottom of the stairs. There were no doors down here. At the end of a short, unlit passageway ahead of them they could see a light. The vague noises they had heard upstairs became clearer now: a muffled human voice and what sounded like a chair being knocked against the floor. Bingo, thought Franco. Bathed in the light emanating from the end of the passageway, he held up his left hand. This was Giovanna's cue to stand still. Leaving her at the bottom of the stairs, he tiptoed down to the end of the passageway, then signalled to Giovanna to cover him before leaping into the light.

He landed in a smallish room. He stood there in the

middle of the floor, stock still for two seconds. First he activated his neck, twisting his head from side to side and up and down, expertly scanning the room for potential danger. There were two people in the room. The woman's eyes were out on stalks. She sat gagged and bound to a chair. He ignored her and turned instead to the second occupant of the room. A young man slumped in an easy chair, engrossed in his phone. Quick as a flash, Franco moved towards him. "Police!" he yelled, pointing his pistol at the young man. By this stage an adrenaline rush was flooding Franco's entire body. It felt like he'd been born for this moment. The young man shook his head, was it denial? Disbelief? Franco didn't care. He was hell bent on an arrest. The police chief watched as his captive looked around for an escape route. But there was no escape.

Within seconds Giovanna appeared on the scene and at Franco's bidding, she deftly removed the phone from the young man before he had even realised what was going on. Franco then wanted to restrain the prisoner. Placing his pistol safely on the floor, out of harm's way, he proceeded to grab the young man's wrists. The scoundrel proved a slippery customer, and an increasingly vocal one. "Get your hands off me!" he screamed. "You can't do this to me! The big man will see that you pay for this." Wriggling his wrists lose from Franco's grip, he started thumping the police chief in the chest. There was nothing else for it, Franco would have to sit on his captive. The force of Franco's body weighed down on the young man and gradually overwhelmed him long enough for Franco, with Giovanna's help, to gag and handcuff him.

Franco knew that they had to act quickly. The last thing he needed was for this young upstart to escape. He needed to make sure that their captive was securely out of the way before the change of shift. Taking a deep breath, he grabbed the younger man under the arms and ignoring his wildly kicking legs, proceeded to drag him away from the room. In another corner of the basement, he handcuffed him to a radiator pipe and removed the young man's shoes.

Giovanna meanwhile busied herself with untying the woman. When Franco came back into the room again, Giovanna was already taking photos of the woman holding up a copy of the Sunday newspaper. It was Roberta Montanari all right. Franco felt relieved.

When Giovanna spotted her boss, she came over to him.

"How is she?" he asked.

"Emotional," replied Giovanna. "When I removed the gag from her, she just wept with relief –"

"And exhaustion?" Franco couldn't help himself. He was starting to feel exhausted himself.

"I've given her a small bottle of water and done my best to tidy her up a bit." continued Giovanna, ignoring his interruption.

"Time is of the essence, Gio. Hold onto those photos you've taken for now, till we check who to send them to."

"No need, boss. I've already checked. Previous photos from here have all gone to the same recipient ..."

On hearing this, Franco had to concede that Giovanna was one step ahead of him.

"All the photos have been sent to the 'big man'," she continued. "Some kind of code name for Bellotto?"

"Ah!" Franco responded without hesitation, "Spot on Gio! In the underworld, Bellotto is known as the 'big man'. Has been for years. Only he's not as big as he thinks he is!"

Conscious of their tight schedule, Franco knew this was not the time for detailed explanation. Again, Giovanna was one step ahead of him. "Don't worry, boss. I'll check that out."

"Good work, Gio. But send the latest photos to Bellotto, sorry the big man, soon. Keep him sweet."

"Talking of sweet, boss. This might be a good time to pass round the Modica!" winked Giovanna.

If truth be told, Franco was not in the mood for humour – he seldom was. But he was feeling ready for a bite of chocolate. And glancing over to Signora Montanari, he could see that she looked even more in need. So he unzipped his jacket pocket and pulled out an unopened bar of organic *arancia rossa* – 60% cocoa.

"Here," he said, handing the chocolate to Giovanna. "Take Signora Montanari upstairs out of the way. Stay with her."

"What about you, boss? Will you be ok?"

Franco looked at his phone – 17.50.

"Go Gio!" he said. "The next guy will be here soon. And check that the safety catch on your pistol is switched on!"

He watched the two women start to make their way upstairs. Signora Montanari did not look steady on her feet. She was needing a lot of support from Giovanna. Don't worry Roberta, he thought, this will soon all be over.

Just a few minutes later a message came through on his phone. It was from the uniformed squad:

WHITE VAN ENTERING BUILDING SITE NOW. ACCOMPLICE #2 ON HIS WAY?

The sound of a vehicle brought everything into sharp relief for Franco. He listened as it pulled up outside the house. And if he was not mistaken that was the sound of someone whistling. Someone's in a good mood, he thought. Sure enough, the second captor came bounding down the basement stairs, positively beaming. "Hey

Guido! Not long now!" he called out before reaching the lit room. "Just one more win tonight and …"

Franco pounced, assailing him from behind. He held the younger man by the neck, in a tight grip. "Good evening, Bruno!"

But Bruno Mangiafico was not in the mood for social niceties. He retaliated with his fists and elbows, winding Franco with a blow to the stomach. The police chief was forced to release his grip on Bruno's neck. The two of them wrestled for supremacy. Like raging bulls they charged at each other, crashing into the walls of the small room, smashing the abandoned wooden chair where Roberta Montanari had been sitting. In the melee, a mobile phone dropped onto the floor. Gotcha! thought Franco, kicking the phone into the dark passage. But in that split second, the younger man seized his opportunity and viciously punched Franco to the ground before sitting astride his chest. Then, just as Bruno raised his fist, ready to strike again, Franco detected a tall, dark figure enter the room right behind Bruno. He couldn't quite make out who it was. Until he heard the unmistakable voice.

"Police! Put your hands in the air and step this way. Now!"

Bruno slowly lifted his heavy body from Franco's torso. And Franco breathed again. Never had he been so pleased to see his deputy. An apology for a smile in Giovanna's direction was all he could manage before struggling to raise his exhausted body off the ground. He felt absolutely spent.

"I've got this, boss. Take your time," called Giovanna, still holding Bruno at gunpoint as she placed him in handcuffs. Then carefully placing her gun back in her holster, she tightly bound up his feet with some of the rope that had been used to tie up Roberta.

Franco suddenly remembered Roberta.

"And Signora Montanari? Where is she?" he gasped, doing his best not to squirm from the shooting pain that he felt in his ribs.

"Don't worry, boss. Roberta is safe upstairs."

Giovanna looked intently at the *commissario*.

"Backup are on their way, boss," she declared. Then added, "And you need to get seen to. You've taken some nasty blows."

He could tell from her tone that she meant business. "You take care of Roberta, go with her to the –"

"Safe house?"

Franco nodded but flinched as he did so. "Give me the two phones …" he groaned.

"Where is the second phone?" inquired his deputy.

Franco nodded painfully in the direction of the passageway where he had kicked Bruno's phone.

"OK, I can handle that, boss. You want me to send the photos I took, and make sure that Bellotto won't suspect anything, right?"

"OUCH!" said Franco, nodding.

"I'll do that before I leave with Roberta. That way if the message is traced, they'll know it –"

"Was sent from here. Good thinking Gio."

He could hear the noise of thumping feet clattering down the stairs to the basement. Backup had arrived. And that was the last thing that Franco remembered before passing out.

CHAPTER 13

"Eat up, Dani! You're going to need that energy tonight!"

Dani Montanari looked up at the smiling face of his teammate Miguel Ramos, who was sitting opposite him at the table in the hotel restaurant. "Yeah, Miguel, you're right." With that, Dani poked his fork into the huge bowl of spaghetti carbonara in front of him, then ate a morsel.

"Come on! We can't wait all day for you to finish lunch! We'll be practising again in half an hour."

Dani checked the clock on the wall facing him: midday. Seven hours until the Sunday evening match in Kentucky between the Bats and the Kats – the game that could determine the fate of his mother.

"Sorry, Miguel. I was just thinking about things. It's been difficult to concentrate this past week." Dani wouldn't have been as candid as this with the Bats' coach. However, he felt more comfortable talking with Miguel. Although the two of them had been competing for the role of main pitcher over the past couple of years, they had developed a camaraderie. Partly this was because they both understood the challenges and rewards of this high-profile role. And partly because they were both continuing to adjust to life in a new country: Miguel had moved to the US from Mexico and Dani from Italy.

"Gee, I know, it's been a turbulent time!" Miguel glanced at the surrounding tables before continuing, this time in a low voice, "Is there anything you want to talk about?"

"No, Miguel," sighed Dani. "I've never been in this situation before, with all the pressure from the fans, the media, the sponsors, everything. It just takes time getting used to."

"Tell me about it!" replied Miguel, who returned to gobbling up the final few pieces of spaghetti.

Dani looked back down at his plate, moving the fork slowly back and forth. Etched in his mind was the photo that had been sent to him on WhatsApp just half an hour earlier. The photo of his mother holding a newspaper; this time, it was the Sunday paper in Siracusa. It must be around 7 pm there now, he thought, calculating the time difference between Kentucky and Sicily. In a way he had been pleased to receive this photo: it proved that his beloved mother was still alive. But the accompanying message had chilled him: *YOU KNOW WHAT YOU HAVE TO DO!* Miguel was scheduled to start tonight's game, but Dani might well be called upon to come on as relief pitcher and close out the match. Could he really let the Kats win without making it obvious that he wasn't trying? And, even if he could, should he do this?

The sudden vibration of Dani's phone interrupted his thoughts. Quickly he took the phone from his pocket and looked at the screen: *NUMBER WITHHELD*. For a couple of seconds he wondered what to do, then he pressed the answer button.

"*Pronto*? Dani?" Dani heard a woman's voice, not one he recognised. "*Sì*", he responded.

The voice continued in Italian, "Dani, my name is Giovanna Campisi. I am a detective with the police in Siracusa. Can we talk privately please?"

Dani looked up at his teammate. "Sorry, Miguel, I've got to take this call. I'll be right back!" Miguel said nothing, but from the expression on his face, Dani guessed that his colleague understood the seriousness of the situation.

Dani stood up and moved quickly towards the door of the restaurant, passing his teammates who were now finishing lunch. "Hey! Dani," one of them called out, "if you've you left something in Bakerside, it's too late to go back now!" Dani ignored the wisecrack and accompanying laughs. Instead he breezed out the door and into the warm autumn sun, unable to bear the thought of what the detective might be about to tell him.

He put the phone to his ear and switched to his native tongue. "We can speak now. What's happened?"

"I've got good news," said Giovanna. "We've freed your mother! She's safe and well."

Dani let out a muffled cry. "What! She's free! Can I speak with her, please?"

"Just a moment," said Giovanna. As Dani heard the phone being passed over, an unpleasant thought crossed his mind. Was this all a hoax? Were the kidnappers playing games with him?

"Dani! It's me." His mother's warm voice shattered his doubts into a million pieces. "The police have rescued me," she continued. "Thank God!"

"Mamma!" By now Dani was nearly in tears. "It's wonderful to hear you! I'm so happy!"

CATCH!

Over the next few minutes, mother and son spoke intensely of their love for each other and about how they were feeling. Roberta explained that the photo Dani had received within the past hour had been staged, to convince those responsible for her abduction that she was still being held captive. Then the detective came back on the line.

"Dani, your mother is in a safe house now. Our operation is continuing. For now, please do not tell anyone that your mother had been abducted or that she's been freed. We'll contact your father, but for now we need to keep her release a secret."

"Of course," replied Dani. "I've got to go now, I've got a big match tonight. Speak soon, mamma!"

"Go, Dani, go!" his mother shouted down the line.

After saying their goodbyes, Dani put his phone away. This changes everything, he thought. Pushing out his chest, he strode back into the restaurant, intent on eating every last piece of carbonara – no matter how cold it might be by now – before giving it his all on the practice ground. Kats, watch out!

It was now late Sunday evening. Officer Mikey Ricci was delighted to be back at police headquarters. His week at the launderette had seemed to pass slowly; indeed, very slowly some days. He had been itching to spend more time with his colleagues but had no idea when that might happen. So, he had been taken aback when Giovanna Campisi had rung him a couple of hours earlier and instructed him to return to police HQ.

"*Fantastico!*" had been Mikey's response when Giovanna told him that she and Franco had freed Roberta. However, Mikey had been concerned to hear of Franco's injuries. "Don't worry," Giovanna had told him. "The boss will need to stay in hospital overnight for observation, but he should be back on duty tomorrow."

Nevertheless, as Giovanna went on to explain to Mikey, the beating that Franco had suffered during the raid had disrupted the plans that he and Giovanna had devised for the second part of their operation. She would now deputise for *Commissario* Spina, but someone else would need to fulfil her role. When Giovanna had told Mikey that he would be working alongside her, he had been over the moon. In contrast to the petty crimes that Mikey had been assigned to since arriving in Siracusa, this meant he would now be centre stage in a major criminal investigation. No sooner had the call ended than Mikey rapidly closed the launderette, jumped into Totti and raced over to police headquarters.

Following his arrival there, Giovanna spoke with him at length about the approach that they would take in interrogating the two men arrested during the release of Signora Montanari from Villa Santa Panagia. The main priority was to secure the evidence needed to arrest Alfonso Bellotto. "We're confident that Bellotto is the person behind the abduction of Signora Montanari," Giovanna said. "The people we've taken in were talking about the 'big man', which is how the criminal fraternity here refer to Bellotto. Also, Signora Montanari was being held in a house being built by Bellotto Construction. However, when we looked through the messages on the phones that we seized during the raid, none of them mentioned Bellotto by name. It'll take some hours before our technical whizz kids can track down the owner of the phone that the captors were communicating with. It could be tomorrow morning before we can confirm the number is linked to Alfonso Bellotto. If, in the meantime, Bellotto discovers that his henchmen have been arrested, then he'll probably throw away the phone and get his lawyers to claim that he's somehow been framed for the abduction."

"Couldn't we get the magistrate to issue a warrant for Bellotto's arrest now, so we could get our hands on his phone?" asked Mikey.

Giovanna sighed. "Ideally, but you have to remember that we're talking about arresting a high-profile person. Someone who could be the mayor of this city in a few days' time. The magistrate will want more than circumstantial evidence before issuing a warrant. What we need is for one of the accomplices, Guido or Bruno, to spill the beans on Bellotto – and to do it soon, before Bellotto realises that we're on to him."

On hearing this, Mikey's shoulders dropped. He had been thinking about Alfonso Bellotto over the previous few days, after hearing about the way that Bellotto was exploiting migrants mercilessly for his own ends. Mikey also recalled the scenes of violence that had unfolded near his home on Saturday afternoon, and seeing the big man himself at San Valentino that morning, soaking up the adoration of his well-heeled supporters. Mikey could feel his blood pressure rising. Surely Bellotto can't escape justice, he thought. There must be a way to put him behind bars – mustn't there?

"Do you have a print-out of the phone messages between Guido, Bruno and the 'big man'?" asked Mikey. Giovanna passed this to Mikey, who sat down at a desk and immediately started to look through them. As he read through the messages, his thoughts turned to Enzo. Mikey had been shocked earlier that day when Flavia revealed that the parish priest was being blackmailed by Bellotto. Could the big man be brought to Police HQ and interrogated about this claim, wondered Mikey. However, he doubted whether this would work. The police would first need a statement from Don Enzo but Mikey was unsure whether the priest was prepared to talk. Following the service at San Valentino, there had been no answer when Mikey had rung Enzo's number. So he had left a voice note for his priest friend. "Sorry I had to dash off earlier. Hope you're OK. Maybe we can have a chat." But Enzo had not got back to him.

"What are you thinking, Ricci?" Giovanna's question brought Mikey back to the present.

"Just mulling over a few things," replied Mikey. "Who do you think we should question first?"

"I'm inclined to start with Bruno. He might be closer to Bellotto than Guido is. After all, his sister is Bellotto's partner." The second part of Giovanna's statement caused Mikey to breathe in sharply.

Mikey's mind raced, as he tried to link this news to the phone messages he had just started reading and to events earlier that day. He recalled his meeting outside the church with Vito Lupo. That meeting had prompted Mikey to phone a police contact in Catania. Stoking his moustache, an idea slowly formed in his mind, then –standing up – he exclaimed: "EUREKA!" Mikey thought even Archimedes, Siracusa's most famous citizen, would have envied the plan that he had just devised!

"Are you feeling OK, Ricci?" Giovanna had a concerned look on her face.

"Never better!" Mikey excitedly explained his idea to Giovanna. Once he had finished, she was silent for a moment, then responded: "Do you really think this will work?"

"I think we should give it a try," replied Mikey. "This could be the way to get Bruno to talk."

Giovanna took time to think over his idea. She did this, pacing back and forth in the office for what seemed to Mikey like an age, even though it was probably less than a minute. Eventually she turned to him. "OK. Come on Ricci, let's do this! But we'll need to get a move on."

Full of anticipation, Mikey walked together with Giovanna into an ante room. There they looked through a one-way window into the interrogation room. At a table facing in their direction sat a large man, probably in his late 30s. Mikey spotted several bruises on his face and a large plaster on his forehead, just below a mass of curly black hair. The man was glancing around the otherwise empty room with a scowl on his face.

"He's been in the wars, hasn't he?" said Mikey.

"He certainly has," responded Giovanna. "He and the boss really slogged it out!" With that, the two officers moved swiftly into the interrogation room and sat down at the table, opposite the man with the scowl.

Giovanna spoke first. "Bruno Mangiafico, we will be questioning you later about the unlawful abduction of Signora Roberta Montanari and the assault on *Commissario* Franco Spina. But first, ..."

"I want a lawyer!" Bruno's deep voice reverberated around the interrogation room.

"A lawyer's on their way," responded Giovanna. "They'll be here when we question you about Signora Montanari and *Commissario* Spina. But before that, we need to talk about the big man. Who is he? Who are you working for?"

"No comment." Bruno sat back in his chair and folded his arms.

"It's Alfonso Bellotto, isn't it, Bruno? It's Rosa's boyfriend you've been working for."

Mikey could almost see daggers flying out of Bruno's eyes as he responded, "Keep Rosa's name out of this!"

Now it was Giovanna's turn to sit back in her seat. "No, Bruno. Until we've questioned Bellotto under caution, we can't rule out the possibility that Rosa was involved in the abduction of her neighbour, Signora Montanari." Giovanna moved forward again and looked Bruno fully in the eyes. "Don't forget that we have your phone and Guido's too. We'll soon be able to confirm that the person you've been calling and messaging is Bellotto. So, why don't you make it easier for everyone, Bruno? Come on, admit it, Bellotto planned the abduction, didn't he?"

Bruno pursed his lips and said nothing.

Giovanni turned towards Mikey, "Officer Ricci?"

This was it. Mikey took a deep breath, pulled out his phone and – after some scrolling – placed it on the table in front of Bruno.

"Do you recognise this man?" asked Mikey, pointing at the photo displayed on the phone.

A trace of a smile crossed Bruno's face. "Maybe."

"That's a yes, then." Mikey pointed once more at the man in the photo. "Vito Lupo. He's an interesting character! I was speaking with one of my colleagues in Catania this afternoon. Vito's well-known there. They call him the 'wolf'. Linked to multiple crime rackets, from extortion to illegal gambling. Outwardly charming, but utterly ruthless if you cross him. Vito hasn't been seen too much around Catania in recent times, so my colleague was interested to hear that he's now based in Siracusa."

Bruno's face was impassive.

Mikey continued, "I've been looking through the messages on your phone. The big man refers several times there to 'muzzling the wolf'. To 'keeping the wolf happy'. Even, in one message, to 'giving the wolf what he's asking for'. And all these messages were interspersed with chat about the abduction of Signora Montanari and holding her against her will. How's the wolf involved in all of this, Bruno?"

Again Bruno showed no emotion.

"Here's what I think, Bruno. Correct me if I'm wrong. I think that the big man, Alfonso Bellotto, owed money to the wolf, Vito Lupo. Maybe Vito gave Bellotto money to help with his election campaign, maybe Bellotto ran up gambling debts." Mikey shrugged his shoulders. "Whatever. The bottom line is that Bellotto needed a lot of money and he needed it quickly. Not only did he have Vito breathing down his neck, he had the mayoral election coming up. What was he going to do?"

Mikey paused. Still no reaction from Bruno.

"Perhaps it was a remark from your sister that started this. She may have mentioned in passing to Bellotto that her next-door neighbour was the mother of a famous baseball player. A player who was about to play a central role in the World Series, one of the world's leading sporting competitions. A competition that would attract huge global interest and for which many people would bet big money on the outcome. So, Bellotto comes up with this plan: to kidnap Signora Montanari and blackmail her son to play badly in the World Series. Then, before the competition starts, the big man places a large bet on the underdogs – the Kentucky Kats –and collects huge winnings when the Kats do win. Was Rosa in on this?"

"No!" The response from Bruno was immediate.

"OK, so Rosa didn't know about the scheme. Maybe it was just you, Guido and Bellotto who were in on this. But you didn't count on the wolf. You see, Vito frequents the area around the launderette. I spoke to him there shortly after I started working there and he's often at the bar at the top of the street. My guess is that Vito realised early on that something was afoot, particularly if Bellotto had just assured him that Vito would get his money soon. Vito is no fool: he would have seen the news about the World

Series and how poorly Dani was playing, and wondered if there was a link to Signora Montanari's unexpected absence."

From Bruno's intent look, Mikey felt that he was now the recipient of the daggers' treatment.

"Of course," continued Mikey, "Vito would have mixed feelings about all of this. Not because he cared about Signora Montanari – he lied to me about that. No, Vito would have thought about all the money he and his gambling cronies might have made if only Bellotto had told them about his plan in advance, before the start of the World Series."

Mikey sensed that Giovanna was looking at him. Time now to go for the kill.

"One of the things I learnt from my colleague in Catania is that Vito likes to have a network of trusted henchmen who can keep him informed. Men like this one." With that, Mikey contracted the photo on his phone, to reveal a man standing next to Vito. "Do you recognise him?" asked Mikey, pointing at the man in the photo.

There was a sharp intake of breath as Bruno's mouth dropped in astonishment.

"This," said Mikey, "is Silvio Tacchino. You know him as Bellotto's chauffeur. But he and Vito go back a long way. Vito himself told me that today, around the time that I took this photo. And Silvio Tacchino is definitely known to the police department in Catania. I sent this photo to my colleague there. And guess what? He got back to tell me that Silvio has multiple convictions for assault. He's a very nasty person."

Bruno was now breathing deeply. Almost there, thought Mikey.

"When I saw him this morning, Vito told me he would really like to meet Rosa. And Silvio indicated that he could help arrange this. Why would he do this, Bruno? What do you think is going on?"

Bruno flung his hands into air. "It's lies! All lies!"

"No it isn't." Keep your cool, Mikey thought to himself. "Vito knows that the World Series could still go either way and that the Bats could beat the Kats. In which case, Bellotto's scheme to settle his debts would go up in smoke. So, Vito wants to keep the pressure on Bellotto, to make sure he gets his money. And since Bellotto thought that abduction was a good way of extorting money, why shouldn't Vito do the same?"

Bruno shook his head from side to side. He doesn't want to believe this, thought Mikey. Then he continued, "I think that Vito is planning to abduct Rosa, as security. If the Bats win tonight, which is likely since Dani Montanari now knows that his mother's been freed, then Vito – with Silvio's help – might even take Rosa tomorrow morning, ahead of the final game. There's only one way to stop this, Bruno. You know what to do."

"NO! NO!" shouted Bruno.

Mikey turned to Giovanna, who lent forward and spoke.

"You clearly care deeply for your twin sister, Bruno. But you need to tell us about Bellotto, so that we can arrest him and take Rosa to a safe location, away from the claws of the wolf. And provided that Bellotto cooperates with us, we'll be able to muzzle the wolf, once and for all. Just tell us, Bruno."

Bruno raised his head, let out a pained scream, then looked straight at Giovanna and, in a hesitant voice, he talked. And talked. And talked.

Flavia was at home, still puzzled. Earlier when she had been sitting outside Bar Stella, she could have sworn she had heard Enzo's voice inside the bar. What was he doing there? And why had there been no sign of him when she'd looked inside? Maybe Fabio was telling the truth and Enzo had never been there at all? And then there was Vito. How come he had left the bar out of the blue like that? Everyone knew he was a regular at Bar Stella, but Flavia had been sitting outside for over an hour and not seen him go in.

She had planned to phone Enzo to find out more. But wondered now if it might be better to have that conversation in person. She wandered over to her front window, overlooking the street below, to see if the rain had finally stopped. On opening the shutters, she saw the dark, wet night outside and grimaced. And then, quite unexpectedly, in the distance she thought she recognised the familiar luminescent flash of Enzo's trainers. She looked again. Yes, it was definitely him and he was heading down via Brescia in her direction.

Without giving it a second's thought, Flavia dashed downstairs and out into via Vicenza. The whole place seemed deserted apart from the solitary figure of the parish priest, making his way from the church to where she stood. "Enzo!" she called and waved frantically in his direction. Dressed casually as he was, no one would know he was a priest. He's left his cassock at home, observed Flavia. And he looked like he was in a hurry. Flavia assumed he was rushing to escape the wet weather. But where was he going? It was only when he was standing right next to her, that she noticed something else.

"*Ciao* Enzo! No Rocco tonight?" she asked.

He shook his head, "Rocco's having a night off."

It was unusual for the priest to be out without his dog. Flavia waited for him to say more but he didn't. "Do you want to come in for a bit?" she asked, breaking the silence.

Again, he shook his head. "Sorry Flavia, that's kind of

you, but I need to get going."

"Going where?" she blurted.

This time, he shrugged his shoulders and looked away.

It felt like the conversation was leading nowhere. Meanwhile, the wetness of the pavement was starting to seep through her sock feet. Flavia had had enough.

"Listen Enzo, were you at Bar Stella this afternoon? Only, I was sitting outside and thought I could hear you inside talking with someone."

He turned his head to look Flavia straight in the eye.

"Maybe you were mistaken," he gently replied. "Sorry Flavs, I'm late. I need to get going."

And with that, he started to make his way up via Vicenza.

She called after him, "Why don't you tell me what this is all about? There's something you're not telling me..." Her voice tapered off as she realised her friend was not going to turn back.

Watching him head off into the darkness, she reflected on what had just happened between them. Something was affecting Enzo. It was not in his nature to close up like this; he was not his usual exuberant self. What had been going on that afternoon at Bar Stella? For some reason, Flavia wondered if it was linked in any way to the blackmailing that he had mentioned to her at the rally ...

By this point, Enzo was nearing the top end of via Vicenza close to Bar Stella. Flavia could just make out his tell-tale trainers. He seemed to hesitate, then went into the bar. Flavia gasped.

Mikey glanced at the time displayed on his phone: 02.06. Normally he would be fast asleep at this time on a Monday morning. But this was unlike any other morning Mikey had experienced since arriving in Siracusa.

He showed the time on his phone to Giovanna, who – like him – was crouching in the shadows of a residential street in the centre of Siracusa. Ideally, they would have arrived there a couple of hours or so earlier, following their interrogation of Bruno. However, there had been difficulties tracking down the magistrate late on a Sunday night. Eventually, though, they had received the warrant they needed.

And the delay had some advantages. The rain had stopped now. Plus, over in Kentucky, the latest game in the World Series had just started; Giovanna and Mikey agreed that this would be a useful distraction. Shortly before leaving the police headquarters, Mikey had checked the sports news and heard that Miguel Ramos – chosen as the opening pitcher for the Bats – had injured his arm during the warm-up. Apparently, Dani Montanari had insisted that he would start the game in place of Ramos and the Bats had agreed to this. Dani's mind must be swirling with so many emotions, thought Mikey.

Giovanna nudged Mikey and pointed towards a light coming from an upper floor in an otherwise dark apartment building, just across the road from them.

"Let's invite ourselves in!" she whispered.

Giovanna pulled a phone out of her pocket. Even under the dim street lights, Mikey could see that the screen was cracked; not surprising he thought – it probably got damaged during the fight at Villa Santa Panagia. Looking over her shoulder, Mikey saw Giovanna typing a WhatsApp message:

CAN I POP BY? GOT TIME BEFORE GO BACK TO HOUSE. WANT TO SEE START OF MATCH!

Giovanna pressed the send button. A few seconds later, the screen lit up and Mikey saw the reply:

SURE! SEE YOU SOON.

Giovanna turned to Mikey and smiled. "Bingo! Let's go."

Mikey was amazed by Giovanna's stamina; how could she have done an overnight stake-out, taken part in the raid at Villa Santa Panagia, and still be composed enough to lead this operation, all in the space of just over 24 hours? That question, however, could wait for another day.

Silently they crossed the street. Once they reached the entrance to the apartment block, Giovanna turned to her left and held up her hand, showing all five fingers. The message to Pappalardo and the two uniformed officers hiding in a nearby doorway was clear: give us five minutes.

On entering the bottom of the stairwell, Mikey noticed that the lights didn't come on automatically. Good, he thought; if there were any CCTV, it would be unlikely to pick them up. Swiftly they mounted a couple of flights of stairs, guided by a few threads of light shining through some small windows on the stairwell. Then they were at the door. Giovanna knocked twice.

"Come on in!" A woman's voice made itself heard above the muffled sound of people shouting. "The door's open."

Is this a trap, thought Mikey. Giovanna pulled out her pistol and slid off the safety catch; Mikey followed her example. Then Giovanna turned the handle and pushed the door fully open.

In front of them they saw a hallway in darkness, save for a light coming from a door at the far end. The sound of shouting was clearer now. Giovanna stepped forward, holding her pistol above her head, and motioned for Mikey to follow her. Slowly they edged forward towards the door at the end of the hall. Suddenly, Giovanna leapt into the doorway and shouted, "Police! Arms in the air!"

A second later Mikey was at Giovanna's side, taking in the scene in the room. Covering much of the wall on the far side was a massive TV screen. As Mikey had guessed, the shouting was coming from fans at the baseball game in Kentucky. On the screen, a young man was standing at the plate, preparing to pitch the ball. In front of him, a massive guy was swinging his bat effortlessly, as though it were a branch from a pine tree.

There were two people in the room. One of them, a woman in a comfy chair, turned towards Giovanna and Mikey, open-mouthed. After a moment's silence, she said, "What's going on? Where's Bruno?"

"Bruno couldn't make it tonight, Signora Mangiafico," said Giovanna, smiling. "He's otherwise occupied."

Mikey gazed at Rosa. In a dressing gown and without make-up, she looked very different from the woman who had strutted into San Valentino on Sunday morning.

"But .... but ... Bruno contacted us just a few minutes ago," responded Rosa, with a tremor in her voice. "He said he was coming here."

Giovanna pulled out a phone from her pocket and held it in the air. "This is Bruno's phone. He mislaid it ... when we arrested him!"

Rosa shrieked and turned towards a tubby man, dressed in loungewear, lying on a large sofa, facing the large, wall mounted TV screen. "SHHHH!" he said to her, maintaining his focus on the screen. "This is important!"

All four people in the room looked at the TV as the pitcher hurled the ball. Mikey saw the name written in capitals on the back of the pitcher's shirt: MONTANARI. The striker swung the bat with all his might and ...

"YES!" Mikey shouted as the striker missed the ball and was given out by the umpire. "What a pitch!"

The players ran off the field for a break and the TV

adverts started. Only then did the man on the sofa sit up, turn towards the police officers and speak. "What's all this nonsense? Who are you?"

"Signor Alfonso Bellotto, I am arresting you for the abduction of Signora Roberta Montanari." Giovanna's voice was ice-cold.

Bellotto looked nonplussed but said nothing. Rosa spoke first. "What are you talking about? Roberta's my neighbour. Why on earth would Alfonso abduct her?"

Then it was the turn of Bellotto. "Ignore this, Rosa. It's all nonsense! The police have clearly decided to thwart the will of the people. They don't want me to become mayor of this great city!"

Mikey glanced at Giovanna, who was continuing to stare intently at Bellotto. "I have a warrant to arrest you, Signor Bellotto," she said calmly. "I repeat, put your hands up!"

Bellotto sighed. "Why should I? We're not a threat to anyone. We're simply having a quiet time watching some sport. Look, the teams are coming back out." He turned back towards the TV screen.

Giovanna nodded to Mikey and said, "Handcuffs. Now!"

Bellotto spun around, his face turning crimson. "You'll do NO such thing. I'm ringing my lawyer!"

"That can wait until we get to the station. Ricci, take his phone!" Giovanna betrayed no emotion in her voice.

As Mikey moved forward, Bellotto stood up and moved away from Mikey, towards the TV. "Ah!" he said. "That's what you're really after, isn't it? My phone. Well, I will hand it over to you – but only after I've wiped all the messages on it. Nothing sinister, but there's some personal material here. Isn't that right, Rosa?" She nodded.

"Put it down!" Giovanna ordered, as Bellotto started to

press buttons on the phone.

It all seemed to happen at once then. Mikey heard footsteps behind him, racing towards the room. A huge WHACK came from the TV's loudspeakers, as a baseball was struck high into the dark Kentucky sky. And an ear-piercing squeal filled the room. Bellotto stopped and looked around, apparently confused.

This was Mikey's chance. In one continuous movement, he put the safety catch back on his pistol, threw it underarm to his colleagues who had reached the door of the room, took three steps forward and flung himself at Bellotto.

There was a massive CRUNCH as the two men collided and Bellotto's phone flew into the air. Mikey and Bellotto fell to the floor, then one of them reached up a hand – and caught the phone.

"Great catch, Ricci!" Giovanna's voice was still steely, but there was no disguising her delight. "Pappalardo, handcuffs!"

Within a few seconds, Bellotto had been handcuffed. Mikey, feeling a bit shaken but uninjured, got back on his feet and placed Bellotto's phone in a bag to be taken down to the station. Giovanna then explained to Rosa that – for her own safety – it would be best to take her to a secure location. "What about Lola?" asked Rosa.

Just at that moment, Mikey realised the source of the squeal. On the far side of Rosa's seat, he saw a large, fluffy cat sitting proudly on a table, purring. "Don't worry, Signora Mangiafico," replied Giovanna, "Lola will be fine. Roberta will be delighted to have her back!"

A shout rang out from the TV. Mikey glanced at the scenes in Kentucky, then spoke to Bellotto. "Dani's playing a blinder! You've got to admit, the Bats are running away with this – they're bound to win now!"

Bellotto scowled but said nothing as he was taken away.

MONDAY 30TH OCTOBER

CHAPTER 14

Flavia stood staring at the sign: *LAUNDERETTE CLOSED UNTIL FURTHER NOTICE.* Why had Mikey not mentioned anything to her yesterday about the launderette closing? It was only yesterday, wasn't it? That she had been sitting in there next to him? Persuading him to go with her to San Valentino's, for Enzo's last Mass before All Saints Day?

This year All Saints fell on a Wednesday. That and the following day, All Souls Day, were holidays in Sicily. Not that Flavia was particularly religious, but she did enjoy having two days of public holiday. She looked forward to spending time with her family, relaxing. They would have lunch together for sure; and weather permitting, they would sit outside at one of the fish restaurants overlooking the large port in Ortigia. Most of all she enjoyed the opportunity to get dressed up, to go out and be with other people who had also made an effort to look their best. Public holidays were prime people-watching time for Flavia. It was fun. And she took a keen interest in the diverse ways that different people expressed themselves through the clothes and the jewellery that they chose to wear. It fascinated her how endlessly creative people could be.

She looked down at the bulging bag of dirty washing at her feet and sighed deeply. Those clothes would not wash themselves. Feeling properly irritated, her attention returned to the sign. Why? Why? Why did it need to close? But she knew there was no point thinking about that right now. There was a holiday coming up and she had clothes to wash – and a shop to open up.

By 10 o'clock Flavia had reviewed her wardrobe options for the week ahead. Rolling up her sleeves, she put on her long, pink rubber gloves and set to work. The first job was to clear the sink of dishes and debris from the night before. Then she used the sink to hand wash a couple of tops as well as some essential undies and hung them all out on her balcony drying rack. She was ready now for a large coffee and a cheeky almond paste cookie.

Miles purred at her feet, as she sat perched on a stool at the kitchen bar. Picking him up for a cuddle, her thoughts returned to the launderette closure. What did it mean 'until further notice'? Absent-mindedly she fingered the cat's lovely, silky fur and started twisting his hair with her fingers. Suddenly Miles yelped in pain and in his eagerness to spring down from her lap, dug his claws into Flavia's thighs. Flavia screamed. The peacock blue silk dress that she was wearing was in shreds – or so she had first thought. In fact, when she stood up to inspect the damage, she could see that just one or two of the threads in her dress had been pulled. The silk material itself was still intact. PHEW! That had been a close one! But the incident had well and truly woken her up. She glanced at her phone, it was time to open up.

One hour later, business had not been great. It never was on a Monday at this time of year. The window display was good for another couple of weeks and there was a limit to how many times she could tidy up the shop counter. Flavia was contemplating closing early for lunch, maybe popping down to the launderette again or perhaps messaging Mikey to find out what was going on ... All of a sudden she heard the sound of the shop door ringing. In that split second everything changed.

"Flavia!"

"*Mamma mia!* Roberta! Is it really you?"

Flavia ran to hug her friend. She soon noticed the bruising on Roberta's forehead, but tried not to draw attention to it.

As they hugged. Flavia sensed Roberta's need to cling onto another human being. They stood in a tight embrace for some minutes. By which time, Flavia felt something warm and watery seeping down onto her shoulder from Roberta's face. Flavia slowly raised her head. That was when she spotted Mikey. He was standing just a metre away from the two women, smiling benignly. Without giving it a second thought, Flavia smiled back at him.

When the two women finally broke their embrace, Flavia continued to hold Roberta's hand. She could see more clearly now that what she had felt on her shoulder had been tears, happy tears of relief and joy. Still, the bruise marks were concerning. Flavia hoped it was nothing serious. Perhaps Roberta had bumped into something or lost her footing and fallen. Both women were temporarily lost for words. Fortunately, Mikey came to their rescue, suggesting that they all sit down. Of course! Why hadn't Flavia thought of that!

Minutes later, all three were sitting upstairs in Flavia's

flat. Miles, who had been forced to evacuate the comfy armchair, took refuge in the corner of the room, from where he surveyed the goings-on through wide, alert eyes.

"Ladies," started Mikey, looking enthusiastically at the two friends now sitting side by side on Flavia's brightly patterned sofa, "there's something I need to share with you."

Flavia was all ears. She watched Mikey take a deep breath.

"First of all, I don't actually work for EasyWash." he began. "My name is Mikey Ricci, Officer Mikey Ricci. I'm an undercover police detective."

What! Thought Flavia, that's a bit of a bombshell! She was eager to hear more. "So, what's this got to do with Roberta? And why were you running the launderette?" she burst out.

"You were running my launderette? But why?" A gobsmacked Roberta joined in.

Both women watched intently as Mikey leant forward in his armchair. Bit by bit, he slowly filled them in on the events of the past week. He told them how the police had first been alerted to Roberta's unexplained disappearance. He explained that the story about Roberta being on holiday for a few weeks had been a ploy to avert suspicion, and it had been the perfect pretext to bring in Mikey, posing as an EasyWash operator, to cover for her.

"I knew it!" Flavia couldn't stop herself, she jumped up. "I knew you weren't actually on holiday, Roberta. But where were you really?" Then noticing the look that Mikey was giving her, she sat down again. "Sorry. Please continue the story, Mikey," she said sheepishly.

Both women listened as Mikey went on to elaborate. During his stint at the launderette he had been working undercover, getting to know the local community, following up possible lines of inquiry that might explain Roberta's disappearance and more importantly point to her whereabouts. After all, Roberta had last been sighted at the launderette and she had left her car there.

Is that all I was? Thought Flavia indignantly, a possible line of inquiry? This time she kept her thoughts to herself. Doing her best to compose herself again, she asked: "But how did you find out where Roberta was?"

Mikey smiled: "That's a long story. But long story short, it was Enzo's friends at Villa Santa Panagia who were key, not me! Those guys helped us track down the house where Signora Montanari was being kept captive."

"Captive!" gasped Flavia, turning now to her friend. "Oh my God! That's awful!"

Roberta shook her head and quietly said: "I never want to go through that again." Flavia realised now that the bruise marks were more sinister than she had first realised. Clearly Roberta had been through a lot. Please God she hasn't been abused or suffered permanent psychological damage, prayed Flavia, putting an arm around her friend.

Mikey picked up the story again, starting with the building site where Roberta had been held.

Quick as a flash, Flavia interjected: "Villa Santa Panagia you say? Isn't that where that brute Bellotto has a housing development? Don't tell me he was involved in this?" She asked, looking pointedly at the bruise marks on her friend's forehead.

Mikey nodded. "Bellotto had heard about Signora Montanari from his girlfriend, Rosa Mangiafico. So, he knew about Dani –"

"But Rosa is my neighbour! She wouldn't hurt a fly. I trust her," exclaimed Roberta.

Mikey continued, talking now in a gentler tone, "It must be difficult to take all this in, Signora Montanari. But we have arrested Alfonso Bellotto, he will be charged with your abduction. And Rosa is currently under police protection, her life may be in danger."

"Enzo will be over the moon when he hears the news of Bellotto's arrest," said Flavia. She couldn't wait to break the news to her friend. Already, she was calculating what this would mean for him. Surely he would now be free to help his migrant friends. The bishop could no longer place any obstacles in his way.

"Yes, I'm sure Enzo will be happy," replied Mikey, adding: "But first I need to tell you more."

Flavia begged him to continue.

"Turns out that Bellotto had instigated the abduction as part of a gambling scam. He and his cronies had stood to gain millions from a World Series swindle, masterminded by Bellotto himself. But," Mikey stressed, "everything depended on the Kats beating the Bats to win the World Series."

The revelation stunned both women into silence. Flavia was utterly flabbergasted. But somewhere in her brain she managed to make a connection between Dani, basketball and the Bakerside Bats. Had Dani been in on the scam she wondered?

"Signora Montanari, are you ok?" asked Mikey, finally breaking the silence.

Flavia turned to her friend. She looked distressed more than anything else.

"Roberta, are you ok?" repeated Flavia, taking her friend's hand.

"What about Lola? Rosa was looking after her. And if Rosa is under police protection, what's happened to Lola?" Roberta looked on the verge of tears.

Flavia held her friend tight. "Don't you worry, Roberta. I'm sure Lola is fine. We'll find her. We can go together if you want. It won't be a problem."

Roberta didn't reply but smiled back at Flavia.

"How about a nice cup of coffee?" volunteered Flavia, standing up, "and a lovely almond paste cookie."

"That sounds great!" replied Mikey, with a twinkle in his eye. "I just need to pop out for a moment, I'll be back soon – keep one of those cookies for me!" Not again! thought Flavia, he's always shooting off or popping out! But before she could say anything, Mikey had disappeared.

Flavia gave her undivided attention to Roberta. Over coffee, the two friends started talking again. Both of them trying to digest what Mikey had been telling them.

They were on their second cup of coffee when someone buzzed the intercom downstairs. True to his word, it was Mikey. Flavia pressed to let him in, then returned to Roberta in the lounge. They heard footsteps coming up the stairs. Then the partly open lounge door was gently pushed further ajar. Expecting Mikey, both women looked over to the door. Suddenly Roberta shrieked with delight: "Lola!" Whereupon a fluffy ball of white fur bounded over to the sofa and jumped up onto Roberta's lap. For the second time that morning, Roberta was in tears. Through glistening eyes, she turned to face Mikey: "Thank you so much, *dottore*. I am so happy to have Lola back. Thanks a million." And with that she picked up her cat and smothered her in kisses and caresses.

Meanwhile, over in the corner, Miles was relaxing his tense body and the twitching that Flavia had noticed earlier disappeared. Leaving his corner, he padded over towards the sofa, slowly opening and closing his eyes. He looked for all the world as if was blinking in Lola's direction. Flavia was curious. Could it possibly be that love was in the air? But Mikey's voice interrupted any further speculation on the subject.

"Sorry, I need to leave you ladies. When you feel ready, Signora Montanari, please give us a ring on this number and a colleague will come and take you back to the safe house." Mikey handed a card to Roberta. "Maybe see you both later?" he asked looking at Flavia.

"Later?"

"Tonight! It's the big match!"

Flavia hadn't a clue what Mikey was talking about, but she could tell that he was keen. Roberta, on the other hand responded with gusto, "Oh my God, it's tonight isn't it? When Dani phoned me this morning after the match, he told me all about the Bats big win last night. Now they're just one win away from winning the World Series. Imagine that – winning the World Series!"

Flavia was confused by the reference to 'this morning after the match'. But there was no confusing the enthusiasm that was radiating from her friend.

"This will be the biggest match of Dani's career!" Roberta continued. "Of course, I'll be watching it! But first I'll need some sleep – I don't think the match starts till 2am Italian time."

"Great!" said Mikey, "Why don't I pick you two up around 1am?"

"Sure!" said Flavia, still not quite grasping what this conversation was all about but it sounded fun. Then, out of the blue, she remembered, "Hang on, I must tell Enzo the good news!"

She broke off there, captivated by Mikey's million-dollar smile. "You're not the only one, who wants to talk with Enzo." He winked.

Meanwhile, over at the police station, a rather fragile Franco Spina stood before the one-way window that allowed him to look into the interrogation room. Against doctors' advice, he had released himself from hospital a couple of hours earlier. With bandaged ribs, a strong dose of pain killers and a massive helping hand from Giovanna he had been transported across town to police headquarters. Through the glass, he watched his foe, Alfonso Bellotto. Franco stood there for a few minutes, relishing the prospect of permanently puncturing that vulgar, overinflated ego. There was no doubt about it, that nasty piece of work belonged behind bars. And yet, Franco would not be fully satisfied with that as the outcome of the investigation. Much as he loathed and despised everything that Bellotto represented, Franco was prepared for a possible trade-off – if it meant that the police would be able to nail an even more villainous crook.

He turned to his deputy. She and Ricci had done a terrific job, not only bringing in Bellotto but also salvaging so much vital evidence from the phones they had confiscated. It humbled him to think that at least he had slept in a bed last night, god knows when Giovanna had last had any shut-eye. And yet, she was still keen and eager to be part of the interrogation. "Wouldn't miss it for the world, boss," she had told him earlier. He took confidence from her strength. Together they were going to crack this.

"Come on, Gio! Let's do this!" he announced, leading the way into the interrogation room.

Franco opened the door to the room and strode purposefully up to the empty table. Sitting down, with Giovanna at his side, he placed a bulging manilla folder on the table in front of him. Bellotto sat there, sprawled on a plastic chair, dressed in grey, velour loungewear that looked at least two sizes too small for his repulsive, overweight body. The two police officers ignored the defiant scowl that faced them. Next to Bellotto sat a young man in suit and tie, pen and notebook at the ready. Franco caught the young lawyer's eye and greeted him with a civil *"Buongiorno"*. But the latter said nothing in reply. Unperturbed, *Commissario* Spina proceeded to remind Bellotto of his rights.

Then Franco began the job of informing Siracusa's would-be mayor of the actions he was alleged to have committed and of the evidence gathered against him so far. Opening the folder, he started by pulling out various photos of Signora Montanari that had been sent to her son, Dani. They showed Roberta, held prisoner in a house on Bellotto's development at Villa Santa Panagia. There was even a photo taken outside the building, of a large sign bearing the words 'Bellotto Construction'. Franco spread them out across the table right under Bellotto's eye. The big man didn't bat an eyelid. Gaining his co-operation seemed a very distant prospect, when every question that Franco asked him met with the same mechanical "no comment" response. Of course, he was perfectly entitled to remain silent. However, as Franco pointed out, before handing over to Giovanna, if Bellotto persisted in not co-operating this could affect the decision of the court when deciding on his sentence.

Giovanna changed tack. She read out parts of Bruno's statement, which clearly pointed to Bellotto's involvement in the abduction. *"It was all the big man's idea,"* she quoted, *"he needs money to pay off his gambling debts."* Franco could have sworn he saw Bellotto twitch on hearing these words. But his attention was momentarily distracted by an odious smell that seemed to be coming from across the table. Vile, thought Franco, curling his lip in disdain.

Giovanna was relentless in bombarding Bellotto with questions. "You ordered the kidnapping of this innocent woman, didn't you Signor Bellotto?" "You had her tied up like a sack of potatoes in the basement of one of your properties at Villa Santa Panagia, didn't you?" "You extorted her son, Dani Montanari, for your own financial gain, didn't you?" But it was like water off a duck's back. Bellotto looked completely uninterested.

On hearing Dani's name, Franco decided to intervene. "Talking of Dani," he began nonchalantly, "that was some game last night." He paused there, before carefully placing on the table a selection of headline news that had been copied from the Internet: *BATS DRAW LEVEL IN THE WORLD SERIES; BRILLIANT BATS COMEBACK; BATS ON COURSE TO WIN WORLD SERIES.* This time, Franco did notice a reaction. It was clear from Bellotto's face that he had not been informed of last night's result. Turning abruptly to his lawyer, the big man barked, "Did you know this? Why didn't you tell me?" True to form, thought Franco looking on. The lawyer shuddered, speechless.

"You don't look too happy about that, Signor Bellotto," said the police chief.

Bellotto snarled back at him.

Feeling the wind in his sails, Franco continued, "The Kats chances of winning are not looking good, are they? Looks like you're going to lose all the money that you gambled on them winning the World Series. Not only that, you can also say goodbye to all the money that you'd hoped to win. All the money that you need to pay back your gambling debts to Vito Lupo. And Lupo's really not going to like that, is he?"

"No comment," growled the big man.

"Maybe you should think again about that." Franco

produced a photo of Bellotto's chauffeur. He placed it on the table and looked in the big man's direction. Their eyes met. Undaunted, Franco held his stare. Then he continued talking, "Unfortunately this man, one of your most trusted employees, has been reporting back to Lupo, keeping him informed of your basketball scam."

The surprise on the big man's face, was unmistakable. "Oh, didn't you know that Signor Bellotto? Didn't you know that Silvio Tacchino and Vito Lupo go back a long way? Worked together in Catania. So, you see, Lupo is fully aware of your predicament. And believe me, Signor Bellotto, you really are in a predicament – big time."

Franco waited for that to sink in, before turning to Giovanna. He beckoned her to carry on.

"Signor Bellotto, I think we all know that if you can't pay back Vito Lupo all the money that you owe him, it will be curtains for you. The wolf will be out for you, irrespective of where you are. At this moment in time, it is looking very likely that the Kats are going to lose the final game of the World Series. All the smart money is on a Bats win."

Bellotto shuffled around a bit in his seat. The grey velour loungewear merging with rolls of body fat, conjured up the picture of a heavy, weary walrus in Franco's mind. Nicely done, Gio, he thought. Now for the bid to clinch the deal. He had every confidence in his deputy.

"But you're a lucky man, Signor Bellotto. You don't have to fall prey to Lupo. We know from your phone records that you've been wanting to muzzle the wolf for a long time. Now you can work with us and help **us** put Lupo behind bars once and for all. "

Franco detected the slightest tweak of interest in the big man's face. Certainly, the young lawyer looked interested.

For the first time that afternoon, he gave Giovanna his undivided attention.

"Let me explain, Signor Bellotto," she continued. "If you testify against Vito Lupo, then your custodial sentence may be reduced or even waived by the judge. Instead of looking at 20-plus years behind bars, you could be living outside of prison, under house arrest. You could lead a pretty decent life, with the security of knowing that the wolf would not be able to harm you or your family."

Franco watched Bellotto. He was listening to what Giovanna was telling him. Now he would need some time to process this information, talk it over with his lawyer. Franco decided this was a good point at which to adjourn the interview for a few minutes. From his own point of view, he was ready for a good coffee and some fresh air.

Advising Bellotto and his lawyer to think over what Giovanna had just said, both police officers left the room.

"Well done, Gio. We can't do any more at this stage. Come on, let's get a drink," said Franco, beckoning Giovanna to walk with him down the corridor to his own office. They had just turned the corner outside the interrogation room, when a mane of dark curls came bobbing along the long corridor towards them, waving a sheet of paper. "*Dottore! Dottore!*"

Franco blinked, then blinked again. Sure enough, it was police officer Ricci. Wasn't he supposed to be off duty today, after Bellotto's arrest in the early hours of the morning?

Franco stood still. "Ricci. Slow down man. Have you got something for me?"

A breathless Ricci came to a halt next to Franco and Giovanna.

"Sorry, *dottore*. There has been a development. A very important development."

Ricci certainly was a master of the unexpected. Franco was intrigued to find out more. So intrigued in fact that all thoughts of coffee disappeared from his mind.

"Well, don't hang about, man. Spill the beans!"

"It's Don Enzo, the parish priest. He's made a statement, testifying to Bellotto's blackmail and –"

"His links to gambling?" This time it was Giovanna who interrupted.

Franco looked from Ricci to Giovanna, then back again. Ricci was nodding enthusiastically. "Whose links to gambling?" bellowed Franco.

"Bellotto! Enzo!" replied Giovanna and Ricci in unison. But it was Ricci who explained to the police chief how the priest had run into difficulty when managing the church accounts. And how he had secretly taken up gambling as a way to get more money. To start with Don Enzo had enjoyed a winning streak, and soon became a regular at Lupo's gambling club, located in a back room of Bar Stella. That was where he had first come across Bellotto. Within a few weeks, however, both of them had ended up with excessive debts. The winning streak had been short lived.

It seemed to Franco that, in the past 24 hours, the investigation had moved forward faster than even he could have imagined.

"So, Lupo was extorting money from both of them? And now Don Enzo has broken his silence about the gambling debts that Bellotto had built up? But in order to do so, Don Enzo must have come clean about his own gambling as well?" Both Ricci and Giovanna smiled and nodded in response to Franco's questions. The sense of satisfaction that the three of them shared was almost palpable. Franco smiled benignly at both of his officers and allowed himself the luxury of a few seconds to savour the moment. This was a new feeling for him.

However, it wasn't long before his analytical brain clicked back into gear. Time was now of the essence. Bringing to justice the prospective mayor of Siracusa was one thing. But Franco had his eye on an even bigger prize. They would need to act swiftly if they were to arrest the wolf before his informants got to him first.

"I'll need a copy of Don Enzo's statement for the next stage of the Bellotto interview," said Franco, reverting to his normal, business-like tone.

Ricci handed him the paper he had been holding.

"Great work, Ricci. Now go home and get some rest, man. That's an order!"

Minutes later, and a couple of squares of Modica chocolate to the better, Franco and his deputy were ready to return to the interrogation room. This time, he had a definite spring in his step. A stench of sweaty feet and stale breath hit them like a nauseous tidal wave when they entered the small room. Unfortunately there was no window to open. But even this could not detract from *Commissario* Spina's eagerness to resume the interview.

Looking Bellotto in the eye, he began by asking the big man for his response. Had he decided to take up the option of testifying against Lupo in exchange for a more lenient custodial sentence? Without batting an eyelid, the big man retorted, "No comment." Franco looked over to the lawyer. But the young man had his head turned downward. Probably out of embarrassment, thought Franco.

It was time for Gio to produce the killer blow. They had agreed that she would lead on this. In all fairness, Franco felt that to do otherwise would be to steal her thunder. He didn't want to undermine her, his trusted deputy. After all, she had done so much to help build up the case against Bellotto. She deserved to see it through. Quite apart from which, Franco's painkillers were starting to wear off. He was happier taking a backseat for now. But nothing was going to stop him from being there. He had waited most of his career to see Alfonso Bellotto brought to justice.

Giovanna looked over to Franco. He gave her a nod. And she started.

"Signor Bellotto, blackmail is a very serious offence. Blackmailing a priest of the Roman Catholic Church is very serious indeed, about as serious as it gets."

During the pause, Franco scanned Bellotto's face. The big man was nonplussed but failing to hide it.

Gio continued, placing a copy of Don Enzo's statement on the table.

"Don Enzo, parish priest in Ortigia, is known to you." She didn't wait for Bellotto to comment one way or the other. "We have a signed statement from Don Enzo, testifying to your blackmail of him."

At this stage, Gio didn't hold back. She read aloud key sections of Don Enzo's statement: the gambling club at Bar Stella, the extortion, the exploitation of migrants working for Bellotto Construction, the confiscation of their papers.

Franco watched as Bellotto's head sunk into his hands, seconds later his upper body lay prostrate across the table. It was time for the Head of Criminal Investigations to step in.

"The game's up, Bellotto."

After the excitement of the past 24 hours, Mikey had appreciated the opportunity to catch up on a few hours' sleep during the early part of Monday evening. After all, he had another long night ahead of him. Thanks to a couple of espressos he had gulped down at Antonino's café shortly before it closed for the night, he was sufficiently awake to head off in Totti around 1 am. First, he picked up Signora Montanari and Lola from the safe house, before continuing to Ortigia, where he collected Flavia, then Marco. Mikey had asked Enzo earlier whether he would like to join them, but the parish priest had declined politely. Not surprising, thought Mikey; Enzo had a lot to sort out after finding the courage to denounce Bellotto.

During the drive to his flat near Piazza Santa Lucia, Mikey told the others the news that he had been itching to relay. "Guess what! Bellotto's confessed. Not only that, but he's squealed on Vito Lupo! I heard that the wolf was arrested a few hours ago. He's been charged with a host of crimes, from illegal gambling to racketeering."

"What!" exclaimed Flavia, who was sitting in the back, next to Roberta. "I thought there was something dodgy about Vito, but I never saw him as a gangster! What a world!" She paused, then continued in a quieter voice, "By the way, Mikey, is there any more news of Enzo? I spoke with him this afternoon and he told me that he had been at the police station with you."

Mikey looked in his rear mirror and saw that Flavia was wearing the same necklace she had been wearing when they first met, just a week ago. He smiled inwardly, recalling how she had frantically run down via Verona chasing the beads when the necklace broke.

"Enzo's fine," he said, "never better. I rang him earlier this evening. He passes on his best wishes, but he wants to stay at home tonight. It's been a difficult time for him."

"That's right," said Flavia. "He told me all about it earlier, about his visits to Bar Stella and the gambling. I had known that something was going on, but it was a shock to hear this! I'm just so pleased that he finally opened up."

Mikey looked again in the rear window and gazed at

Flavia's smiling face and her sparkling brown eyes. This shouldn't be the last time that I see her, he thought.

His musings about when he might next visit Flavia's boutique were interrupted by Roberta's voice. "Is there any more news of Rosa?" she asked.

"Yes, Signora Montanari, there is!" he exclaimed.

"Oh please, call me Roberta! All my friends call me Roberta," a beaming Roberta interjected.

"In that case, please call me Mikey! Any friend of Flavia's is a friend of mine!" Mikey responded in a flash, with a cheeky wink in the mirror directed at Flavia. And then he continued to share the news, "I've heard that Rosa should be able to return home soon; possibly even tomorrow!"

"Wonderful!" exclaimed Roberta. "It'll be lovely to see Rosa again; Lola will be delighted too!"

A few minutes later, they arrived at Mikey's flat and sat down in front of his small TV. They were just in time to see the start of the final game of the World Series. It was Tuesday 2am local time – Monday 7pm in Kentucky. The following few hours passed in a flash for Mikey: the Bats tore into the Kats, with Dani, who had been chosen as the Bats' starting pitcher, dismissing Kats' batters at will. Each of Dani's successes was greeted with whoops of delights, and Marco jumping up from his chair, punching the air. Every so often, Mikey heard a knock on the wall from his neighbour, clearly upset at being disturbed during the early hours of the morning. When Dani was replaced at the end of the 7th innings, he was greeted with enthusiastic high-fives from his teammates. By then, the Bats had a commanding 8-1 lead and the deafening silence in the Kats' stadium contrasted starkly with the raucous cheers thousands of miles away in Mikey's flat.

By the time that the Kats' final innings edged towards

its conclusion, it was nearly 5am in Siracusa. Mikey turned towards Flavia and Roberta, who were sitting on the sofa next to his chair. "My neighbour's going be even angrier soon – when the Bats win!" he joked. Flavia laughed loudly, tossing back her long black hair, while Roberta smiled and stroked Lola, who was sitting contently on her lap. Mikey thought that Roberta looked tired – not surprising after everything that had happened over the past week – but her cries of encouragement throughout the game demonstrated her unwavering support for and belief in her son.

"Look!" said Marco, who was sitting on the other side of the sofa from Mikey. "The new batter for the Kats is nervous, I can tell!"

Everyone focused their attention on the TV screen. Miguel Ramos – who had recovered from injury and had taken over from Dani as the Bats' pitcher for the end of the match – was staring intently at the huge Kats player holding his bat. Ramos composed himself, then flung the baseball towards the batter.

WHACK!

The ball flew into the night sky, then dropped. Down, down, down. A Bats fielder raced forwards, then flung himself full-length with his arm outstretched.

"Catch it! CATCH!!" Roberta's shouts drowned out even Lola's squeals as the cat jumped down from her owner's lap.

"YES!!!!!" All four viewers screamed and rose to their feet in unison as they saw the ball nestled safely in the fielder's huge glove. Roberta and Flavia embraced each other in tears. "What a catch!" said Mikey, as he watched the Bats players ecstatically celebrating their triumph. No-one looked more ecstatic than Dani, who was held aloft proudly by his team-mates.

"Bravo, Dani!" Roberta turned towards the screen, clapping enthusiastically. Mikey suddenly felt Flavia's arms around his waist in a warm embrace, just as the bells of the Basilica of Santa Lucia rang out for 5 o'clock. Not even his neighbour's volley of bangs on the wall could ruin this moment for Mikey. Perhaps the bells are a sign, he thought. Maybe he should stay in Siracusa after all.

EPILOGUE

"Two espressos please!" Franco paid for the coffees at the counter of his favourite bar, then took them to a nearby table where he sat down. Opposite him was a man wearing a dark shirt, with a cinnamon-coloured dog by his side. "I can recommend the coffee here, Don Enzo," said Franco, as he emptied a sachet of sugar into his cup.

The parish priest smiled. "Thank you, commissario! I always appreciate a good espresso!"

Franco nodded, whilst carefully stirring the spoon in his cup, intent on dissolving as much of the sugar as possible. Was it only a week ago, he thought, that he had been in hospital, recovering from his brutal encounter with Bruno Mangiafico at Villa Santa Panagia? Bringing the cup up to his lips, Franco downed the espresso in one, then savoured the taste. So good, he thought. Almost as good as knowing that Guido Cavallaro, Bruno Mangiafico, Alfonso Bellotto and Vito Lupo were all now in jail, awaiting trial.

The priest continued, "And thank you for what you did today, commissario. It's a great idea of yours to issue a press *release, telling the guys' side of the story. It means a lot to them."*

Franco had visited Villa Santa Panagia an hour earlier, where he had met Don Enzo for the first time, along with a group of the migrant workers who were working at the site. "That's no problem," he replied. "It's important that people in Siracusa and elsewhere hear their stories. About how they've been exploited. And about how brave they were in reporting something that wasn't right. It's because of their actions that we were able to free an innocent woman from captivity and put some very evil people behind bars."

Don Enzo drank his espresso, then responded, "Absolutely! The guys acted as good citizens and they deserve the chance to build a life in this country. We need to change the narrative."

Franco nodded and thought back to his conversation with Amelia following the riot. "You're right, Don Enzo. To be honest, up until recently, I knew very little about the lives of migrants in Sicily. It wasn't a priority for me. But I'm better informed now, and other people need to be too. We all need to speak out whenever we see injustice, of whatever form, whoever is responsible."

"Thank you, commissario. The guys' lives won't change overnight, but you're giving them hope. You're showing a lot of courage, speaking up." Don Enzo hesitated before adding, "I need to do the same."

"Are you referring to Bellotto's cousin, the bishop?" asked Franco.

"Yes, in part." The priest sighed. "Archbishop Argento will be weakened by Bellotto's arrest and I know that I can and should stand up to him. But it's more than that. I've seen many bad things within the Church – corruption, merciless pursuit of money and power. Plus, I need to admit my own failings, my gambling. These are things I should have spoken out about earlier. And I need to say them now!" said Don Enzo, banging his fist on the table.

"I'm sorry, commissario," he said shortly afterwards. "I sometimes get a bit carried away." There was a pause, then he continued. "By the way, is there any more word about the rioters?"

Franco's mind was instantly filled with images of the mass disorder from that Saturday afternoon in Piazza Santa Lucia. A peaceful demonstration that was violently overturned by racist thugs. "Well," he replied, "we've arrested about 15 of those involved. Hopefully they'll be brought before the courts during the coming week. But this is just the tip of the iceberg. It's clear from social media that these thugs have many supporters. There may be more trouble ahead." As he spoke, Franco reflected on the spectre of hate hanging over the city, over the island and beyond.

Don Enzo leant forward. "Commissario, there many more good people in the world. Many, many more. We must always remember that."

Rocco barked again. "I'm sorry, but I need to go now," said the priest. "Thank you again, commissario. We'll be in touch about the press release." Standing up and shaking hands with Franco, he continued: "And you should know how much I appreciate what Mikey did. Please pass on my sincere thanks."

After they said their goodbyes, Franco left the bar and walked towards Ortigia, reflecting on the conversation. Who would have thought that he would have much in common with a parish priest? However, he had taken an instant liking to Don Enzo and realised that they both needed to confront corruption within the organisations for which they worked. Don Enzo's parting words had also convinced him that Mikey Ricci was indeed an asset to the force. Perhaps Mikey could be Giovanna's deputy, if Franco were promoted and Giovanna took his position as commissario in Siracusa?

Franco's thoughts turned to Catania and to the vacant post of Chief of Police, which would shortly be advertised. Promotion to this role had been a long-standing dream for him, both for his *own career and for the opportunity to spend more time with Amelia. But he understood now that Amelia might not see her future in Catania or even in Sicily. Like many of her generation, she may well decide to make a life for herself either on mainland Italy or further afield. He accepted that, but hoped that wherever his daughter found herself, she would remember the island on which she had grown up.*

As the sun fell, Franco looked to the skyline and saw the shimmering outline of Mount Etna in the distance. He took a photo of the volcano in all its glory, then sent it to Amelia with a WhatsApp message:

CIAO, AMORE! ETNA WILL ALWAYS BE PART OF US ☺

Printed in Great Britain
by Amazon